FOR A MODEST FEE

FOR A MODEST FEE

FREDA JACKSON

TouchWood
Editions

TouchWood Editions
www.touchwoodeditions.com

Library and Archives Canada Cataloguing in Publication
Jackson, Freda, 1942–
For a modest fee / Freda Jackson.

Print format: ISBN 978-1-926741-08-6
Electronic monograph in PDF format: ISBN 978-1-926741-74-1
Electronic monograph in HTML format: ISBN 978-1-926741-75-8

I. Title.

PS8619.A243F67 2010   C813'.6   C2010-902781-7

Editor: Marlyn Horsdal
Proofreader: Sarah Weber
Design: Pete Kohut
Cover images: Nurse: Michal Rozanski, istockphoto.com.
Train: Peter Zelei, istockphoto.com.

We gratefully acknowledge the financial support for our publishing activities
from the Government of Canada through the Canada Book Fund, Canada
Council for the Arts, and the province of British Columbia through the
British Columbia Arts Council and the Book Publishing Tax Credit.

Mixed Sources
Cert no. SW-COC-001271
© 1996 FSC

FSC

The interior pages of this book have been printed on 100% post-consumer
recycled paper, processed chlorine free, and printed with vegetable-based inks.

1 2 3 4 5 13 12 11 10

PRINTED IN CANADA

To five generations of nurses in my family

Kristina Haldorsdatter Olson, Midwife
Elleanor (Amy) Stoness Gravert, R.N.
Theresa Robinson Wright, R.N.
Judy Potter Oliver, R.N.
Christine Jackson Hutchings, R.N.

ONE

Elizabeth sat in her darkened parlour and accepted a cup of tea from a massive woman in an ill-fitting dress. More strangers jabbered in her kitchen, snooped through her cupboards and swiped at spills with her linen tea towels. Was there no end to it?

He couldn't be gone so quickly, without warning. But Elizabeth Evans, who had studied nursing in order to be by her father's side, to share his life and this insane adventure, knew what all good nurses know: a heart attack can, and does, happen that quickly.

She hadn't needed Dr. Burns from Calgary to tell her that. "Fifty-two years old you say? Prime age for heart attack. I'm surprised he came out west at his age."

Then he'd stared at Elizabeth as though he expected her to justify her father's decision to begin a new medical practice thousands of miles across the vastness of Canada. She had no likely explanation for it herself.

Two years earlier, a mild flutter of interest had reached their home in Toronto; Canada had two new provinces. Elizabeth had been more interested in events closer to home, like the prospect of a symphony orchestra set to begin concerts the following year. Most of Ontario was more excited about having a professional hockey team.

A year later they were in Alberta. Now, as the summer of 1907 faded into autumn, she sat alone—no father, and certainly no symphony, although there had been some shinny hockey on the frozen river last winter.

To her left, the Methodist preacher, Reverend Matthews, sat like a bump on a log with scraps of cake lodged in his scraggly whiskers, while his wife, Theodora, chattered on and on in that affected British accent that became more pronounced each day she was away from her precious homeland. An odour like mouse droppings hung around the pair of them. Didn't that musty smell have something to do with the plague?

Elizabeth's cup clattered from her trembling fingers into the saucer, bringing to a halt the murmur of voices in the parlour. She looked up to see them all gawking at her. Some, like the Porters from the hardware store, appeared concerned, but most stared with rude curiosity. The grief they voiced was for her father; not many of them had any real concern for her. They turned back to their chatter.

Through the arch to the dining room, she saw Herbert Schneider sidle around the mahogany dining table to reach her housekeeper, Mrs. Montgomery. Elizabeth heard snatches of what he said. "With the good doctor gone now, if you need work, anything at all—that hotel of mine will be finished soon and I'll need help."

His wife, Beatrice, stood apart from the crowd, dressed in a shapeless maroon thing that did nothing at all for her mannish features, which today were dark with anxiety. What possessed Herbert to bring her to a funeral? It could set her off for days.

A fly threw itself stupidly against the window screen, its frantic buzz adding to the confusion of accents from God-knows-where as people came by to mumble a few words. Elizabeth nodded, said thank you and wondered if there was any point in trying to remember names. Perspiration trickled down her spine and collected at the waistband of her petticoats.

"Will you have a sandwich at least, Elizabeth?" Only Mrs. Montgomery used her given name. Everyone else called her Miss Evans or just plain Nurse.

Elizabeth shook her head. "I can't, thank you." Her lips felt dry and tight as she looked up into the housekeeper's sad grey eyes. She had proven to be a real find—smart and clean, and good at "keeping secrets," as her father had said.

The housekeeper pried Elizabeth's clenched fingers from the cup and saucer. "I'll stay when they're gone and clean up for you."

But they lingered on, steaming up the parlour with their sweaty Sunday woollens. Had none of these people heard of linen or cotton?

Finally, she heard Mrs. Montgomery say, "No, no, I'll tidy up, thanks all the same. There's no need for any of you to stay."

Then, blessedly, they were gone. Elizabeth let her head sag onto the back of the blue horsehair chair, closing her eyes and listening to the house, to what her father had called their last concession to civilization. It sounded empty, as empty as the bank account and the cash box in the desk drawer.

When she had found her father slumped over his desk four days ago, she thought the worst thing in the world had happened. Then she had tried to pay for the coffin and the undertaker, and found that, no—things could get worse. She had no money, not even enough to pack up all her beautiful belongings and get back to Ontario. She opened her eyes and lifted her aching head, looking around at what she could sell or barter for a train ticket.

"How may I help?"

Elizabeth jumped. "Oh, Mrs. Montgomery, I didn't know you were still here."

"Is there anything I can do to help?"

"Help?" Elizabeth asked. She heard a touch of hysteria in her voice. It would never do to lose control in front of a servant. It would never do to crumble in front of anyone, at least that was what they had taught her during training. She wanted to snatch the tea towel from Mrs. Montgomery's hand and scream.

"No, thank you," she said instead. She looked around the room again, at the polished mahogany mantel clock and the dainty jardinière, then rose and walked stiffly into the wide front hallway with its rattan chairs and matching table. Sun filtered through the leaded-glass window in the door and reflected back from a gilded mirror. This is where patients waited in comfort to see her father. Used to wait.

Elizabeth stepped across the hall and into the immaculate white room that had been her father's office, sniffing the antiseptic air that hung over everything, realizing again that if there was one corner of this horrid wilderness that she didn't hate, it was this room. She touched the heavy wooden desk, ran her fingers over the white enamel cart with the tidy, wrapped bundles of sterile instruments, counting rolls of gauze, trying to put a figure to the sum of all that surrounded her. She should have paid more attention to these details. The house and everything in it had probably cost quite a lot. What was quite a lot to a busy physician? She didn't have the faintest notion.

"He always bought the best," Mrs. Montgomery said quietly from the doorway.

Elizabeth swayed under a wash of desperation. "Of course he ordered the best. What did you expect?" Then, to her dismay, hot tears slid from her eyes and dribbled down her cheeks.

Mrs. Montgomery took her none too gently by the wrist and pulled her into the kitchen. In that distant way she had, the housekeeper said, "You need to eat something and then get out of those hot clothes and have a nice sponge bath. Relax for the rest of the evening and try not to worry too much."

"Not worry?" Elizabeth heard her own voice screech and break. "Do you know what 'worry' means?" Then she forgot her promise to herself and broke down in front of her housekeeper.

Mrs. Montgomery folded her arms around her own ribs in a hug, then withdrew by taking one tiny step back. "I know what worry means."

"I want ..." Elizabeth began, then took a shaky breath. I want that hug, she almost wailed aloud. But there would be no such comfort coming from that quarter. She calmed herself enough to sit at the table.

"You want?"

"I don't know ..." She sank back in the chair.

"Something to eat?" The housekeeper slid a plate across the table, heaped with more sandwiches than Elizabeth could gag down in her lifetime, then poured a cup of tea that had stewed too long in an ugly brown pot that didn't belong in this house. One of those women must have brought it, making themselves at home the way they always did. Elizabeth peeled one of the thick sandwiches open and inspected the greying slab of ham inside.

"It won't hurt you."

She nibbled the dry bread and salty meat. "What's to become of me?"

Mrs. Montgomery swiped her skirts aside and perched on the edge of the chair opposite Elizabeth.

"I'm stuck out here without a friend to my name," Elizabeth went on. "It's possible that I have very little, if any, money, and there may even be some bills to attend to. I'm afraid to get the mail or go into the general store." She glanced up.

The housekeeper nodded.

"All I have is this wretched house and everything in it. How much could that possibly amount to?"

"I'm not sure. In a small town and late in the season, it's hard to say." Mrs. Montgomery spoke in the manner of someone who had already given considerable thought to that very question. "I do know that you haven't slept in days and that you should try to eat. I could stay another night."

Elizabeth responded without interest, "If you like. Perhaps I'll have that sponge bath now."

* * *

An hour later, Ann Montgomery started down the knoll from where the doctor's house stood at the northeast corner of town. She listened to the grasshoppers and a few children who had managed to stay out to play. Aspen Coulee spread before her, wearing a mantle of evening quiet. Glinting in the late sun on her right, the steel tracks of the Canadian Pacific Railway connected them to the rest of the world, and to her left, somewhere beyond her sight, it carved eastward through stands of aspen, poplar and miles of unclaimed grassland.

Instead of heading to Main Street, which ran perpendicular to the tracks, she took the long way, passing the toy-sized Methodist church, giving herself a few extra minutes to deal with her own thoughts.

It had all been too good to be true. Only a year ago, she had landed in this unlikely settlement to take up the improbable job of housekeeper to the local doctor and his daughter. She had let herself become accustomed to the clatter of a bursting railway town with its clean smells of fresh sawdust and prairie wool. Her ease had ended with the life of Dr. Evans and she caught herself searching faces again, wondering when her past might step down from the next train.

Arriving at what the locals called First Avenue, the long thoroughfare that ran parallel to the tracks, Ann turned right onto the boardwalk and covered four blocks, glancing now and then at the many empty lots and raw cellars, past the heat from the laundry, not enjoying the smells from the bakery as much as usual. Near the west end of the avenue stood a long, narrow clapboard building with an unused front door opening directly onto the boardwalk. She bent to unlatch a low gate at the side, then picked her way down a dusty path that separated Bertha's Boarding House from its ravaged vegetable patch. Most of the produce from the garden had already disappeared into quart sealers, now stored in the dirt cellar under the house, or into the gullets of the dozen or so men whom her landlady managed to cram into the second-floor bedrooms.

Ann eased the screen door open and shut, tiptoeing to her own cramped room at the back of the main floor. Day and night, summer and winter, the smell of boiled potatoes hung in the house. Quietly closing the door behind her, she lifted her skirts and deftly slid a key from a pocket in her petticoat. At the foot of her bare metal bed stood an ancient, carved Chinese wedding chest, the red-stained lions having faded decades ago to the colour of dried blood. Newer burn marks already blended into the complicated carvings. She had only enough time to slide the secret panel aside, snap the lock open, lift the lid and return the key to her pocket before the hinges scraped on her bedroom door.

"Why do you keep that heathen thing?" Bertha Severson never knocked and rarely expected an answer to her demanding queries.

Ann, leaning over her trunk, filled her lungs with incense and expensive scent. She lifted a cheap white shirtwaist and a cotton nightgown from the top tray.

"I told Elizabeth I'd stay on for another night so I'll need some clean work clothes."

"You mean to say that you still have to dress up in that Frenchie uniform now the doctor's gone?"

"I will, for Elizabeth's sake. After all, when she hired me down in Calgary, she said that she had two rules: I was to wear real maid's clothing and I couldn't live in. She didn't want anyone talking about her dear father and I sure don't need any gossip about me." Ann dropped the lid of the trunk with a solid *thunk* and the lock caught automatically, magically.

Bertha's gaze slid from Ann to the trunk as though the dragon-shaped handles would come to life and bite her. "Well, she puts on too many airs for folks hereabouts, even under these sad circumstances. That watered-silk dress she wore today—now that must o' cost more 'n most men earn in a year, don't you think?"

Ann took a simple navy serge skirt from a peg on the wall; in the nightstand that used to be an apple box, she found a fresh white bib apron and two pairs of neatly folded cotton stockings, remembering her frenzy in Calgary when she had tried to find what might be considered maid's clothes, spending a few dollars of her precious stash of money on the things she held. She jammed everything into a carpetbag from under the bed, then straightened.

"What's she going to do now, in that big house all by herself?" Bertha asked.

"I don't know. I'd better get going in case she needs my help." Ann brushed by Bertha and through the screen door once more.

Bertha's final warning followed her down the garden path. "You're crazy to try to help that one. She won't thank you or give two pins for anything you do. And that's all I have to say on that subject."

Ann thought Bertha was probably right, but she remained quiet. The doctor, rest his soul, had tolerated Ann because she could keep secrets—she certainly hadn't had much else to offer—and Ann had been thrilled to work in the safety of Dr. Evan's household. Now his pampered little girl had money problems, and Ann Montgomery still needed to work. Bertha hadn't given her time to count the money in the yellow silk bag in her trunk, but she knew it wouldn't get her far enough east to open a shop of her own.

She glanced up in time to see a tweed belly protruding from the door of Schneider's General Store. Her worst nightmare in a celluloid collar. She turned sharply left and cut across the baked ruts of back lanes, passing chicken coops, heaps of lumber and half-built houses, angling her way toward the northeast edge of town where the last slice of setting sun caught the Evans house, lighting it up like a beacon.

* * *

Herbert Schneider had seen Mrs. Montgomery go into the boarding house and had slid over to his open door to wait for her. He heard her steps coming his way.

He had two thorns in his side: Bertha's Boarding House gobbling up the money his hotel should be making if he could get those lazy carpenters to work, and the Evans house. He was sick and tired of listening to Beatrice whine about Elizabeth Evans having the best of everything. Overhead, he heard his wife's heavy tread thumping back and forth in their living quarters, and felt a stab of annoyance and dread. His sweaty palms stuck to the wool as he slid his hands into his pockets and rocked back and forth on the balls of his feet, his thoughts turning to the Widow Montgomery.

There was something too closed about the woman. Widows who looked like that, moved the way she did, and a housekeeper to boot, well, everyone had heard stories about housekeepers taking care of more than the house.

She should be here by now. Herbert peeked around the doorframe. A clump of dry sagebrush tumbled across the street, spooking a lone horse in front of the new post office.

"Damn it." He pulled his hands out of his pockets.

"Pardon?"

"Nobody's talking to you. Get back to work," Herbert snapped at the young clerk who had stayed on to stock shelves.

The boy gave him a surly look and took his own sweet time unpacking bottles of vanilla.

On the way to his cubbyhole office at the back, Herbert scooped up a handful of soda crackers from the nearly empty barrel and stuffed them into his mouth. Merchandise was getting low again; every train spilled half a dozen families and twice as many single men looking for work or free land. Between the thought of more trade and the salt of the crackers, he started to feel a little better.

Leafing through the neat stack of papers on his desk, Herbert came across his copy of the survey map of the town. He had penciled in who owned which lot and marked the ones that were still available. Several good business plots along Main Street and First Avenue were unclaimed. The Railroad Land Department had recently decided that any building on these prime lots had to be worth one thousand dollars or more. Herbert chewed on that with his crackers for a minute, caught between his yearning for faster growth and his love of neat, well-constructed buildings. He knew they were right—they always were—but it slowed things down considerably.

There was a quarter section across the tracks and down a bit from the new roundhouse, just out of town where a boggy stream ran toward the river in the spring, but it was worthless—wet on the low parts and pure sand on the high ground. Not fit for farming and too expensive to drain for building.

That meant that any residential expansion would have to go back from First Avenue, straight north of the existing town site. The place was bound to grow. He could feel it in his bones. Now was the time to quietly get his hands on more land and sit on it.

He ran his forefinger over the grid pattern of the map. Dragging his fingernail to the northeast, he stopped abruptly and swallowed his pleasure with the last doughy mouthful of crackers. Four large, prime lots belonged to the doctor. The local businessmen had decided that a doctor would need to keep his own horse, so they'd sold him enough land for a stable and a small pasture right in his own backyard. Herbert had agreed, so anxious was he to have a medical man in town. Homesteaders set down where their wives felt comfortable, and there was nothing like a charming doctor to make women feel at home.

Now that big property and the house on it belonged to the doctor's sassy daughter, thinking she was so modern, bouncing up and down the dirt roads on a bicycle, of all the fool things.

Annoyance tightened his neck muscles as he recalled Beatrice's whining voice; it always sounded as though she had a head cold. "If we're going to maintain our position in this town, we should have a real house like the doctor. We could order it from one of those catalogues; they come with all the pieces numbered, like a big puzzle." On and on about that house.

Finally he'd blown up at her. "What do we need with a big house? We're never going to have any family to put in it, are we?"

Her yellow skin had turned a mustard colour under her blush. He'd jerked his head toward the bedroom and her eyes bugged out of her head.

Her voice had broken into a weak squeal. "It's daylight."

Now, in the shadows of late afternoon, Herbert rolled the map into a tight sausage and smacked it on the palm of his hand. Lately he'd been wondering if there was more to her barrenness than he had thought. She could be a sly one, no doubt about that.

TWO

Banging awoke Ann and battered her nerves as she fumbled to get dressed in the unfamiliar guest room. She struck a match and swiped it across the wick of the lamp, replaced the globe and started down the stairs.

One shadow wavered behind the glass on the front door. No, maybe two. Elizabeth came down behind her, drawing on a blue wool robe that matched her suede slippers. The mantel clock chimed twice.

"Who is it, Mrs. Montgomery?"

"I can't recognize them through the glass."

Holding the lamp high, she opened the door, letting the yellow spill of light fall onto a dark young man with a child beside him, a little girl about five years old, who shivered in a thin cotton frock and bare feet.

"Dock-tor?" the man asked.

"Oh, my." Ann studied the man, then the child, before looking to Elizabeth.

Elizabeth took a long, shaky breath. "Are you sick, child? Or hurt?"

The girl shook her head and stated flatly, "Mama."

"Dock-tor?" the man repeated, then prodded the child between her narrow shoulder blades.

"We need the doctor, please. For my mama." She formed the unfamiliar words carefully, as though she had been rehearsing them. Her eyes were dark in the shadows of her small oval face.

"But, the doctor," Ann began, then shifted her attention to the man. "Haven't you heard? Dr. Evans has passed away."

"Passed?" The child looked confused and frightened.

The man frowned and shook his head.

The girl twisted her skirt in her hand and looked imploringly at Ann. "The doctor is gone? When he will be back? We will wait?" Her bottom lip began to tremble.

The young man looked at the housekeeper, a furrow deepening between eyes as dark as the child's. "We wait for dock-tor."

He pushed by Ann and entered the wide hall, then sat ramrod straight on one of the rattan chairs, planting his fists on his knees, watching Ann as though he expected her to produce the doctor from the cool night air. Like a shadow, the little girl followed one step behind, then leaned into his thigh and began worrying a strand of dark hair. There was no mistaking the family likeness.

Ann looked at Elizabeth, so pale and drawn. "I don't believe they understand."

Elizabeth squeezed her eyes closed, then opened them. "What Mrs. Montgomery is trying to tell you is that my fa—the doctor— d-died recently. The doctor is dead."

Ann nodded, staring back into his black eyes. "Dead."

The little girl sucked in her breath, stopped twisting her hair and touched the man's hand. They looked at one another without a word.

Elizabeth was able to ask, "What is your name, child?"

"Eva. Eva Gregorowicz."

"What's wrong with your mama?"

"The baby comes. Is not good."

The man watched Eva's lips move and nodded in agreement or encouragement, Ann wasn't sure which. "Not good," he repeated.

Elizabeth's voice strengthened. "Would a nurse be of help? Would your mama like to see a nurse?"

The girl's face lit with hope. She started to speak to the man, but he stood abruptly. "Ah, yes. Nurse."

"I'll have to come with you," Ann said with a sense of foreboding. Dr. Evans would never have let his daughter wander around in the middle of the night with strangers.

Elizabeth nodded, as though she expected no less. "We'll come," she told the child. "Wait here."

The man put his hand on the girl's shoulder. "A nurse," he murmured to the anxious little face.

Elizabeth came back downstairs buttoning the black silk dress she had worn a few hours earlier. She carried a linen drawstring bag which she handed to Ann with the curt order, "Keep it clean." From the office she grabbed her father's medical bag before heading toward the door. The young man reached to take the bag from her hand but Elizabeth held on and pulled back. Ann took Eva's hand but could not leave the house with the two of them blocking the doorway, yanking the doctor's medical bag back and forth. "Elizabeth, he's just trying to help."

"No one touches it but me," Elizabeth said through clamped teeth.

This would have been laughable under any other circumstances, Ann thought, but right now she felt like giving them both a smack. Her nerves weren't up to one of Elizabeth's dramatic scenes.

"Go fast," the man glared down at Elizabeth from under the heavy dark hair that fell over his eyes.

"He's right, Elizabeth. It might be faster." Then pointing at the man, Ann asked Eva, "His name?"

"Is Stefan."

"Let Stefan carry the bag, Elizabeth. You take the child's hand and I'll carry this." Ann held the linen bag to her chest. "Now, let's go." She placed the lamp on the hall table and blew it out, then pressed them all onto the wide front veranda.

Stefan led the way, walking with easy strides under a fading moon, across a swath of dew-drenched prairie wool that dragged at the women's hems. Mosquitoes swarmed out of the grass in ghostly grey waves, launching a bloody attack on hands and faces, burrowing into the warmth of their necks. Eva slapped and danced to protect her bare ankles and feet, tried to keep up, but finally whimpered to a stop. Stefan shoved the contentious bag at Elizabeth and hoisted Eva onto his hip, tucking her skirt around her feet. Without a word, he marched on.

They headed south and crossed the railroad tracks east of town, then followed an old buffalo trail toward the river, coming to a new colony of squatters that had sprouted on the banks above the stream. Soddies built of clumps of dirt loomed shoulder height in the moonlight like trolls. Ragged tents, and shanties constructed from discarded wood and tarpaper, had been thrown up at random. A dog snarled. Someone called, "Who goes there?"

When Stefan pulled back the sack that covered the doorway of one of the soddies, Elizabeth muttered something that her father probably hadn't taught her. Ann stepped into the old-cellar smell, didn't duck low enough, and felt soil tangle in her hair and trickle down the back of her neck. She had to take a few seconds to adjust to the gloom, the earth walls sopping up what little light came hissing from a lantern.

Eva ran two steps to a rusty metal bed that had been propped against the dirt wall. Lost in the hollow of a grimy tick a woman panted, a shabby sheet twisted around long, thin legs. She turned to look at Eva, tried to smile then bit down on her lip, her teeth startlingly white against grey skin.

In the corner Ann saw the ghostly outline of two faces, a man and a woman, sitting cross-legged on the floor on a piece of crimson carpet that must have been Asian in origin. She had a fleeting memory of Chinatown, green tea and Jingfei Chiu. She heard click-clicking and thought it must be chopsticks and that she'd surely lost her mind, as so many did out here, then realized it was the sound of rosary beads in the older woman's hands. She heard the thirsty whine of a million or so mosquitoes that darted in and out at will, and, overriding it all, an animal-sounding groan rising from the battered cot. The older couple shuddered together and turned their faces away.

Elizabeth squatted by the bed. "What's her name?"

"Mama's name is Hilde," Eva said.

"Bring me the lantern. I'll need some hot water. Get a fire going." Elizabeth looked at Ann with exasperation, holding her hands high, palms up. "How can I . . . ?"

"Stefan?" Ann turned to ask the man for help, but he had not entered the soddy with them. "Where is the father?"

"Disappeared," Elizabeth said. "Hilde, I need to examine you."

"Disappeared," Ann repeated in exasperation. "Wouldn't you know it? Eva, where is your father?"

"Father?" The child paled even more, staring at Ann with haunted eyes.

Ann's nerves were strung to the breaking point. She was going to witness a birth for the first time in her life and it didn't excite anything but dread in her. "Go fetch your father. We need his help."

Eva started to weep, then crossed herself. Her mother muttered a worried question, but the child only shook her head.

"Your father? Stefan?"

"Stefan?" Eva repeated with a frown. Then her little face cleared with understanding. "Stefan?" She pointed toward the door. "Stefan is father's brother. Father dead." She crossed herself again. "Like doctor. Dead."

With a look of determination, Elizabeth said, "We'll have to have Eva with us to translate, but keep her at the head of the bed, please, Mrs. Montgomery. She shouldn't be here at all, but what can we do?"

"Do you think you could call me Ann, please?"

Elizabeth opened the bag and carefully withdrew a large white apron. "Ann it is. This doesn't look good, I have to be honest with you." Elizabeth tossed Ann one of those woman-to-woman looks that even she, deprived of female company for most of her adult life, found easy to understand.

From the bag Elizabeth pulled a crisp white cotton square. She shook it open and folded it into a triangle which she tied low on her forehead and knotted at the nape of her neck, covering her hair. "Eva, are those people your grandparents?"

"Yes."

"They must leave." Elizabeth pointed at the door. "And Eva, ask your uncle to bring us lots of water. Quickly."

Without argument, Eva stood and went to her grandparents. She took each one by the hand and pulled them toward the door, speaking to them as though they were children.

Stefan soon returned with a battered bucket, took one look at Elizabeth, decked out in her head covering and long sterile sleeves, and bellowed, "No! No nurse."

Elizabeth and Ann stared, stupefied.

"You wanted a nurse," Ann managed.

He poked Ann on the shoulder. "You nurse."

"Oh, for evermore," Elizabeth said.

Ann laid a firm hand on Elizabeth's arm. "Nurse," she explained to Stefan. "Elizabeth Evans. Nurse." Then she pointed at her own chest and said, "Ann Montgomery. Housekeeper. Helper."

He looked Elizabeth up and down. "You nurse? So little, like a girl?"

The young man was saved from a tongue-lashing by a cry from the bed that brought Hilde to an upright position.

Elizabeth placed her hand on the woman's forehead. "Get Eva in here."

The next hour was a revelation to Ann, and an education she would rather have done without. In only a few minutes her opinion of Miss Elizabeth Evans was altered forever. This would be the Miss Evans who had won the grudging respect of one or two of the locals, people who found no incongruity in resenting her uppity ways. Hard work was a common denominator everyone understood.

Ann managed to get the rickety stove going with kindling and dry grass. Stefan followed her directions quickly. Water steamed and Elizabeth made everyone in the room scrub their hands with strong antiseptic soap, even Eva, who bravely translated every one of her orders.

At a point that could have been minutes or hours later, Elizabeth addressed herself to Eva. "Your uncle, Stefan, he will have to go now."

Stefan dropped an armful of wood and fled.

"Help me get her out of these clothes," Elizabeth said to Ann, and as gently as possible, the two women stripped a dank, clammy shift from Hilde's body and quickly draped her with a sheet.

"She's so thin," Ann whispered.

"Not as bad as some I've seen. That isn't her biggest problem, though." Elizabeth spoke in undertones. "There's something else wrong here and I'm not sure what it is."

Using a flannel rag, Ann washed Hilde's face, then averted her eyes and swiped under the sheet at the damp neck and chest. That would have to do. I can do this, Ann promised herself. She took deep breaths and tried to steady her hands.

"You've seen a birth before?"

She shook her head.

Elizabeth lifted Hilde's hips and placed a folded sheet on the dirty mattress. "Try to stay with me, Ann, but if you have to leave . . ."

"I'll stay. Of course, I'll stay."

"Eva," Elizabeth asked, "did your mama hurt herself recently? Did she fall?"

Eva had curled herself around her mother's shoulders like a cat. She shook her head.

Elizabeth opened her father's bag and took out a sterile package, setting it carefully on the corner of the bed. "Was she sick? Did she stop eating? What has happened here in the last few weeks?"

"Not eat?" The huge eyes filled with tears. "Only when Papa . . . when he died."

"Of course," Elizabeth said. "When was that?"

"July tenth, nineteen-oh-seven," the child recited.

Elizabeth looked up from her work and blinked. "July tenth?"

"Is on his grave," Eva said. "July 10, 1907."

"You can read?" Ann interjected.

"Just the grave. I go to English school soon."

"That would have been about six weeks ago. A shock could do this." Elizabeth ducked her head under the sheet and came away looking grim. She unwrapped a strip of gauze and wound it around her nose and mouth.

There was one more shuddering screech from Hilde, then just an exhausted moan that went on forever.

"Eva, leave now," Elizabeth ordered.

But the child resisted. "No. I stay with Mama so she won't die."

"Eva," Elizabeth began again, then motioned to Ann. "Get some more towels and some of the gauze from Fath—from my bag." She hiked her skirts and knelt on the end of the bed.

Ann grabbed the last of some grey-looking rags from the edge of the stove where they had been warming and hurried to join Elizabeth, then froze in horror.

From between Hilde's thin thighs poured a sticky stream of dark blood, black in the smoky light. Then, with wet plop, the racked body expelled a gelatinous mess. Bile rushed into Ann's mouth as the hot stench of putrefied flesh rose from the cot. Elizabeth coolly caught the stillborn infant and folded it quickly inside the old towels.

The room swirled and faded. Blackness closed in on Ann and her knees buckled. She realized that she was crying, mucus dribbling down her face.

"Get out," Ann heard from a tremendous distance, like the voice of God shouting into a rain barrel. "Get outside, into the fresh air."

Ann grabbed a wailing Eva and staggered out the door on legs that had turned to pudding.

Stefan paced the few steps between the dirt house and the small tent that he called home, propelled by the muttering and moans from inside. He froze when he heard the bossy little person who claimed she was a nurse yell, "Get out." Then Ann stumbled in front of him, dragging a screaming Eva with her.

"Mama's dying." Eva's cries echoed through and around the other shacks and soddies. He crouched to hold her. Ann sat heavily on a wooden crate, gulping for air, fumbling to loosen the top button of her dress. Eva pulled at her own clothes and wailed into Stefan's face. She didn't go to her grandparents for comfort.

Stefan shook his head, ran his hands down Eva's arms to try to calm her. It wasn't possible. Hilde came from strong peasant stock. Women like Hilde didn't die from birthing.

The nurse shouted more orders from behind the sack door. "Put your head down, Ann, between your knees. I can't take care of both of you."

Both meant two. Stefan heard a thin whine of grief from Hilde but no baby's cry. He felt a knot of fury build just below his rib cage, a ball of helplessness like bad food, undigested, a sickness that he'd suffered since the first day he set foot in this empty land. He held his dead brother's little girl and looked at his father, slumped like a worn-out old man against the dirt house. His mother huddled there too, worrying a rosary between her thin fingers. They had become as dependent on him as Eva. More so.

"Shh." He stroked Eva's hair, listening for any further sound from the nurse or Hilde. Ann flopped forward, her head on her knees as Elizabeth had said. A band of sky lightened in the east, heralding the false dawn. In the Old Country, this part of the night, when darkness held on for a few minutes, not wanting to give in to the light of day, was thought to be the time when people died, when their souls took flight from their bodies. He shivered and became even angrier with himself for thinking like those superstitious old fools. He had been so lucky to study at the university and here he squatted, thinking old-fashioned thoughts.

Stefan stared blankly at the sack door, his mind not able to work, to think what to do next. Finally the nurse came out with black-looking smears of blood staining the pure white of her apron. She stripped soiled white sleeves down over her arms and shoved them into a bag, then peeled white gauze from her face.

She knelt before Ann. "Better now?"

Ann wiped at her eyes and nose with a handkerchief. "I'm sorry to be a nuisance. How is—everything?"

The nurse started to speak in a very tired voice, then turned to include Eva and Stefan. "Eva, I'm sorry but the baby was, well, not alive. Had not been alive for some time. Can you explain to your uncle and grandparents?"

Eva continued to shiver and snuffle inside the circle of Stefan's arms. "My uncle understand English good, but he don't like to talk it much."

Elizabeth looked directly at Stefan. "Do you understand me?"

He nodded, then tipped his head toward his parents. "I tell them."

"How is Hilde?" Ann asked.

"Resting." Then the nurse turned to Eva. "Eva, your mama is asleep now, but you can go in and watch over her for me. Would you do that?"

Eva disappeared into the dirt house.

"Stefan, do you need a priest or something? Would Hilde or your parents want a priest?"

"Oh, God," Ann said.

"A priest? For Hilde?"

"No, Hilde should recover if she doesn't become feverish. She needs a lot to drink—milk, clean water, boiled would be best. I'm thinking of the, uh, infant."

Stefan muttered and crossed himself. Ah, God. Of course, another one left in the black soil of this lonely country.

Stefan spoke quickly to his parents, then told them to go inside and make tea as more light softened the horizon and a robin called, "*Cheerup, cheerio.*"

"We don't have priest here. Nick, my brother, is buried back in another town. I ask some person—someone—what we should do. I take care of it."

She nodded. "The Roman priests travel around a lot, you know, to the Indian reserves and other places. If you can't find one, the other clergy will help you. The undertaker in town is called Faraday. Hilde needs to stay in bed for several days and not lift anything or do any heavy work."

Stefan wondered if he could find a few pennies for milk. He had seven more days of work before he would get paid: would the undertaker wait that long?

When his parents were settled and Eva had fallen asleep beside her mother, Stefan walked the women home and this time, the nurse didn't argue when he carried the leather bag. The dew from the night melted into mist in the low areas and then dissolved as the sun climbed higher. There was something soft about the early mornings in this hard country and Stefan, up early every day, usually didn't mind the two-kilometre walk to work. But today he might be late, might lose his job to someone just off the train. Then what would happen to them all?

The house that had intimidated him last night looked even more impressive in the perfect light of a new day. Square, two storeys, with wide windows all around and a broad porch both front and back. Simple and beautiful. The stable and outbuildings in the big back-yard were all painted yellow to match the house. A gentleman's house.

His father and brother had pulled him away from his studies and friends in the Old Country to find a better life, to have their own land, maybe to live in a grand house like that. But where did they end up? In a dirt shelter, like the animals.

THREE

By the time Elizabeth turned toward home for supper the following evening, a thunderstorm that had been brewing all day had boiled in from the southwest. Lightning sizzled out of black clouds and gusts of wind whipped the wolf willow. Daisy flattened her ears and stretched her dainty legs into a trot. Wilted and weary, Elizabeth let the horse have her head and trusted the little mare would avoid the gopher holes.

They turned into the yard at a brisk pace, nearly running over Stefan. Saw in hand, he had the beginnings of a pile of wood cut from a heap of logs dumped on the ground.

"Whoa." He stepped back and grabbed Daisy's bridle before she could trot into the stable, buggy and all.

Elizabeth passed him the reins. "Why are you back here? I just came from attending to Hilde and she is doing well."

He had offered his hand to help her down, but stopped and she realized that she had offended him. He's a prickly character, she thought.

He straightened, drawing his shoulders back. "I come back—came back," he corrected himself, "—to cut wood for the stove. I cut trees for the construction crew and they let me have them so I bring for you. To pay for your help." He seemed to have to force himself to look directly at her, but as he did, she noticed his gaze take in her blue-and-white-striped uniform and the silver brooch with the familiar red cross and the words Queen Victoria Hospital.

Elizabeth raised her voice against the storm. "I see." She didn't, but she was too tired to deal with more of his awkward explanations. "You'd better get home. Leave the wood for another day."

Together they put the horse away for the night. As they left the stable, the wind tore at Elizabeth's skirts and slammed the door out of her hands. Stefan grabbed it and shoved the bolt into place. They parted without another word.

Elizabeth crossed the porch and entered the back door of the house through the spacious washroom with its blue enamelled washing machine and pulley-operated drying racks. She dropped her soiled linens into a large wicker basket and turned right into the kitchen where fresh peas, new potatoes and more leftover ham sandwiches waited on the table.

"How are your patients?" Ann asked.

"Hilde is better. A strong woman, I think, after all is said and done. Mrs. Weyman will only get worse. The tumour in her abdomen is growing at an alarming rate and I don't know what more I can do."

"They're lucky to have you. What more could anyone, even your father, do for Mrs. Weyman?"

Elizabeth sank onto the chair. "Nothing. But I'm not sure I should be giving narcotics to anyone."

"Narcotics?" Ann sat opposite her.

"The medicine that I took to Mrs. Weyman today is made with opium. A narcotic."

"Opium? Surely not?"

Elizabeth nodded and poked at her food.

"You have opium in this house?"

Elizabeth looked into Ann's strained face, surprised at the unusual display of emotion. "A small amount. Why, what do you know about opium?"

"Only that it's very habit forming. Aren't you afraid Mrs. Weyman will become dependent upon it?"

"I know she will. In the end, she will."

"You know that and still—it's a terrible thing," Ann said, "Isn't it?"

"What does it matter in this case? The alternative is unbearable pain for her."

A flash of lightning lit the kitchen, followed instantly by a crack of thunder that tore open the sky to let the rain fall in sheets outside the window, pounding the roof and slashing against the windows.

Ann felt the hair stand up on her arms. She rubbed them briskly; it must be the storm. "You know what you're doing, I'm sure."

"I don't," Elizabeth said. "That's the point. I'm not certain when to increase the amount or by how much. What will I do for Mrs. Weyman when I run out?"

Ann reached for a China teapot. "Maybe you could contact someone. What about the police surgeon? Wasn't there one through not too long ago? Maybe he could help."

"Yes, a friend of Father's. Sergeant Ewan McRae. They stayed up most of the night drinking brandy and trading tall tales. But police surgeons wander the whole district and I don't have any notion how to contact one of them."

"Could you write to them in Edmonton or Calgary and leave word that you need help? It may take a while, but someone will get your message eventually. The train comes tomorrow—a letter would go right away."

"Ah, yes. The train." Elizabeth stood and carried her half-empty plate to the dry sink under the window, then leaned on the edge.

Ann followed with her own plate. "Why don't you get ready for bed and let me do the dishes?"

"Do you like your work?"

Startled, Ann looked at the dirty dishes in her hand. She was pleased to be able to say, "Very much. I like working in this house more than anywhere I've ever worked."

Elizabeth stared at the rain as it sluiced down the glass. In an almost-inaudible voice, she said, "I don't know if I can afford to keep you much longer. When you mentioned the train, it reminded me that I have to go to Calgary myself. I have to see the lawyer, Mr. Macdonald. See to my affairs, I guess people say."

"I wondered. I didn't like to ask, but I have to admit I wondered."

"Could you stay at least until I get back? I don't like to leave the house empty."

"Stay? Of course I'll stay," Ann said, stopping short of screaming, Where would I go?

* * *

"Nice rain last night, wasn't it?" Alf Porter asked.

Herbert Schneider nodded. "Freshened things up." As the train thundered into town, he felt the power of the locomotive vibrating under the soles of his feet, humming up his legs and through his body. It made him smile, as though he had invented this modern wonder himself.

The conductor opened the coach door with a clang and the first of the newcomers stepped onto the bustling platform. They were well dressed and toting a pile of handsome luggage. He heard some of them speak, recognized the Midwestern twang and grunted with satisfaction. Money and good old American know-how. An unbeatable combination. To add to his pleasure, Herbert saw Alf watch in dismay as they unloaded a heap of farm equipment. They wouldn't be spending their money at Porter's Hardware Store, but everyone needed groceries and dry goods on a regular basis and Herbert could fill that bill. "Likely-looking bunch of farmers, don't you think?" He rocked on the balls of his feet.

Alf tried to put a good face on it by doffing his hat as the group passed by. "Yep, they are."

Down the platform, Bertha Severson prattled with Ann Montgomery and the Evans brat. Herbert stopped rocking.

Alf plunked his hat back on his head. "Did you come to say how-do to the new teachers, too?"

"Teachers?" Herbert lied. "No, no. We hired them, now it's up to the women to see they get settled." He saw Bertha moving forward as two women stepped down from the train.

"Still think we should have held out for men," Alf went on.

"Well, you will recall, Mr. Porter, we weren't able to get men to come out here for what we pay the women. Men get half again what a woman is paid. And that's as it should be," Herbert hastened to add. "But with nearly fifty students now, we needed two teachers and we couldn't afford two men."

"Appear to be sensible women, don't you think? Older than I thought they'd be, but that's fine. Handle the big boys better. Well, someone from the school board better say hello." Alf doffed his hat again and left Herbert standing there.

A couple of other people stopped to greet the teachers, then gradually everyone moved on.

* * *

It wasn't until after supper two days later that Ann and Elizabeth found time to visit Hilde again. Butterflies drifted amongst the buffalo beans, and bees swarmed to the thick perfume of purple clover.

By the time the women had crossed the meadow, the cacophony of the grasshoppers had given way to a haunting sound drifting over the hills. They looked at one another, puzzled. At the top of the ridge that would lead them down a wide coulee to the river, clear, pure notes of music had stilled the birds.

"A violin?" Ann whispered.

Elizabeth nodded. "Liszt."

"What?"

"Liszt is a composer. Hungarian, I think. I took piano lessons for a short while but my teacher persuaded Father to let me give it up. I was too impatient, he said. Being impatient has never stopped me from enjoying music, though. It was one of my favourite holidays with Father—a trip to New York for shopping and concerts."

By the time they entered the camp the tune had changed to a faster piece, an exotic melody that felt exactly right, dancing on the smoke of the campfires, drifting downstream with the muddy river.

"He's good," Elizabeth said as they drew closer. "Whoever this musician is, he's good."

Even though it was mid-week, a Sunday mood of restfulness had settled on the camp. Men, women and dogs lounged around the tents and shanties scattered under the red willow and slim birch trees.

Stefan couldn't see Ann and Elizabeth, with his chin tucked into his shoulder and his elbow high, the bow flying over the strings of his violin. Like everyone else in the camp, they stopped to listen. The grandparents sat on the scrap of red carpet and rested their backs against the dirt wall, eyes closed.

For fully five minutes, the two women stood and listened. Lost in another world, or at least another country, Stefan seemed totally oblivious to his audience. He wore a clean white shirt, a loose garment that looked like a blouse, open at the throat and rolled back over brown arms. His trousers were the patched work clothes of every day, but the hands that had wrestled brush out of the ravines wooed the instrument with tenderness as he brought the piece to a lingering close.

Stefan did not acknowledge the scattering of applause. He adjusted the strings and prepared to play again before noticing Elizabeth and Ann. Without pretension, he lowered the violin and stood, bowing slightly. "Good evening."

"That was lovely," Ann said. "Please don't stop for us."

He nodded. "Thank you." But he didn't sit down to play again, standing instead until they had entered the soddy.

They stepped from the mellow evening, fresh with music, into the dank hut. Hilde sat in her bed, a grey blanket over her knees and a plum-coloured shawl around her shoulders, looking a great deal better than the last time Ann had seen her. Elizabeth suggested a few minutes in the fresh air before bed so they bundled her in a robe and the blanket before steadying her, one on either side.

"Look who's here." Elizabeth kept her arm firmly around Hilde's waist.

Stefan offered the crate he had been sitting on. His father stood and someone in Stefan's audience called, "Glad you're feelin' better, Missus."

The grandmother disappeared, then returned with her hands full of tiny, exquisite crystal glasses and an amber bottle. She offered the first glassful to Elizabeth who took it hesitantly, peering into the thick, murky liquid.

"Is just wine." Stefan passed a glass to Ann.

"Oh?" Elizabeth held the glass up to the light with a sardonic twist to her mouth.

Stefan offered the next glass to Hilde, but raised his brows at Elizabeth first as if needing her permission.

"Yes. A bit of wine will be fine."

The grandfather raised his glass and, in a beautiful, deep voice, pronounced what appeared to be a grand toast.

Ann wet her upper lip with the wine and then licked. Sweet. Sticky.

Elizabeth sipped as well, then wrinkled her nose. "It's not like any wine I've tasted before."

Stefan looked at her sharply and Ann realized that, in spite of his problems with the language, he was easily offended.

"It's very nice," Ann said quickly. "Did you make it?"

"No." Stefan tossed back the rest of his drink and then pointed across the camp with the empty glass. "Some people there—give to us."

"How kind of them," Elizabeth said dryly.

Ann handed her empty glass to Stefan and spoke before Elizabeth could insult him outright. "Will you play the violin for us again?"

"No. I put away—it away."

"Ah. Well, it is late, I suppose. Thank you for the music and the wine." Ann patted Hilde on the shoulder. "Good night, everyone."

"Yes." Elizabeth handed her half-empty glass to Stefan. "Thank you for the wine."

He took the glass from her with an exaggerated version of his earlier bow that elicited a small chuckle from Elizabeth, this time in fun. The sadness lifted from her face for a few seconds, making her look even younger.

"You will take some vegetables?" Hilde asked. "The beans, they are needing to be picked."

"Vegetables?" Ann asked.

"My mother has a big, big garden," Eva bragged.

"We enjoy vegetables," Elizabeth said.

So Stefan took them to the garden where they filled their pockets with beans.

Ann wandered through the rows, stepped over the onions that bulged from the earth and checked the ears of corn. "Your sister-in-law is a wonderful gardener, Stefan. I've seen some fine gardens at the coast, gardens that provided a living for families of six or eight. Everyone says the soil is good here on the prairie—dry, but good. If you could get water to it . . ."

Elizabeth straightened from the bean vines and dusted her hands against one another. "It's late. We'd better go before it gets too dark."

"I walk with you," Stefan said.

Ann continued to talk about the garden. "This land belongs to the railway, I think."

Stefan nodded. "Was the only place for us when we leave the train. My brother had just died and we had to stop somewhere and this"— he waved his hand—"is where."

"But one day, any day, they can ask you to leave."

"Maybe we are gone by then. Maybe I have enough for a house, somewhere better to live."

"You really should find something before winter. That place is not healthy," Elizabeth said.

She looked at Stefan with her bright, clever eyes and he felt a wave of shame for the way they had to live. He had always thought he could put up with all the ugliness in this barren country as long as no one from their old world saw them living like animals. He had hoped it didn't matter what anyone out here thought.

"I save money," he said stiffly.

Her expression didn't change. "I know."

"Why haven't you taken a homestead, Stefan?" Ann asked, walking on ahead and leaving them together, face to face.

He opened his mouth to answer, but Elizabeth said it for him, "He's not a farmer."

"I am not a farmer," he repeated, looking down at her.

"But Hilde is, isn't she?" Ann's voice trailed back to them. "She didn't learn how to make a beautiful garden like that in just a few weeks."

As they followed her across the field, Stefan had to admit the truth. "Hilde found the garden already started. Someone left it to dry up, when they moved to their own land, maybe."

"But Hilde saved it. Where did she learn to do that?"

"Her family for many, many years have worked the land, but always the landlords take away more—more land and more money for taxes. Same for all the families in our village. When my brother Nick married Hilde and Eva was born, it was too many people for only a little land.

"My father was teacher in the Old Country and at night he made secret classes for our Ukrainian language. Then they caught him and he had no more teaching job. We come here because Nick hears there is free land for everyone. He had big dreams for this country." His voice died away as discouragement overcame him. His own dreams were still back in the Old Country and had nothing at all to do with digging in the soil.

Ann stopped and looked at him with a frown. "But Elizabeth is right. You're not a farmer, you're a musician."

He nodded. "When I am little boy, our priest heard me play piano in the community hall. I had no lessons then, but," he shrugged, "I could remember songs and play them. The priest found ways to get me lessons and then into university in Kiev."

In front of them, the doctor's house reflected the setting sun. The nurse walked faster. "Well, just because *you're* not a farmer doesn't mean Hilde can't have her farm. Women can file too, you know."

Ann stopped when they reached the steps. "They can?"

"Women file?" Stefan looked from one woman to the other.

Elizabeth marched up the steps. "Of course they can. Especially a widow. You can ask at the post office, but I'm quite certain I'm right."

Ann explained carefully. "File is the word used to claim ownership of a homestead. You need a little money, ten or fifteen dollars, I think, and then you have to live on it and take care of it, of course."

"I know what file means. Women can do this?"

The nurse stood in the open door looking down at Stefan. "And why not?"

He shrugged. "I didn't know."

"I'll look into it tomorrow. Then I'll talk to you and Hilde about it. How is that?" Ann asked.

Elizabeth disappeared into the house.

The housekeeper moved to follow. "Good night, Stefan. This is good news, isn't it?"

Stefan took his time walking back to the camp, following the flicker of the campfires through the dusk. He couldn't share any of Ann's excitement or Elizabeth's conviction. Many of the people at the camp talked of having their own homestead one day. And most of them did—moving to an isolated piece of land many kilometres from town and other people. Not for him or his parents, the lonely empty spaces without the noises and movements of other people. But Hilde? Could he let Hilde do such a thing by herself? With a little girl? No. The two women meant well. But it could never be.

FOUR

The next evening Bertha's husband, Pietr Severson, arrived with Ann's red chest and she had to face the fact that her situation had become even more precarious. If Elizabeth found a way to sell her house, Ann would be homeless: the teachers now occupied her room at Bertha's.

She had four days while Elizabeth was in Calgary, days of relative ease, and she decided to enjoy every moment of being alone. From the depths of her trunk, she lifted a black lacquer tin with an inlay depicting peaches and tangled green branches. Longevity.

Downstairs, she pushed the kettle on to boil and arranged a silver tray with a dainty teacup and a sugar cookie. With a half-smile, she pried the lid open on the inlaid tin and brought it to her nose, inhaling deeply. Buckshot tea.

Scooping a generous portion of leaves into the pot, she smothered it with scalding water, watching them swell until they saturated the kitchen with their musty aroma. She checked that the doors were locked and took her tray upstairs.

A light breeze lifted the lace curtains and freshened the guest room with the smell of new-mown hay from somewhere nearby. But the tea—ah, the tea came from the other side of the world.

She leaned back on the embroidered pillows, nibbled at her cookie, savoured her tea and smiled at the little holiday she had created for herself. A book lay unopened on her night table; there were words and tales enough in her mind, strange stories in a carping old voice, the voice itself a big part of the magic.

"What do you think of my little party, Mother?" she asked aloud.

The answer came to her with a snort, as clearly as if it had been spoken at the foot of the bed.

You always too easy to please. I tell you many times, don't be satisfied with so little.

For the next two days Ann scrubbed and washed, dusted and polished, until everything looked and smelled immaculate. Even then, she wandered from room to room, looking for anything that might need attention, until a rap sounded at the door.

Jake Durham was the foreman of one of the railway construction gangs. His words came muffled through nearly closed lips. "Have thith bad toof. Real bad."

"The nurse isn't here today, Jake. She went to Calgary."

His eyes, dull with anguish, dared to meet Ann's. "Not here?"

Ann shook her head. "She'll be back tomorrow afternoon."

"Not here," he repeated, his hand going automatically to his jaw.

His expression was patently easy to read; he'd spent all day building up the courage to have a tooth pulled, and now he would have to suffer another twenty-four hours and work that courage up all over again.

"We have some drops that may help if you'd like to come in and try that?" Ann opened the door and stood back.

He crept into the house, looking all around. Ann took pity on him and pointed to one of the rattan chairs. If he had to go into the treatment room he would faint for sure.

"Wait one minute," she said before going to find the bottle of oil of cloves.

He nodded his head, his cheeks pulled in as he sucked on his tender tooth. When she returned, he opened his mouth obediently for her to swab the broken tooth with a liberal dose of medicine.

"I've put a wad of cotton in there with the drops on it. Leave it in as long as you can. Try to keep your tongue away from it. It's hard, I know, but that just makes it worse."

"Fanks," he mumbled as he stood to leave. Then he poked his hand in his pocket and came up with a fist full of coins. He held them out to Ann and raised his brows. "'Ow muff money?"

"Oh. Money. Ah, well." Ann reached into his palm and took a silver five-cent piece. "That should be enough, thanks. I hope the tincture helps."

Ann looked at his retreating back and then at the coin in her hand. She thought of the pile of wood Stefan had cut for them and an idea began to form in her mind. Maybe there would be a way to stay after all.

Don't be satisfied with so little.

The following afternoon, Ann passed the new schoolhouse where the teachers sat on the brown painted steps, eating sandwiches.

Lydia Turnbull, tall and slender with a dreamy, faraway expression in her pale green eyes, would teach the older children and her partner, Iris Tanner of the round solid appearance and booming voice, would take charge of the little ones.

"Come and see what we've done with our school." Lydia rose and led the way inside.

It was cool and dim and smelled pleasantly of new lumber. The two rooms opened off a central cloakroom with two rows of hooks along the walls. A wooden stand with a water crock, hand basin and slop bucket stood at the far end.

Miss Tanner showed Ann her scant array of double-seated desks made of rough-hewn pine. "We're expecting more any day now."

"I'm meeting the train soon," Ann said. "Why don't you come with me? Your desks may be on it."

The polished bench in the shade of the station was already full, so they had to stand with about a dozen others amongst the cream cans and egg cartons. At last, they heard the faint call of the whistle and saw a slight glint of sun on the silver cowcatcher.

"Here she comes," someone said.

The train appeared about a half mile out of town, making good time as it topped a small rise. It would slow down and turn a bit south, then disappear into a small gully for about two minutes, following a grade that had been dug into the side of a bog.

"It won't be long now," Ann said, sharing the anticipation with everyone else.

You too easy to please.

* * *

Elizabeth felt the train lean into the curve and could see the station in the distance. Her heart sank. She propped her forehead against the window, the tears she had been fighting back all day threatening to embarrass her. The ugly brown plains and stunted aspens passed by outside the window with the same lonesome monotony as the stark telegraph poles. The sun reflected off the still water of a slough that the locals called Brown's Lake. She couldn't understand what possessed Ann to wander these hills in her time off, but wander them she did, returning with bouquets of wild roses or a clump of mint. She appeared to have an obsession with clean houses and even cleaner smells.

Some small corner of her mind had held onto the hope that Mr. Macdonald, like her father in the past, would have all the answers, solve the problems of money and the sale of her house in Aspen Coulee. But he hadn't produced a magic wand. In fact, he had gently informed her that bad business practices were the real reason her father had uprooted them from Ontario. Your father liked nice things, Mr. Macdonald had stated.

Well, didn't everyone?

Mrs. Macdonald had tried to soften the blow. Didn't Elizabeth have someone back home? An uncle or a cousin of the male persuasion, a man to take her under his wing? No? Ah, well then, a suitor perhaps? At the admission that she hadn't really had many suitors, and hadn't encouraged the few who came around, both Mr. Macdonald and his wife had been straightforward with their advice. Sell the house to the highest bidder, take only those things most essential to a frugal existence, and get back to Toronto.

Sell to the highest bidder? In Aspen Coulee? She didn't know whether to laugh or cry.

The train jolted and she smacked her forehead against the window hard enough for her to see stars. A general muttering broke out in the passenger car.

"What's he think he's doing?"

"Did the engineer fall asleep up there in his cab?"

Then came a grinding and the clash of steel on steel. Elizabeth sat up, alert. That didn't sound right.

A gentleman with an important manner heaved himself to his feet and stepped into the aisle. "Conductor!"

"Sit down," Elizabeth said. "You'll be safer sitting."

He drew himself up in a huff. "Now see here, young lady . . ."

He didn't have a chance to finish.

* * *

"Where are they?" Alf Porter stretched up on his toes and looked south. "They should be in sight by now."

"I thought I heard some clanging down that way. We should hear the whistle again by this time," Kenny Hogan, from the livery stable, responded.

All faces stared south. No one spoke again for a moment or two, then an odd grinding and crunching noise drifted toward them. A black burst of crows screeched straight up into the clear sky. People looked at one another with raised brows.

The birds disappeared on the horizon, leaving an eerie calm.

Then mournfully, chilling them all to the bone, the wail of the train's whistle. Not the short, cheerful toots they were waiting for, but a long pitiful call that did not stop.

"My God," Pietr Severson said softly. "It didn't, did it?"

"What, Pietr? What is it?" Ann asked.

But he didn't have to answer. A railroader appeared down the tracks, running and stumbling toward them, waving his hands over his head. "Gone over—derailed—in the slough."

Pietr responded first. "We got a train wreck. Get some men. Round up as many rigs as you can."

* * *

A baby cried and cried. Not the wail of a sick or injured child, but the petulant whining of a baby unattended or unfed, the whimpering punctuated by moans and grunts from all corners of the car. Elizabeth lay perfectly still, her nose filled with the boggy stink of a half-dry slough. It smelled so good she wanted to laugh out loud.

A spot on her scalp about an inch above the hairline and over her left eye stung and a thick stickiness that she recognized as blood oozed down her temple. With painstaking movements, she took inventory of her body, twitching her feet, feeling a deep pain in her knees like the time she had fallen while skating. She realized her skirts were twisted about her waist and reached to pull them down.

She sat up in a rubble of shattered glass and tangled seats. The car lay on its side at a drunken angle with the front end dipping downward into the slough. Mud had been scooped through a broken window and, along with coarse grass and stagnant water, was churned with shards of glass and bits and pieces from burst luggage.

"Freddy?" A white-faced woman crawled toward Elizabeth on her hands and knees. "Have you seen my boy?"

"Mind the glass," Elizabeth said. "There's broken glass everywhere."

A disembodied voice banged on the wall of the car. Only now the wall was the roof. "Get out. Get out before she slides down some more."

Elizabeth pulled herself up on shaky legs and called back. "How? How do we get out?"

The door above her clanged open, exposing clear blue sky that was immediately blocked by the head and shoulders of a big man. "Pass the youngsters up. There's water enough below, could drown the little ones."

Freddy's mother wailed all the more. "Dear God. Drowned. Freddy!"

"Yes. The children." Elizabeth looked for the cranky baby. It sat beside a blood-spattered young woman who appeared stunned and unable to move.

"Get up." She looked the woman right in the eye. "Do you hear me? Can you understand?"

The woman blinked and drew a shaky breath. She stared stupidly back at Elizabeth but didn't speak or move.

"Come on, folks. Get yourselves over here," the voice from up above ordered.

Elizabeth tried to remember how many people there had been, fifteen or sixteen perhaps, including the children. Most of them started to rouse themselves, calling to each other and choking on the oily fumes of kerosene from the broken lamps.

Stepping over a twisted seat, Elizabeth heard grunting through the tinkle of falling glass. She pushed aside a piece of mahogany paneling and saw the man who had been demanding the conductor only minutes before. More footsteps sounded across the top of the car, then a man dropped beside her. Jake, if she remembered correctly.

He bent his knees to look at Elizabeth's head. "You hurt bad, Nurse?"

"I don't think so. There's a missing boy by the name of Freddy and this fellow here appears to need help. Other than that, I'm not sure. There seem to be a lot of cuts."

They heard an ominous sucking sound.

"I think you should get out first," Jake said. "Then I'll get the others moving."

Another head poked through the door. "Need help down there?"

"Yup. I'm going to pass the nurse up to you, then start handin' up the youngsters." He put his hands on Elizabeth's waist. "Pardon me, Miss, but this will be the fastest."

Elizabeth felt herself being lifted as easily as one of the children, then arms from above wrapped around her and she sat with a thud on the top of the wrecked train car, blinking in the sunlight at a crowd of worried faces. She crawled on raw hands and knees around broken windows to the edge of the car and had a brief glance at the terrible mess before more hands reached to help her down.

Ann ran hard for the first time since she had been a very little girl. Her breath wheezed from her lungs and her mouth felt dry and gritty. Men, women and children swept around her, but she managed to keep up with most of them. They topped the knoll above the slough and stopped as one.

Three freight cars had toppled like dominos onto one another and into the slough. Splintered boards and broken cartons were scattered over the bog, along with the new desks for the school. Of the two passenger cars, only one had tipped and now lay on its side.

Ann pressed her hand to her heaving chest, searching for Elizabeth's navy travelling suit. Passengers spilled out of the car that remained upright and milled around the hillside, waved back by several men who appeared to be rescuing people from the fallen car. The locomotive had been unhitched and now sat impotently, ten yards from its battered charges.

Pounding hooves and the clatter of harness brought the first of the wagons, a homesteader with a hayrack. Pietr motioned him forward where he stood over two figures on the ground. Ann glanced at them and then searched again for Elizabeth, but her eyes wandered back to Pietr and the people at his feet. Something was familiar about the small form, sprawled on the ground with her head on the chest of a child. A woman stood over them, wringing her hands.

Ann started forward. "Elizabeth?"

Blood had congealed on Elizabeth's forehead and cheek, and one eye was already swelling shut. More blood and dirt caked her clothes. She pushed her hair back and stared up at Ann with a dazed determination.

"Miss Evans." Miss Turnbull knelt beside her. "You're hurt. Your head is bleeding, and your hands, too."

Elizabeth looked at her knuckles as though they belonged to someone else.

Herbert Schneider arrived, out of breath and genuinely alarmed. He stood with Alf Porter and John Woodside, the stationmaster, staring first at the devastation of the train wreck, then at the bleeding passengers as they staggered up the side of the hill, and finally at Elizabeth Evans, crouched beside the injured child. More men got there, looked from one to the other, then appeared to come to the same conclusion.

Herbert shrugged his shoulders and left it to Alf to approach Elizabeth. "Miss Evans, would it be possible to use the doctor's office for the injured passengers?"

Elizabeth sat back on her haunches, surveying the faces turned her way. "This boy goes first. He's alive, but unconscious. And then the heavy gentleman they just dragged out. Keep them both as still and flat as you can."

Without any further questions, a farmer backed his rig up and the men began gently lifting the two patients onto the hayrack. Freddy's mother climbed aboard and cradled her son's head.

"Elizabeth, wait," Ann said with a light touch to her arm. "You're hurt, too."

But Elizabeth shook the hand off as if it were a fly. She closed her eyes. "Let me think. I'm trying to remember. Once, at the hospital in Ontario, we had a disaster like this. Part of a new store collapsed and about a dozen people were hurt." She opened her eyes and looked intently at Ann. "What other injuries are serious? Who else needs attention?"

Ann turned to Pietr. "Miss Evans won't be able to do it all alone. She will need help."

"I need help," Elizabeth agreed.

"Mr. Woodside has already gone back to the station to send a telegram," Pietr said. "I think the railway will have to send someone."

"But it will be hours before anyone can get here," Ann said. "Look at the tracks. They're all torn up."

Elizabeth tried to stand. Hands reached to help her and hold her until she steadied herself. "Thank you, Jake. Let's get everyone up to the house. Everyone who is hurt in any way. Can you help, Miss Turnbull?"

"Of course." The teacher hoisted herself onto the side of the flatbed and Pietr picked Elizabeth up and set her as carefully as a teacup beside the pale boy.

"Hup."

The team started toward town.

FIVE

In the long hours that followed, Elizabeth wondered if everyone in town and half the people in the province were tramping through her house. Freddy lay, too still, on her davenport, his mother crouched on the floor beside him. The heavy man she had found under the boards had been put, complaining profusely, on the cot in the treatment room. His name, appropriately enough, was Mr. Bedlam, and to the best of Elizabeth's knowledge, he had a broken collarbone.

One by one, the passengers paraded by, dragging the mouldy stink of the bog on their boots. Those with scrapes that needed cleaning and a dab of iodine were passed on to Ann and Miss Turnbull. Elizabeth pushed back a throbbing headache and tried to sort broken bones from sprains and bruises. In the end, she put a young man called Charlie, barely old enough to shave, on her parlour chair with his leg propped on a footstool and pillow. The bad angle of his foot led her to believe his ankle was broken. Once again, women filed into her kitchen with the smells of coffee and spice cake.

Elizabeth arranged an enamel tray with catgut and needles, and put a heap of bandages on her father's desk. She thought of all he had told her and shown her about wounds, especially those on the face. She squinted through her swollen eye and slowly, painstakingly, pressed the ragged edges of skin together before carefully imitating his tiny, perfect stitches to try to lessen the scarring. She willed her hands to be steady, mechanically washing them in carbolic after each patient, wincing as the strong solution bit into her scraped knuckles.

Now and then she asked one of the women to empty the porcelain basin and refill it with fresh, warm water.

By the time the last of the passengers got to the house, darkness had fallen and Ann came in with lamps. Elizabeth left the office now and then to check on the broken limbs and the unconscious child. She said very little, leaving reassurances to the other women who floated in and out of her muddled vision like moths. Her stomach fluttered and she knew that she would have a terrible headache if she stopped to think about it.

At some point during the long night, she thought perhaps she should be keeping an account of the patients, their names or the number of sutures. Her supply of sterile needles had long run out so she disinfected them in carbolic solution for a minute or two because she didn't have the thirty minutes necessary to boil them properly. Her hands turned a dull red.

At last she looked up and saw only Ann, who asked, "Will you eat something?"

Elizabeth shook her head and reached for clean bandages. She blessed her father's overestimate of supplies. "Who's next?"

"That's it. There is no one else. I've never seen so much blood in my life."

Elizabeth looked at the housekeeper's exhausted face and splattered clothes, then around the room. She stood and stretched her aching back and groaned out loud. "The broken windows did most of the damage. Where have you put everyone?"

"They're all around town, wherever we could find room for them. Won't you at least have some tea?"

Elizabeth didn't have the energy to argue. "All right."

She followed Ann into the kitchen and sank into a chair. Bertha handed her a cup of tea and slid a plate of bread and butter toward her. Jake and Stefan came and went, filling the woodbox and water buckets. Herbert Schneider and John Woodside stared grimly at her stained clothes but said nothing.

Her respite was short-lived. Freddy's mother yelled from the parlour. "Nurse!"

Elizabeth saw her own fear reflected in Ann's eyes.

Before they could move, Lydia Turnbull came in with a tired smile. "The little boy has regained consciousness."

Everyone in the kitchen followed Elizabeth into the parlour where she checked the boy herself before collapsing on a chair, near tears with relief. Through the window beside her, dawn, heedless of their ordeal, turned the dark hills to silvery green.

From the treatment room came Mr. Bedlam's quarrelsome voice. "What's all the racket? Where's that goddamn nurse? I need more medicine."

"Oh, be still!" Bertha bellowed back.

At her comment, Elizabeth felt her tears turn to hysterical laughter, then the solid clunk of boots on the front porch stopped the gaiety.

"Now what?" Elizabeth asked the room in general.

"What now?" Ann repeated. The nurse's battered face shone sickly pale in the thin light of early morning. How much more could this pampered little girl take, Ann wondered.

Before she could open it, the door swung in and a man entered from the hallway.

He was tall—as tall as Jake—but lean and lanky. He pulled a sloppy felt Stetson from his copper-coloured hair with one hand and a grubby white canvas bag from his shoulder with the other. The blue trousers with yellow stripes and the dusty scarlet coat told everyone in the room that the help Elizabeth so desperately needed had arrived.

With the lilt of the Highlands in his voice, he said, "I'm told ye're in need o' a doctor here."

Elizabeth struggled up from her chair and went to meet him. "Oh, Dr. McRae. I'm so glad you're here."

He stood looking down at her from his great height. "Aye, lass, I'm here. And I'm sorry fer the loss o' yer father. But just look at ye. Dinna no one ever teach ye proper? Ye have tae take care o' the nurse, afore ye can take care o' the patients."

Elizabeth's frame sagged. Her eyes filled with tears and her chin began to tremble. Lydia, blowing out lamps, stood frozen to the spot.

Ann could scarcely believe her ears. She stepped quickly between Elizabeth and Dr. McRae. "Now see here, you have absolutely no right to speak to her like that." She jabbed a finger into his chest and had the satisfaction of seeing his sleepy eyes widen. "You don't know what Elizabeth has been through tonight. I won't allow you to speak to her like that. I just won't allow it. Do you understand?"

Absolute quiet settled over the house as Ann stared the doctor down. His mouth seemed to twitch a little, but under such a long shaggy moustache, who could tell for sure? From the corner of her eye, Ann saw Bertha and Lydia steal back into the kitchen.

Then a scream rang out. Everyone jumped except, Ann noted, the laconic Dr. McRae. She left him where he stood and raced into the kitchen. "Heavens to Betsy! Now what? Lydia, have you hurt . . . ?"

Two steps into the kitchen, she stopped short with Jake and Elizabeth piled up behind her. Lydia stood with her backside pressed to the chrome bumper on the range, one hand clutched to her bosom. Squatting on the floor, looking baffled and terribly put upon, were three half-naked Indians. They filled the kitchen with the smells of wood smoke and horse sweat.

"I've told ye before, Horse Child, ye need tae knock at a white woman's door. They're sore touchy 'bout things like that."

Ann turned to glare at the doctor where he lounged against the doorframe. No doubt about it, he was having a private little laugh at their expense.

He raised his bushy brows at her filthy look. "They're my men. I sent them 'round back tae put our horses in the wee stable. We've been out west wi' their chief for nigh three days and nights now—congestive heart—then a rider came with word from the railway. They rode with me all night."

Ann took a closer look at the strain on the man's face. She should have been able to recognize exhaustion by now. Maybe a small conciliatory gesture would be in order.

She turned back to the men on the floor. "Why don't you sit up and let Bertha get you something to eat? Some coffee? Bertha, what do we have to feed them?" Bertha was the last woman in the country to swoon over a couple of Indians with bare bellies.

"Oh, biscuits are easy. And some scrambled eggs? I'll get something right away."

Ann nodded wearily, but the three Indians stayed on the floor and looked up at her with their hurt brown faces. "With jam?" she asked them desperately.

The one called Horse Child grunted.

One of the others spoke in injured tones. "Even left our pants on, this time. Hot in these houses. Left our pants on like the sergeant said and still white womans scream at us."

Jake chuckled. Ann twirled round and glared at him. Elizabeth smiled crookedly. Over the nurse's head, Ann saw Dr. McRae watching her and the lines around his eyes creased a little more. All her righteous fury came boiling back.

She turned back to point at the Indians, then slammed her open palm on the table. "Sit up to the table! I don't have the time or the patience to pamper the childish feelings of grown men. Let Bertha move around the kitchen so she can get you some food. And keep your damn pants on!"

Jake burst out laughing so she aimed a finger at him. "You. Stay here. I don't want to hear any more screaming from this kitchen. Is that understood?"

The Indians got up and sat at the table, their backs as straight as arrows. The tallest of the lot, the one with long dusty braids and smears of rust-coloured mud on his bare chest, grunted at length in a characteristic monotone.

Horse Child interpreted for Ann. "Shot-On-Both-Sides, he think you fine, big white woman. He thinks you talk bad, sometimes, maybe, but he don't beat you much for that. He has many horses. Can pay good price for woman. Fine-looking white woman." He nodded his head up and down emphatically but Ann was sure she saw the same infuriating twinkle in his black eyes as she had seen in the doctor's.

Not one person in the kitchen moved so much as an eyelash. Even the big grin on Jake's face disappeared. Ann sucked in her breath and without a glance at anyone, turned to stalk from the room. Dr. McRae pried himself out of the way so she could pass.

Elizabeth didn't dare look Lydia in the eye, never mind Jake, for fear of laughing. It was just about the most outrageous scene she had ever witnessed. She wanted to pinch herself to see if she was awake, but her headache reminded her of that. "Dr. McRae, if you could look at Freddy for me? He was unconscious for hours and I'm sure he has a concussion at the very least. And Mr. Bedlam . . ."

"Bedlam?"

She led the way. "He's the clavicle in the treatment room. And that really is his name."

"And this lad?" He stood over Charlie.

Elizabeth looked up at the doctor hesitantly. "A fractured tibia?"

He didn't even look at poor Charlie's ankle, just stared down at her instead. She must have done something wrong. Probably everything.

"Your daddy had an office, I believe?"

"Uh, yes, of course. I d-didn't use it for Charlie, I had so many s-sutures, you see."

"Sutures, now is it, lass?"

"Y-yes. There was broken g-glass everywhere."

He took her by the shoulders and nudged her ahead of him. "Let's get ye into the office."

Ann followed close on their heels. Dr. McRae stood in the middle of the office and looked at the mess of bloody lint that overflowed the wastebasket and lay scattered around the floor. He swept the clutter from her father's desk onto the floor, and plunked his bag on one corner. He turned to Elizabeth, shaking his head, then picked her up and set her on the other corner.

A tear plopped loose from her swollen eye and trickled down her cheek. "Would p-people please stop p-picking me up?"

For some reason, that got a smile from Dr. McRae and she recognized the quiet, funny man she had met last Christmas.

"Ach, child, would ye shut yer wee gob now?" He took her face between his long hands and parted her hair where it had been bleeding earlier.

She flinched. "Ouch."

"I'd be grateful if ye dinna yell too loud, lass." He tilted his head at Ann who stood close by, watching every move he made. "Yer broody hen here dinna take well tae screamin', now does she?"

Elizabeth sagged with relief. She didn't have to do it all anymore; in fact she didn't have to do anything but sit here and let someone else take care of things. She glanced at Ann to see how she had taken the remark, and saw grim determination and not one bit of humour on her face.

"Maybe someone could get me some warm water?" Dr. McRae asked no one in particular. Ann exited in a swirl of skirts. He chatted pleasantly as he waited to wash his hands. "And the pet rooster ye have in yer henhouse, the big one in the kitchen called Jake, he might take offence too, dinna ye think?"

Elizabeth smiled back as Ann returned promptly with the water. Her housekeeper was evidently prepared to think only the worst of the police doctor and his half-naked Indians. Elizabeth wished she weren't so tired and sick; she could enjoy it all more. "I don't have any roosters."

"I'm sorry tae hear that, I surely am. I'm going tae have tae sew up that wound on yer head. It's a deep one."

"I don't know if there are any needles left."

He opened his canvas bag and took out a clean dressing case. "I carry m'own surgery with me."

She heaved a sigh. "I was afraid you might."

Next he flashed a pair of scissors. "And I'll have tae cut a bit from those lovely long locks."

Tears welled again. "Are you sure?"

"Let him do what he needs to," Ann said quietly near her elbow. "It will grow out in no time. You'll see."

Dr. McRae waggled his brows at Elizabeth. "There now. Could ye get a finer recommendation than that?"

Ann snorted.

Elizabeth thought it might be time for these two to meet. "This is Mrs. Montgomery. She's our, that is, my housekeeper."

"Maybe she could find me some antiseptic and clean lint?"

Elizabeth gritted her teeth while Dr. McRae put eight tiny stitches into her head. Then he reached into his bag and drew out a murky blue bottle with a dropper. "Open wide."

Elizabeth pressed her palm against the medicine. "Oh. That reminds me. I need to talk to you about Mrs. Weyman. She has a tumour. I've been giving her a sedative, but I don't know if the dosage is correct."

Dr. McRae heaved a deep, exasperated sigh and removed her hand from the dropper. Still looking at Elizabeth, he said, "Mrs. Montgomery?"

"Take the drops, Elizabeth. You can talk to Dr. McRae about your patients later."

She opened her mouth and took the opiate on the back of her tongue.

"Now then," the doctor said, looking directly at Ann. "I want you tae get our wee Nightingale tae her bed afore that draught takes hold, tuck her up in her nest and keep her there for two or three days. Would ye see tae that for me?"

When she returned to the confusion downstairs, Ann found the doctor kneeling on the floor by Freddy, talking in his quiet way to the mother. "He should stay here for two or three days. Let the ladies take care o' both of ye."

"But I should get home," the woman fretted.

"I dinna think the trains will be running for a time anyway."

Next he went to the dining room where he flattened his palms on the middle of the beautiful oak table and shifted his weight forward. He gripped the edge and shook it, then nodded his head.

"T'will do. D'ye think we could find a blanket or two?"

"I can," Bertha said, but looked at Ann for permission.

"Of course, Bertha. Give him what he needs," Ann said. "On the top shelf in the washroom."

"Let's get you settled first, lad," the doctor said to Charlie.

Horse Child took a lamp and a dirty cup off the table and handed them to Lydia without a word, then crumpled the lace tablecloth into a ball and dropped it on the floor. He folded the blankets in half and spread them lengthwise, one atop the other, on the table.

The doctor nodded at Horse Child and, as carefully as they could, they lifted Charlie under the arms and knees and put him on the table. The boy's eyes filled with tears and his bottom lip started to bobble.

"We have chloroform, Doctor," Ann suggested, "and a proper applicator, but I've never been called upon to use it."

"Horse Child, would ye get the chloroform that Mrs. Montgomery so kindly offers? Horse Child has been my assistant for four years now. He's given more chloroform and helped set as many bones as I have. Well, nearly." The doctor tossed his coat in the direction of a chair and rolled the sleeves of his combinations up past his elbows before opening the dining-room window as wide as it would go. "Let's have some air afore you open that canister, Horse Child." he said. "Tired as we are, we'll be asleep afore the lad."

In no time Charlie was asleep, his trousers removed and the leg of his drawers cut up to the knee. Ann didn't flinch until the grating crunch of bones being moved back into place made her a little light-headed.

"Bertha, would you go to the kitchen and ask Jake to bring a folding cot from the stable, please? It's up in the rafters. We'll put Charlie in near Freddy."

As Ann helped Dr. McRae prepare the table for their next patient, she realized a few things about him. She determined, for instance, that in spite of first appearances, the man possessed an abundance of charm which he spread around indiscriminately and his hands on his patients were as steady and true as Dr. Evans's had been.

He didn't need to waste his charm on Horse Child. The two men worked as a team, the Indian's face impassive, his eyes half closed. And yet he knew when the doctor wanted a splint or a roll of gauze without ever having to be asked, and when they were finished, he rolled Charlie in the top blanket and carried him like a babe to the cot in the parlour without so much as a nod from the doctor.

"Where's Jake?" Dr. McRae asked. "We need him tae help move Bedlam."

Ann turned to leave. "I'll get him."

She blinked at the bright sunlight and the crowd of people in the kitchen. The other two Indians had gone back to their people, Jake told her. He sat at the table with Lydia, and—here her mind balked—Beatrice Schneider. Iris stuffed wood into the range.

"Quite a few people have been by to help," Lydia said.

Beatrice nodded vigorously, her usual morose expression replaced by a brightness that looked almost feverish.

In a couple of days Ann would speculate with Elizabeth about the unpredictable Beatrice's motives for turning up to lend a hand. For now, she said in all honesty, "I'm happy to see you. We can really use your help. Now, Bertha and Lydia can go home to bed."

"What shall we do?" Iris brushed her hands together.

"Well, first of all, Jake, the doctor needs you to help move Mr. Bedlam. When he is cared for, I think it will just be a matter of keeping an eye on everyone."

The women nodded, looking serious and important, so Ann left them and went back to the dining room where Horse Child, Jake and Dr. McRae struggled with Mr. Bedlam.

They had saved the worst for last. Bedlam was obstructive and belligerent and by the time Horse Child had manoeuvred the chrome mask of chloroform over the man's nose, the others were sweaty and short-tempered. When they were finished, Ann had Jake carry hot water upstairs to the room that had been Dr. Evans's.

Dr. McRae watched her as he rolled his sleeves down. "You've near got all yer chicks put away now, haven't ye?"

She was too tired to be baited, if that was what he was trying to do. "Yes I do. I even have a bed upstairs for you, Doctor, and I can find another cot for Horse Child, if he would like that."

"Horse Child hates tae sleep indoors. Except for the dead o' winter, and even then he'd rather not. Nay, he'll bed down in the barn. I, however, would enjoy a soft bed and pillow."

"Just up the stairs and . . ."

"I know m'own way tae bed."

"Very well," Ann snapped, and went to the kitchen to see if there was a drop of warm water left for herself. She started upstairs and tripped on the last step, slopping some of her water. She had heard the expression, "Too tired to pick up my feet," and now she knew the truth of it. Eyes on her jug, she went into her room and was halfway across the floor before she stopped dead still.

Dr. McRae stood by her bed, his suspenders hanging around his thighs and his combinations peeled down over his waist. In the palm of his hand he held her lacquered tea tin. He looked at Ann, then the tin, and then at Ann again.

"I've come tae the wrong room, have I not?" He held the tea up and raised his eyebrows at her, then glanced around the bedroom. "I felt sure I slept in this room when I was here last."

Ann nodded. "You probably did. I've been staying with Elizabeth and using this room."

He turned the tea tin over in his hand once more and then set it back on the nightstand and looked at her wearily.

"I thought you could sleep in Dr. Evans's room. Do you mind?"

"O'course not."

Ann set her water on the washstand. "I'll show you the way."

He picked up his coat and followed her into the front bedroom. She crossed to close the heavy draperies against the sun and heard his boots hit the floor.

"There's water for you, too," she said, but the only answer she got was the creak of bed springs and a heartfelt sigh. Pulling the door closed behind her, she heard the unmistakable sound of a quiet, even snore.

SIX

Ann woke into full awareness, alert to a house full of activity, and scrubbed at the grit in her eyes with her knuckles. At first she wondered if she had slept at all, but the angle of light under the curtain told her it was suppertime. Her shoulders ached and her feet hurt. She got up anyway.

With little thought, she washed in cold water and searched for clean clothes amongst the few she owned that would be appropriate. She had to settle for a dove-grey walking skirt and a white shirt-waist that had more tucks and lace than she would have liked. She peeked in on Elizabeth, who remained sound asleep, then tiptoed downstairs so she wouldn't waken the doctor. No need. Dr. McRae sat at the kitchen table with Horse Child, eating soup and charming Beatrice Schneider. Beatrice, breaking bread with an Indian? Maybe, Ann thought, I'm still asleep after all.

"Mrs. Montgomery, you should have stayed in bed," Beatrice chirped, squirming on her chair. "Miss Tanner and I have everything in hand. Don't we, Iris?"

Above Beatrice's head, Iris Tanner rolled her eyes at Ann. Iris appeared to have learned that it was harder to put up with Beatrice's good days than her dark ones.

Ann went to the east window and pulled the curtain aside. "Daisy, too? Has Daisy been cared for?"

"Daisy? Who's Daisy?" The alarm on Beatrice's face was a reflection of what it cost her to admit she didn't know everything.

"The horse."

Horse Child spoke in his deep slurred voice, sounding half asleep. "I took care of the horse."

Ann studied the homely bronze face and liked what she saw. "Thank you. Sometimes I forget her. She deserves better and certainly needs more exercise."

Beatrice's shrill voice interrupted her. "There, you see. All taken care of, just like I said."

"Have some soup and tea," Iris said. "And Mrs. Nelson brought a nice fruit cake."

Absently, Ann answered, "In a minute." She walked through the dining room, stopping to pick up the crumpled tablecloth. In the office, her shoulders sagged. Where to begin? She fingered the bandages still in the cabinet, counting the new ones, subtracting from what she knew had been there two days ago. "I have an inventory here somewhere," she muttered to herself.

She turned to find Dr. McRae watching her. "A disaster o' this size uses a lot o' supplies. Like war."

"Or an earthquake," Ann said.

They assessed one another for a moment before the doctor spoke. "We have tae be going now. I've written notes for Elizabeth in the book, there. No' that she'll need them. She's a bright wee thing. If ye need me, I've told the big lad, Jake, where tae find me. The railway will let him leave his work tae fetch me. 'Tis their mess after all."

"You're leaving? But Elizabeth has a patient, Mrs. Weyman, who is in a very bad way. They live out of town. Elizabeth sent a letter to find you, in fact, to see if you could come and advise her."

"How far?"

"Oh, it's only a mile, just east of us," she assured him. "Not far at all."

Ann watched a frown work its way across his sunburnt brow, saw him pondering his obligations and knew that his first priority lay with the North West Mounted Police.

"Verra well, then. We'll saddle up that wee mare and give her the exercise ye say she needs. Ye can ride out with me an' show me the way." He slung his bag over his shoulder and went out, calling to Horse Child to help saddle up.

Ann approached Daisy with a forced smile and a few soothing words, knowing she had to do this for Elizabeth and hoping she wouldn't embarrass herself too much. She lifted her left foot to the stirrup and found herself boosted into the saddle by Horse Child's shoulder. She landed with an unladylike grunt and Daisy stepped out to catch up with the doctor and his shaggy pinto. Ann grabbed the reins and the saddle horn at the same time.

Tugging at her skirts, she tried to stay behind the two men so they wouldn't see her knees shaking. The wind lifted Daisy's mane and loosened her own hair, but she wasn't about to take her hand off the saddle horn to tuck it up again. She looked at Dr. McRae and Horse Child, slumped in their saddles, their hands resting slackly on their thighs.

Dr. McRae turned easily. "Ye're the guide, Mrs. Montgomery. Lead on, if ye please."

She gave a stiff nod and let Daisy trip past the two Indian ponies, following a path that cut through the grove behind the barn and away from the back of the house. They followed a well-used trail for about ten minutes, then crossed a field of stooked grain and entered a clearing through a thicket of rustling poplar and a half dozen spindly fir trees.

The Weyman homestead, weathered by a decade of wind and sun and cold, had wormed its way into the undergrowth like blight. Hogs wandered at will through the trampled scrub where a gangly youth whacked at the brush and the pigs indiscriminately, trying to get the animals into a pen for the night. He stopped when he saw them, his arm raised and jaw hanging, gaping at the policeman and the Indian.

"Hello, Boyd," Ann called.

The boy dropped his stick and pelted into the house. "Pa! Pa!"

"He's quite backward," Ann explained to the men.

Orville Weyman came out of the house looking every bit as stunned as his son. Ann couldn't find an excuse this time, so she just looked at the doctor with a shrug.

"Aye. We cause some discomfort wherever we go, Horse Child and I."

They dismounted in front of the homesteader. Boyd scuttled in and out of the house, sidling up behind his father and squinting at them through his crossed eyes.

"Mr. Weyman, Dr. McRae has come to Aspen Coulee to see to the people who were in the train crash."

Orville Weyman shuffled his feet and swatted at a fly, never taking his eyes from the two men.

"You heard there has been an accident?"

He nodded. Boyd grinned and aped his father's nod.

"Miss Evans wanted to have a doctor come to see Mrs. Weyman. That's why we're here."

"Uh, well, I don't know, you see," he paused with a sidelong glance at Dr. McRae, "I don't have the, uh, that is, I never really paid Dr. Evans. Nor Miss Evans, neither."

"Oh." Ann realized she had put everyone in a difficult position. She knew the Weymans paid in kind, like most of the doctor's patients, but Dr. McRae would probably expect real money. She brushed a swarm of sticky flies from her face and wondered what to do next.

Dr. McRae handed his reins to Horse Child and untied his saddlebag. "I get paid by the government. If you want me tae see yer wife I will. Otherwise we have tae be on our way."

"I suppose, then." Orville turned and moved toward the door. "She does enjoy seeing the nurse now and then."

Ann managed to slide from the saddle and led Dr. McRae toward the door. Horse Child took Daisy's reins and wandered off to where a few blades of grass had survived.

The cabin had soaked up the day's heat, and the smell of illness hit Ann with a physical force as she stumbled over a cat that screeched past her ankles. They stood in one room where a canvas partition, the remains of an old tent by the look of it, separated a double bed and a jumble of clothes from the rest of the house. In front of Ann, a cook stove sat on a piece of tin that had grown fuzzy with grease and dirt. They picked their way around a cupboard of sorts, made from old packing boxes, that held a few dishes and cutlery, then past a table with two chairs and a stool. "Good evening, Mrs. Weyman." Ann approached the shrunken woman who reclined on a metal cot that had been pushed under the only window. A pint jar with yellowed water and three sagging tiger lilies balanced on the bare sill. "This is Dr. McRae."

The woman looked in alarm at her husband, then at Ann. The corners of her sunken eyes were crusted with rheum and her yellowed skin stretched dry and shiny over her bones. Her lips quivered. "I don't understand. Orville?"

"The nurse sent him, that's all." He patted her hand awkwardly.

Ann squatted by the bed. "Would you mind letting him see you? The rest of us can step outside if you like."

She took Ann's hand in both of her own. "Will you stay?" she whispered. "Miss Evans always stayed."

Good Lord, no, Ann thought, but what could she do? Orville pushed his son out the door ahead of him.

With few words, Dr. McRae probed the woman's abdomen, looked at her eyes and took her pulse. In the end, the examination was over very quickly.

They left the yard on the trot, relieved to be back in the open air. Ann watched the doctor's profile as she tried not to bounce out of her saddle. "Thank you for coming. I guess there wasn't much point, except Elizabeth needs advice on the amount of narcotics that should be given." When he didn't answer, she went on lamely. "I'm sorry to have wasted your time."

He reined in his horse so they rode side by side. "I've more time than she does. I can advise Elizabeth but . . ."

"But?"

"But it's a terrible place for a woman tae die, dinna ye think?"

In the distance a dusty sunset hung behind the silhouette of the town. The Evans house stood removed on its knoll with a look of permanence, while the rest of the settlement smudged into the poplars, disappearing back into the ancient hills.

Taking a deep breath, Ann cleared her head with the spice of sage and wolf willow gone to seed. "Yes. They don't really want Elizabeth to come. It's the question of money, as you saw. But she goes anyway. How could she not?"

The doctor grunted what could have been agreement.

"They pay with meat sometimes. Bacon or salt pork. I'm afraid Elizabeth isn't very, uh, consistent, in her business dealings."

"But you are."

"Someone has to be," she responded. "I should have known Orville Weyman wouldn't want to part with any money. They were one of the first families into the area and they've done well, but he is known to be very close. I'm sorry about that, too."

"Money has never been o' much concern tae me."

Ann didn't need to look at him to know the words rang true, but she did anyway.

His hat concealed his eyes. "I do get paid by the government, ye know."

But not much, if I know anything about governments, she thought. As they drew closer to the town, they watched the plodding approach of four riders following the tracks from the south.

"And where did ye learn tae manage money, Mrs. Montgomery? From Mr. Montgomery, perhaps? Or a sensible girls' school back East?"

"I'm a widow. I'm from the West—San Francisco—and I learned to pay attention to money in the way many people do, by virtue of never having any of my own."

"Ah, San Francisco. Earthquakes and buckshot tea."

She glanced quickly at his profile, but his attention seemed to be fixed on the four riders who had passed the church and were moving steadily toward the front of the Evans house.

Dr. McRae raised his hand in a casual salute and slowed his horse. Daisy stalled beside him. He turned sideways in his saddle and faced Ann straight on, his features a map of shadows and planes in the fading light. "Buckshot tea is an acquired taste, don't ye agree, Mrs. Montgomery? Wouldn't ye admit, the first time ye sipped it, ye thought someone was playing a nasty joke?"

"The first time I drank buckshot tea," she answered, "I was so fascinated by the tapestries on the wall, the embroidered silk cushions, the incense and God knows what else floating in the air like spirits from another world that I had finished two cups before I even realized how vile it tasted."

His burst of laughter was deep and warm and genuine. He leaned back in his saddle, arms crossed on his chest, regarding her for some minutes before speaking again. "Tell me about your earthquake, Mrs. Montgomery."

"I think the newspapers covered the facts quite well. But actually being in the midst of it"—she paused to take a deep breath—"I'm not sure there is any way of describing that. Like our situation here, there were many, many injuries from broken glass and flying objects."

He sat still, watching her.

"But the fire," she went on quietly, "The fire took a greater toll. It burned for three days and nights, the air was thick with smoke and ashes—and fear. Mothers screaming for their children . . ." Her voice trailed off.

He shifted in his saddle and waited for more.

She glanced his way and shook her head, unable to continue, not willing to relive the nightmare of being driven, with thousands of Chinese, from one part of the city to another, from the waterfront to Nob Hill and back again. They were cast out—no, beaten out—of every neighbourhood, every park and open space, with no chance to pause or rest or think what to do next.

"Nae need tae go on." He turned his attention toward the Evans house. "I know these gents here, particularly the fellow in the too-tight waistcoat. He's my secondary employer, if ye will. The Force contracts my services tae the railway, if by chance I don't have enough tae do. Worker injuries for the most part, a bit o' typhoid in the spring. My biggest obligation right now is tae the Indian tribes along the foothills and that commitment is as much political as it is medical.

"These men will be here tae see tae their precious train and tae make sure the passengers have everything they need. For yer future reference, the usual rate for a nurse is about ten dollars a week, an' that's when she goes tae the patient's house. Ye have three patients and ye'll be giving them room and board."

They approached the back of the house as the railway men entered the front. "And," he went on, "dinna forget tae have them replace yer supplies. All o' them."

In the waning light, Ann gave him a grateful, "Thank you very much."

He tied his horse to the back porch. "I'll let them know that all the passengers should survive, and then I'll go see how our wee nurse is doin'."

"Thank you for that, too," Ann said as she turned her horse toward the stable.

Daisy walked straight into her stall. Ann slid to the ground, feeling childishly proud of her outing, hung the saddle over a railing and flopped the bridle atop it, then gave the mare a pat on the rump. Rubbing her own backside, she took the time to scoop some oats into the manger and check to see that there was water in the trough.

In the kitchen, Beatrice Schneider sat with bright red spots on each cheek as though she had a fever, all traces of her silly smirk gone. Across from her, his thick thighs spread, sat her husband. Ann was hungry and tired and had little patience for either Schneider. She heard Iris Tanner in the parlour and went to join her.

The teacher sat on the end of the sofa at Freddy's feet, reading from Elizabeth's copy of *Huckleberry Finn*. Watching with great interest were the four executives, including the man in the too-tight vest who introduced himself as Gordon Parker. Ann tried to decipher what emotions played behind their eyes and decided in favour of relief.

"Mrs. Montgomery, I presume," Mr. Parker said. "I've been hearing very good things about you and the young nurse from Dr. McRae."

"Yes, well," Ann said, "we're happy to have been of assistance, of course." She considered her choice of words. "But a disaster of this proportion uses a great deal of supplies."

"The doctor mentioned that as well. Would I be remiss in asking for an invoice, Madam? We'll be here for two or three days. My associates will have to look at the tracks and assess the damaged goods. If you could get it to me, say, the day after tomorrow?"

"I'm sure we can have something for you before you leave. Have you found a place to stay?" she asked.

"We brought a caboose with us to the other side of the, uh, mishap, so we'll stay there and do our own batching, as they say. Always do.

We're just renting the horses so as to get around town easier. Kind of you to concern yourself, though."

"Well, I believe there is some coffee and cake in the kitchen. You're most welcome to sit a while."

"That sounds real nice. Thank you."

She showed them into the kitchen but before they had eased into their chairs, Herbert Schneider introduced himself as the proprietor of the *railway* hotel, apologizing over and over that it wasn't ready for them.

So it was true what she had heard, Ann realized. The railway was willing to back local businessmen in order to have hotels built in the towns of their choosing. Lucky for Aspen Coulee. Lucky for Herbert Schneider.

Dr. McRae came through the kitchen with his saddlebag over his shoulder. "Horse Child and I will be goin' now."

"Now? In the middle of the night?"

"Aye. Ye can send someone to fetch me if ye have need. Isn't that right, Mr. Parker?"

"Well, of course, if necessary . . ."

Ann followed the doctor onto the back porch. "Is Elizabeth . . . ?"

"Elizabeth will be better for a day or two in bed, if ye can manage that. She's made o' good stuff."

Ann leaned her shoulder against the pillar. Fireflies danced in the woodpile. "Yes. The town is lucky to have her here."

"And she's lucky tae have you," he said before the night swallowed him up.

* * *

They managed to keep Elizabeth in bed until noon the next day when she limped down the stairs, her eye black and purple, a crooked bald patch beside her widow's peak. It occurred to Ann that Dr. McRae might be an excellent doctor, but he wasn't much of a barber.

One by one, throughout the day, their reinforcements dropped away. The teachers needed to clean the bog from the students' desks and prepare for the start of school on Monday. Bertha helped get most of the laundry on the line, then had to rush home to cook for her lodgers.

By the time they had fed their patients and washed the dishes that evening, Elizabeth collapsed on a hard kitchen chair, her face drained of colour.

Jake stuck his broad face in the back door. "I'm finished my job for the day. Anything need doing here?"

"As a matter of fact, Jake, I have two requests. I wonder if I could get you to carry some things upstairs for me? But first," Ann said, "I think we need to take care of that tooth for you."

An hour later, the open foyer at the top of the stairs had been turned into a comfortable sitting room, with the deep cosy chair and matching stool from the parlour. Ann brought a small oak table up and put a pink-and-green globe lamp on the sewing machine where it spread a warm light.

"When things are quiet we'll have a private place to sit, since we've lost our parlour for a while. I gave the little silver dinner bell to Mr. Bedlam, and Charlie can just call if he or Freddy need anything. What do you think?" Ann looked from Elizabeth to Jake.

"Looks nice," Jake said with his hand to his jaw. "Kin I go now?"

Elizabeth dropped into the chair and flopped her feet on the stool with a deep sigh. "Away you go, Jake. Leave the dressing in as long as possible and then tomorrow you can rinse with warm salt water. And take one of the tablets I gave you as soon as you get home."

SEVEN

On Sunday morning Stefan took his family for a stroll to see the site of the train crash, dawdling over the trampled grass so Hilde would not tire. The air was cool and he dreaded the coming winter, which everyone said could be "a killer." The question of a decent place for them to live still plagued him.

On the hillside above the wrecked train, they sat near another group that had come to watch, the children playing and venturing as close to the tangled steel as they dared before the emergency workmen shouted at them. Stefan leaned back on his elbows, a blade of grass between his teeth.

His father ventured a question in their own language. "What will they do with the broken ones? Will they use the wood and steel again or will it just be thrown away?"

If his father would only go to town now and then, try to talk to a few people, Stefan thought. Such a clever man and now he was confused and afraid of everything. Stefan felt a deep sadness to see him like this.

"I don't know, Papa. I don't think they know themselves." He pointed to the passenger car that had been put right side up. "That car I suspect they can fix and use again. It would be the most expensive one, too, don't you think? With all the windows and things?"

"Dirty foreigners. Won't even try to talk our lingo."

Stefan glanced over his shoulder to see who had spoken, but no one looked their way. He spat the grass onto the ground and stood up, not sure if he was ashamed or angry. He should be used to the cruel things people said, but he wasn't, and he had less and less patience for the lethargy his parents had sunk into, for the futility of their lives. Knowing full well they would be anxious without him, he stalked down the hill, past teams of horses and groups of people in their Sunday best.

Jake sat on a wooden keg, drinking water from a galvanized dipper. He offered it to Stefan. It tasted warm and stale, but he drank anyway because Jake accepted him enough to drink from the same dipper.

Wiping his mouth on the back of his hand, he pretended interest in order to make conversation. "We sit up there and think, what you will do with broken cars?"

"Well, they tell us they can salvage the passenger car and two of the boxcars. The other boxcar will be abandoned, I guess. They'll take the steel off it. Too bad, too. Fine lumber—treated and painted. It would make a good farm building of some kind." Jake stood and stretched. "We can't waste our time on boxcars now, anyway. We have to hurry to get the track fixed an' we're breaking the law by working on Sunday to do it."

Stefan looked at the toppled boxcar. Some boards were broken, the door hung off the side and a mess from torn bags of flour and packages of squashed prunes lay around. But the floor was solid and the roof was intact.

He hurried after Jake. "What does that mean? Abandoned?"

Jake shrugged. "Just left behind. It's on railway property, so maybe someone will come and clean it up some day. I don't know."

"They would let me? Like the trees?"

Jake hoisted a sixteen-pound sledgehammer without so much as a grunt. "Let you what?"

"Clean it up? I clean it up, I keep it?"

Jake rested the hammer on his shoulder and looked directly at him. "Could be. I can ask. You want it?"

Stefan felt something like the weight of the hammer lift from his chest. He didn't know the first thing about how he would do it, but he nodded. "I want it."

* * *

A crew, including a handful of pig-tailed Chinese, left over from a bygone era and looking too slight for such heavy work, had come into town to fix the tracks. Like everyone else, Ann took a few minutes to watch them work, but unlike the others, she was happy to keep her distance. She tried without success to recognize something familiar in the closed faces and downcast eyes of the men in colourless, loose cotton clothes but a great deal had transpired in the past year and a half.

In four days they had the train running. On the fifth day, Freddy and his mother took grateful leave of the nurse and Aspen Coulee. Ann threw the doors and windows open and set Charlie on the back porch to labour through the last few pages of *Huckleberry Finn* by himself. She cleaned and polished the dining-room table but the bloodstains on the wooden floor of the front hall were impossible to scrub up.

Sheets and towels whipped on the clothesline; an old hen stewed on the back of the stove. When Elizabeth came through the front door just before supper, she raised her voice over the whir of the carpet sweeper. "You have mail."

Ann put the large red envelope in her apron pocket and continued sweeping.

By the time the women took their tea and mail upstairs, the sun had slid behind the horizon and Ann needed to light the lamp. Across from her, in the stuffed chair, Elizabeth bent her head over the handful of mail.

"There is an envelope from the Canadian Pacific Railway." Her bruises had faded to small mauve smudges, like crushed wood violets, in the inner corners of her eyes, and there was a purple cross-hatch of lines where she had plucked the stitches out of her scalp while Ann watched and cringed.

Elizabeth pressed a slim piece of blue paper to her chest. "It's a cheque, made payable to me for—can you believe it? Forty-six dollars!"

Ann felt an easing of tension in her neck. She rested her head on the curved wooden back of the rocking chair.

"That's a decent amount of money, isn't it?" Elizabeth asked.

Ann nodded.

"I wonder if Father ever made this much real money in, I don't know, weeks and weeks." She turned the cheque over and over. "It won't be enough to get me out of here, though, will it?"

"No."

Elizabeth sagged in the chair. "Whatever will I do? I can't stay here. I won't stay here!"

"Have you considered . . ." Ann began, not sure her suggestion would be well received, knowing full well that she was thinking more of herself than of Elizabeth.

"Considered what?"

"Well, considered the fact that you have a valuable service to offer the people here, that you could stay and . . ."

"Stay? Here?"

"Just through the winter," Ann hurried to say. "Or until someone who can afford to buy your house arrives in town." She lowered her voice and pointed downstairs in the general direction of Mr. Bedlam. "Like a bank manager? We need to make an effort to have Mr. Bedlam leave us, and the town, with a pleasant impression—or at least as pleasant as possible."

"Another winter here?"

Ann went on quickly. "Jake was willing to pay you whatever you asked to have his tooth taken care of. I have seen at least a half dozen women in town who appear to be in the family way. You could continue with your father's work, in whatever capacity you are able, and get paid for it. It's just something to think about."

Elizabeth opened her mouth to argue.

Ann decided to let the subject rest. "And now it's my turn to read my mail."

Her diversionary tactic worked. "Are you going to share your letter? Why is it red? And with that huge wax seal? You don't see them much anymore, do you?"

"Red is for good fortune. Good joss, in Chinese. It's a long story."

Elizabeth kicked off her slippers and tucked herself into a cross-legged position on the chair.

Carefully, Ann ran her forefinger under the flap and cracked the seal. A chip of wax fell on her skirt and she scooped it up and warmed it in the palm of her hand until it gave off the faintest whiff of beeswax.

She took a deep breath and read aloud. "Daughter. I sit on this foul box with this miserable letter writer and tell him the words to send to you. He is very young and foolish, I think, but he makes the ugly English words crawl across the paper and they look almost pretty when he is done." Ann held the thick parchment toward Elizabeth. "She's right, isn't she? It is a pretty hand. I can just see her, you know. Such a little tyrant with a tongue as sharp as a knife. I'm surprised that she can still find someone to write her letters for her."

"Daughter? I thought your mother had passed away. And why can't she write her own letters?" Elizabeth asked.

Ann took time to think through a cautious answer. "As I said, it's a long story. Her name is Jingfei Chiu and she's at least ninety years old, although she tries to pass herself off as twenty years older or younger, depending on whom she is manipulating and why."

The face across from Ann was full of curiosity, so she continued.

"I lived and worked in an apartment over a warehouse in Chinatown in San Francisco. It was a very lonely time for me. I had no family left and my work, well, it kept me from having many friends or meeting new people. So I got into the habit in the afternoon, when I had time off, of walking through the lanes and alleys, into the pokey little shops with strange, foreign goods and that's where I met Jingfei. She was alone by then, too, and she decided that I would become something of a daughter to her. If you saw her, you would think she is the most unlikely-looking mother in the world. Small, shrivelled and dressed in one outlandish costume or another. But she has been good to me."

An owl called outside the window. Both women jumped, then relaxed. Ann felt lighter for having revealed this much of her past, and heavier for not being able to tell it all. "She doesn't write either English or Chinese. In fact, she told me she has never been to school, even though she's something of a genius with numbers and figures. No one could ever cheat her with money, although I have a strong suspicion that she has cheated a few people herself."

She sat up straight and read the rest of the letter, her heart sinking with the next few words. "This old lady does not stay well. Much pain. Probably dead when you get these words far away there where you are. That is the will of the gods."

"Pain?"

Ann looked up from the page and took a chance. "She had been a concubine since she was little more than a child and suffered severe beatings that plague her still." At Elizabeth's shocked stare, Ann went on, "A concubine is . . ."

"I know what a concubine is." Elizabeth tried to sound sophisticated, but her voice cracked. "You befriended a *concubine*?"

"Yes," Ann answered. "But then, she was willing to be my friend, too."

Elizabeth squinted from Ann to the letter and chewed on the inside of her lip thoughtfully, but said no more.

At the end of the letter, just below the spot at the bottom where Jingfei made the Chinese characters that indicated her name, was a single sentence. "With much respect, this miserable letter writer would like to say, Venerable Mother very sick old lady."

Ann took a deep breath, almost a sigh. It was not unexpected.

"What will you do? Will you go?" Elizabeth asked.

"No. When we parted, we knew we would never see one another again. She can't travel anymore and I will never return. We said our goodbyes."

EIGHT

Herbert Schneider walked from his store to the east end of First Avenue, a satisfying squeak coming from his new boots. He stopped where the gophers burrowed right next to the last house, which happened to be the Methodist manse, and stood and stared at the tumble of boxes, broken toys and rags that looked as though the children had tried to scramble together a tipi. The wildest kids in town belonged to the preacher. Herbert shook his head, then crossed the avenue and followed the railroad tracks back to the station, across from his hotel. He inhaled the early morning air and the feel of industry about to happen.

He couldn't have accomplished any of this back home in Nebraska. All the towns had been well established when his papa had dragged them west, and all the jobs had been gone. So Papa had turned to the bottle and the town had taken to calling them poor white trash.

The pleasure Herbert normally took in an early stroll through town had been diminished by another spat with Beatrice at the crack of dawn. As usual, she had cried in that strange tearless way she had, all doubled up as though her innards hurt. He worried that her bad spells were getting more frequent and more severe, and that he had no sons and maybe no hope of ever having any.

What satisfaction could a man find in being a town father but not a real father? "Overseer" was the title the railway gave him when he was appointed to run the town. He didn't care for that term at all, much preferring "Mayor," but that would mean he'd have to be elected, and the other businessmen in town were content to let him manage things. So he was administrator, secretary, treasurer and sanitation officer all rolled into one. He repeated that to himself a couple of times and it lightened his step considerably.

In front of the station, Herbert clasped his hands behind his back and surveyed the skeleton of his new hotel. It was a perfect location, directly across from the stately maroon train station, on the corner of First and Main. That's where the railway had wanted it and Herbert had jumped at the chance.

Two so-called carpenters wandered from the boarding house to the pile of lumber and barrels of nails that should, by now, have been turned into a simple, three-storey hotel with a front veranda and a tidy balcony off the third floor where he would have his residence. If they saw him, they pretended otherwise. He glared at them anyway.

Across Main Street, on the corner opposite his half-built hotel, was Will Hepburn's Barbershop, Billiard Parlour and Pawn Shop. On the boardwalks, front and side, Hepburn had taken empty nail kegs, cut them in half, and filled them with soil, and now they sat there in the fresh morning air bursting with late-blooming posies. It was a womanish thing to think of but Herbert had to admit it gave the street a nice settled look. He'd have to talk to the carpenters about flower boxes.

Herbert stared at the closed curtains on the parlour window above his store, half expecting the dark fabric to move, so sure was he that Beatrice followed his every move. He gave a little shudder, wondering if her nerves and suspicions could be spreading to him. But the window brought back the source of their latest argument, which once again hinged on her insane hatred of living over the store.

"Daddy never intended for me to live over the store like some dirty Jew. He wouldn't have given you all that money if . . ." Her hand had slammed over her mouth and she'd cringed back, realizing that she'd gone too far, standing there in her bare feet with her hair hanging around her ears in stringy ropes.

Then she'd blubbered on in a flurry of garbled words. "You could have more room for merchandise up here. Think of it—dry goods, bolts of cheap cloth for the farmers' wives. More room downstairs for canned things. That window, that window there"—she'd stabbed a frantic finger at the parlour window that he stood looking at now— "you could turn it into a display window with ready-made dresses and hats."

Sometimes her craziness sounded right close to genius. He'd read that something like that happened now and then. Of course, she still thought she could talk him into the Evans's house although he had already decided on a nice big residence right in his hotel. Any fool settler could have a house. Only rich people lived in a hotel. All the same, he might as well humour her for the time being; let her plan a dry-goods department if it would keep peace for a few weeks. The word "department" had a nice ring to it, too, as in department store. He came back from his thoughts to see Alf Porter and the barber wave for him to join them across the street.

"Coffee time," Will called.

"Thought we'd try the Chinaman's place," Alf said. "Have to encourage new businesses or they'll leave for greener pastures."

"Be interesting to see how he managed to turn that dump into a restaurant," Herbert mused aloud.

One of the Chinamen from the railroad gang, a fellow called Sam Wu, had decided to stay in town and start a café in the low, unpainted clapboard building that stood next to Severson's boarding house and forge. Herbert had always thought of it more as a fire hazard than anything, but the front of the long, narrow building had been opened out to accommodate a fairly good-sized plate-glass window and a red screen door. The fringe of weeds that had choked the patch of dirt out front had been pulled and lay wilted in a pile by the single doorstep. This was the kind of situation the Land Department wouldn't allow anymore.

"Ah, I see Mrs. Montgomery has been in here with her poster, too." Will stopped to look at a message on a long sheet of white paper on the inside of the door.

"So she has. I have one of those behind the till. Excellent idea, I think, with the doctor gone now." Alf stood back to let the other two enter.

Herbert felt his lips tighten and tried to relax his features into an indifferent smile. He hadn't seen a notice in his store. He didn't have time to scan the page before he was inside the cool, colourless interior of the Chinaman's.

They sat at one of the oilcloth-covered tables with mismatched salt and pepper shakers and an old sardine tin for an ashtray. The chair creaked and wobbled under Herbert's buttocks. At the back, the Chinaman himself stacked thick white cups and saucers on a narrow table that had been covered with the same grey, marble-patterned oilcloth.

"Three coffees, Sam, please," Alf called, and in a few seconds the man shuffled to their table bearing a tin tray with three steaming cups of coffee, a jug of cream and a bowl of sugar. With an obsequious nod of his head and quick motions of his long, yellow fingers, he placed a spoon by each cup.

As soon as the thin figure in the dark green smock returned to his work at the back table, Herbert lowered his voice slightly and asked, "How the hell can these people afford to open their own places?"

Will stirred two heaping spoons of sugar into his cup. "He's been working on the railroad for twenty years. They don't get paid much, but if he saved—well, it looks like he did save, doesn't it?"

All three looked around the barren room that echoed back the sound of their voices and the scrape of their boots. There were five tables and perhaps two dozen chairs, a few dishes on shelves, and an old black stove visible through the open door of what must be the kitchen. On each side wall hung a red tasselled banner in a shiny material with the squiggly shapes that made Chinese words.

"He just started this week," Alf said. "Give him time. None of us did it all overnight. We had to work at it."

Herbert took a wary sip of the coffee. Very tasty. "I thought these Chinks sent all their money back home. Heard tell a day's wages here could support a dozen relatives for months over there."

Will leaned back in his chair and crossed his arms over his neat, narrow waistcoat. The pearl buttons down the front of his snowy white shirt winked at Herbert. "Hot for this time of year, isn't it? Think it'll give you time to get your hotel up?"

Herbert took another long swig of his coffee. He didn't get coffee like this at home. "Yup, yup. Coming along nicely."

"Think they'll have the roof on before the snow flies?" Alf asked with a grin.

Herbert steadied his hand as he returned his cup to the saucer. "Long before that. Matter of fact, the wife and I were just talking this morning about our plans to enlarge the store."

He had the satisfaction of seeing Will sit up straight. Even Alf put his cup down and turned sideways to look square at Herbert. "Enlarge the store? Adding on?"

"No, no. But we'll be moving to our residence in the hotel soon. Mrs. Schneider is interested in turning the upstairs of the store into a dry-goods and ladies' apparel department." He let the last phrase roll off his tongue with élan.

"Move? Soon?" Will asked. "Not at the rate they're going." He jerked his thumb in the general direction of the unfinished hotel.

"Like I said, the wife's got her heart set on a ladies' wear department, so I'm bringing in two more carpenters today. Stir things up over there. We want to have everything in place by Christmas."

The more Herbert talked, the more he believed what he said. Then he started to worry because he could see that he would have to turn his boasts into reality. Will had managed to twist his private plans right out of his mouth and, in some convoluted way, Herbert knew, this was all Beatrice's fault once again. The woman was possessed of the devil.

Herbert tried to pay attention as the other two gloated about the fellow who intended to start a newspaper in town. Plainview, their rival town to the west, wanted him but he had made his decision in favour of Aspen Coulee—because of the railway again. Smart money invested where there was a main station, not just a siding.

The Chinaman came back with a dark blue enamel coffee pot. "More coffee, please?" he asked in pretty good English.

"Naw, we gotta get back to work." Will stood to leave. "Let me get it this time," he said, throwing a few coins on the table.

"Thanks. I'll buy tomorrow," Alf said.

Herbert wanted more of that good coffee, and maybe a piece of the pie that the Chinaman had just brought out to cool, but instead he rose, too. "Yup. Busy day ahead."

He parted from the other two on the steps of the Chinaman's and walked through Bertha Severson's garden and across the back lane to Pietr's forge to ask if he knew anyone who needed work. Two minutes later Herbert steamed down the boardwalk, his fists clenched. Damn Swede had got too big for his britches. Too cheap! Who did he think he was, telling Herbert Schneider he wouldn't get any more help in this town until he treated his men decent and paid them well?

He headed for the post office. Sometimes men came through town and checked in there to ask where work could be found. Herbert stopped to admire the new post office; the government made nice buildings. By the time he had entered the neat white structure and walked across the clean-smelling, oiled floor he felt a little better. He would get his hotel taken care of; didn't he always take care of things?

Herbert went to fiddle with the combination on his private mailbox, nodding at a young man who sat at a corner table with a printed cardboard sign on the wall behind his head. It was the Dominion Lands Agent. The fellow would be here for a couple of days, then go back to Edmonton.

Herbert approached Mel Johnson, the postmaster, to ask about workers and at the same time heard behind him the door opening and closing. "I wondered if you had heard of anyone needing work. I want to get that hotel finished sometime before snowfall."

Mel started to tell him that the railway had let the emergency labourers they had brought out to fix the broken tracks go, but Herbert was distracted by the rustle of skirts and the low tones of women's voices. He couldn't be sure how he knew, but he felt they didn't want him to hear what they said.

Mel glanced at the table in the corner, then back at Herbert. "You know where that is?"

"What's that?"

"The shanty town, the one down by the river, not the one across the tracks here. That's where they'd be, if they're still around. I don't know how much good they'd be, if the railway let them go. They generally hire anybody."

"Maybe I'll take a walk out there," Herbert said, but his ears strained toward the conversation in the corner.

As he had suspected, one of the women was the Widow Montgomery. She stood straight and tall before the land agent, a bony, dark woman fidgeting by her side. He figured from her clothes that the second woman must be one of the foreigners from the shack town Mel referred to, but he couldn't for the life of him think what the two women would want with a land agent. He remembered Alf and Will talking about the Montgomery woman and some kind of poster, and decided it would be polite to wait and ask for one for his store.

Ann spoke slowly and patiently, as though she were talking to a child. "I know what the Lands Act says, Mr. . . ?"

"Hudon."

"Mr. Hudon. I came in a few weeks ago and spoke to someone else from your office. Section 32 says 'Every person who is the sole head of a family'."

Hudon looked flustered. "It's just I've never done anything like this before. I've only had to deal with men. They understand these things."

"I understand these things too, Mr. Hudon. And I'm here to explain them to Mrs. Gregorowicz." She held a sheaf of papers and a surveyor's map in her hand. "What more do you need from us?"

The clerk reached a shaky hand to the map on his desk. "Uh, what quarter was it again? Here?"

That's when it dawned on Herbert that these two women actually intended to file a homestead claim. Or, from the sounds of it, the Gregorowicz woman did. They wouldn't get away with that nonsense, would they? He let the smile he had ready for Mrs. Montgomery slide from his face and didn't even pretend he wasn't eavesdropping. He stared at the discomfited clerk and waited for him to find enough gumption to come up with a sound regulation that prevented women from taking free land.

Ann flashed a glance his way and her cheeks pinked up, but her voice was steady as she recited the quarter, township and range. Herbert tried to think where that would be and finally just stepped closer and had a look at the map.

He heard his own voice, even though he had intended to let the clerk handle it. "Why, that's the useless quarter of sand and swamp across the tracks and west a bit from the new roundhouse."

He saw Mrs. Montgomery's lips press together and Mrs. Gregorowicz gape at him with round, frightened eyes.

The widow's cool voice sliced through him. "We're conducting official business here, Mr. Schneider." She didn't even look at him, just prodded the clerk by shoving the filing form across the table.

Herbert took a step back and felt his hand prickle with the urge to swat her right across her perfect face.

"The sole head of a family, Mr. Hudon. We have a letter from Father Laboucane declaring that Mrs. Gregorowicz is a widow and the mother of a little girl and that she cares for her aging in-laws. On top of that, she has a home, ready to move onto the land as soon as possible. So the requirement to establish a dwelling will be met immediately. Two of these letters are testimonials from people who vouch for her ability to . . ."

"The ability to make the necessary improvements, lady?" the clerk asked sarcastically. He had found his backbone at last, to Herbert's satisfaction. "To prove the claim? Break the land?"

Herbert sucked in his breath when, as smug as you please, she plopped the letters on the table.

"Precisely that, Mr. Hudon," she said.

Hudon ran his hands over the letters, read a bit with his lips moving, then looked back up. "There's the matter of a fee, too, you know. Ten dollars. Cash." The last vestige of hope died on his face as the Gregorowicz woman reached into her battered old pocketbook and brought out a handful of paper money.

The agent loosened his collar and messed with his pen and inkwell. He dug through a fat briefcase and came up with business forms. He cleared his throat and shuffled everything on the table once, then twice.

In the end, he had to do it. A few words of explanation by Ann in that cool voice, the official stamp of the Department of the Interior, a receipt for ten dollars and the land—160 acres—belonged to a scrawny foreign woman who couldn't even read and write English well enough to file on her own.

Herbert stood and stewed as Mel looked on from behind his cage. Any notion of entering into a conversation with the widow had been erased from his mind by what had just taken place. He thought of the patch of land in question, wondering if there was something there he had missed. Maybe these women had some inside knowledge that the railway intended to build in that direction. The Montgomery woman had been cosy with the railway officials; it could be she'd offered them more than coffee and cake and got some useful information in return. Housekeepers had ways of getting something in return.

"Congratulations, Mrs. Gregorowicz," Mel said.

Ann's face lit with a rare smile. "By all means. Congratulations, Hilde. You have your farm."

"Like that? Only that?" The bony woman held her receipt in her fist and looked at the agent. He shrugged but clamped his lips together.

"Like that." Ann took the other woman's arm and steered her out of the post office. "Good day, gentlemen. Mr. Hudon."

"Well, if that ain't the damnedest thing," Herbert fumed. "Are you sure they can do that?"

Hudon whitened at the tone of voice, but shrugged again. "I'll look into it as soon as I get back. If they've tricked me somehow, they'll be in big trouble. You can't cheat the Dominion Lands Department and get away with it. No siree."

Herbert snorted in disgust, then pulled his pocket watch out and stared at it. This had turned out to be one rotten day and it was still only ten thirty in the morning. His belly growled and somehow his mind kept returning to the pie at the Chinaman's and that scrawny woman owning a quarter section of land, and all of it together made him feel very sorry for himself. The sweat on his hands stuck to the knob as he opened the door to leave. At the last second his gaze rested on another one of those damned posters. The words on the thick, white paper were printed in India ink and flowed across the page in fluid calligraphy that Herbert envied. He could use a sign writer like that in the store. He read it quickly, and then more slowly to make sure he got the full meaning of it.

ELIZABETH EVANS, EXPERIENCED NURSE AND MIDWIFE
TRAINED AT THE PRESTIGIOUS
QUEEN VICTORIA HOSPITAL IN ONTARIO
OFFERS NURSING TREATMENT IN HER HOME
IN ASPEN COULEE
OR MIDWIFERY CARE IN YOUR HOME
FOR A MODEST FEE

NINE

It was nearing the end of October and Mr. Bedlam had been gone for days, leaving on the train in the company of a young and elegant wife who had stared in horror and disbelief when the nurse refused to accompany them back to Toronto.

"I have other patients to attend to," Elizabeth had said, resisting the urge to throw some things in a bag and join them. "You may be able to hire someone in Calgary or Winnipeg if you think it's necessary. Or, better still, break your journey up. Stop a few times on your way and let your husband rest."

She found the most urgent of her present patients sitting in front of his tarpaper lean-to in the tent camp by the station, a septic foot propped up on an empty case that had once held canned tomatoes. Someone had misjudged and brought a sledgehammer down on his toe rather than the railroad spike. Yesterday she had cleaned and dressed the seeping wound, all the time trying to talk the young man into getting on the train and having it attended to by a doctor in Red Deer or Calgary.

She pulled her fall jacket closed against the crisp weather and wished she'd worn a scarf on her head. "Well, James, the train goes this afternoon. Will you be on it?"

"Naw, I don't think it's that bad. I had a black toenail when I froze my foot as a kid. It was a nuisance until it fell off, but it didn't kill me."

"This is not a bit of frostbite. See here." She unstuck the gauze that had been stained a pinkish yellow with blood and pus. "The whole end of the toe is black, not just the nail."

He started to fuss about losing his job. She was fed up with the railway for putting men in situations where they could get hurt, then dropping them at the side of the tracks along with the rest of their litter when they couldn't use them anymore. This was her third injury in as many weeks. And the most serious. She dropped the soiled gauze into his campfire and watched until it turned to flame.

"James, the end of the toe is black and cold because no blood is reaching it. The infection and bad smell tell me that the tissue is actually rotting."

He twisted on his rickety chair. "Well, I don't know. Got no one to take care of my dog, and . . ."

Elizabeth had reached the end of her patience. "Your dog! This creature here?" She pointed to a small, tan dog that showed traces of collie in her sharp nose and alert ears. "You will risk your life for this mutt?"

That got a heated reaction. "Mutt or no, she's a good watchdog. People will rob the food off your plate in this place." The dog came to his chair to have her ears rubbed. "An' what do you mean, risk my life?"

"If I'm not mistaken, this toe needs to be removed at the first joint, here," she tapped the first knuckle. "The bone is crushed, the tissue is dead and the blood isn't flowing properly. Gases will begin to develop in the wound and death follows very quickly."

The colour drained from his face. He shook his head and stammered, "No, I don't believe . . ."

"I'm not trying to scare you, James. Well, yes I am, but for your own good. Everything I say is true. Would you rather lose the toe or your whole foot—or even your life?" She stood with her hands on her hips. "If you don't believe me, then that's all the more reason to ask a doctor."

She edged onto the empty tomato box and carefully placed his foot on her lap. Taking a pair of surgical scissors, she cautiously cut away the worst of the decayed tissue that obviously had no sensation left, then daubed the wound with iodine.

He continued to hesitate.

"James, I've never done an amputation. Do you want your toe to be my first?"

"N-no."

"Now I'll put a thick, heavy dressing on it for the train ride. I'll even walk you over to the station myself. How is that?"

He sighed and shrugged his shoulders.

Against her better judgment, she added, "And I'll take care of your dog until you return. Or find someone who can."

Elizabeth helped him stuff his belongings into a battered suitcase and his mangled foot into three heavy wool socks. A piece of string around the dog's neck served as a leash. She left him in the relative warmth of the train station with his foot propped on his suitcase, looking as forlorn as the dog that she dragged along behind her.

Stefan was waiting for her outside. Since they had helped Hilde get her quarter section, he had taken it upon himself to be something of a protector to her and Ann, and Elizabeth had to admit that she liked his concern. She was even ready to admit that she liked the man, and when she had a moment, asked herself why. He was, after all, just one of dozens of labourers in town, wasn't he?

"You're not working today?" she asked.

"I have no more work on the bush-clearing job. They move to the east and I can not go that far away until everyone is settled."

"Without work, how will you be able to move the train car and fix it up?"

Stefan took the string from Elizabeth and tugged the whining dog across the street. "I have money for that. Enough for that."

"You don't look very happy about it. I thought you wanted everyone settled by winter."

"What is this?" he asked in exasperation. "This crying dog?"

Elizabeth sighed. "I offered to keep her until her owner gets well."

He bent and picked the dog up. "The string is choking it," he snapped.

"Yes, well, I didn't know what else to do." She glanced at his stormy face. "Don't you want your family settled?"

"Me? I want—I want different for myself. You will think I am very selfish, no? I am unhappy because I don't want to be here in this Wild West, but every day something more comes to hold me here. Some days I feel—what is the word? Trapped?"

She stopped halfway up the knoll and looked straight at him. "I feel trapped, too! I don't want to be here, either. I want to go back home to Toronto."

"Why you don't go then?"

But Elizabeth didn't want to get into money issues. "Where would you go?"

"I have sent letters to music schools in the United States of America. And Canada, too. I could teach, study more. I have, how you say it, recommendations from home." He gave a hopeless shrug. "Is just a dream now."

Elizabeth waved at Ann who stood on the steps of the house watching them approach. They were several yards away when Ann demanded, "Stefan Gregorowicz, I need to speak to you."

"What can I do, Mrs. Montgomery? You need help with something? Some wood?"

She looked him full in the face. "Nothing like that. I've just been by Mr. Hepburn's."

He took a step back and put the dog down.

"Stefan?" Ann waited until he looked at her. "On the glass shelf in the window. It's yours, isn't it? No one within a thousand miles has anything so beautiful."

He nodded.

"Why?"

"I need to make them safe for the winter."

"What?" Elizabeth demanded. "What are you two talking about?"

"So you sold it?"

"No. Just the loan of money. I will get it back."

Elizabeth grabbed the forearm of this man who was not just another labourer. "You sold your violin?"

* * *

Later that week, as Ann and Elizabeth walked home from the Weymans', they saw, in the distance, the broken boxcar being dragged on skids like a giant stone-boat behind two teams of horses. Half a dozen Lilliputian men scrambled around it, pulling on ropes and poking the sides with poles to keep it from tipping over. The women stopped on a rise to watch, their hands to their foreheads shading their eyes.

"I suppose it was worth it," Ann murmured. "They'll be warmer in there at least. Look, it has a chimney already."

"And a floor, I presume. That's what I hate most about those soddies. That old cellar smell. But, his violin . . ." Ann started walking again, shaking her head.

"There are sad stories everywhere out here. Look at poor Mrs. Weyman. I don't see how she can last much longer. She isn't eating anything and she's started to develop sores on her body from lying in bed. Her bones are almost sticking through her skin." Elizabeth sighed.

"Would you eat the messes Orville slaps up? That place is so filthy, it's a wonder they aren't all sick."

"I know. I just hate going there. What a terrible way to die."

Ann stopped walking and looked back in the direction from which they had come. "Dr. McRae made a remark like that when he came out with me. I'd forgotten all about it 'til now. What was it he said? It's a terrible *place* to die. I wonder if he was implying—you don't think he meant . . ."

"Meant what? That we should take her in? Orville would never stand for that. You know how tight-fisted he is."

"No, Orville wouldn't want to pay for that. But I wonder if there is some way we could talk him into it. I just hate to see anyone suffer to that extent. She's so dirty and it can only get worse. Imagine when she can't even get up to use that disgusting bucket and starts to soil the bed?"

Elizabeth narrowed her eyes at Ann. "Do you think we should start offering a service to people who won't pay?"

"Oh, he'll pay. One way or the other," Ann answered thoughtfully. "He'll pay. If we put it to Orville that caring for his wife is women's work and we would be willing to do it, in exchange for some cured pork, say, or potatoes—whatever I can wheedle out of him."

"Ann, honestly, you're shameless. And," Elizabeth continued, "do you realize what that will entail for us?"

"A little, I do, yes, and I'm willing to learn. Who else will do it? Someday, somewhere, I hope someone will do the same for me."

* * *

Ann's shock turned to irritation and then to downright anger. Elizabeth's face showed a tight-lipped determination to get the job done. Cats stalked across the dirty dishes on the table and hissed from shadowy corners. Now that the weather had turned cold the house crawled with them, and not one of the squalling bunch appeared to be house trained.

Elizabeth perched on the edge of the dirty bed with Mrs. Weyman's hand in hers. "This is best for you. You'll see—we'll have a nice time, the three of us." She looked up to include Ann.

Ann nodded and tried to smile, but Mrs. Weyman continued to weep weakly, sparse drops trailing down her cheeks as though she didn't have enough of life's juices left to even make a decent batch of tears.

"Why are you taking me out of my home?" She looked at Elizabeth with hurt and disbelief. "Where's Orville?"

"He's bringing the wagon around. We've fixed a nice pallet for you and we have lots of blankets. It's turned cold since you were last outdoors." As Elizabeth spoke in her calm, professional voice, she folded Mrs. Weyman into a heavy man's cardigan, as though she were wrapping a baby in a grey shroud.

"But why," the woman whined. "I don't understand. Why can't I stay here?"

"We want to make you more comfortable. And make less work for Orville and Boyd." Elizabeth put a faded felt hat on the stringy hair and then wrapped a long wool scarf around Mrs. Weyman's head and neck.

At that moment, Orville came in, in a burst of fresh air. His wife reached her arms toward him, her scrawny fingers opening and closing, trying to clutch onto something. "Let me stay, Orville. I won't be a bother, I promise. I want to be in my home. Please?" More moisture was squeezed from her rheumy eyes.

Ann had to look away, but not before she saw grief and doubt and something else pass in waves across Orville's face. The something else looked rather like relief. Boyd twitched anxiously behind his father, his emotions clearly visible. Sorrow and fear. He understands, then, Ann thought.

Mrs. Weyman drooped forward onto Elizabeth, her small reserve of strength spent. She continued to cry in small breathy gulps while Orville stood with his hands hanging by his sides, looking down at the bundle of bones that had been his wife. What is he thinking, Ann wondered, and felt some of her anger seep away. She hoped he had a store of better memories than this to last him through his life.

"Ann, hand me the quilt there, will you?" Elizabeth asked. "We'd better be on the trail before it gets too late."

Boyd clutched the meagre bundle of his mother's belongings, Ann carried extra blankets, which she hoped would be left in the wagon and not brought into their clean house, and the nurse helped Orville with Mrs. Weyman. He didn't need help. He lifted her wasted body easily and in three steps was out the door.

"Oh!" Mrs. Weyman gasped in shock at the cold air. Her husband tightened his grip and held her closer, dipping his face to shelter hers from the wind. They were eye to eye, their cheeks brushing—hers, emaciated and yellow, his, unshaven and ruddy—and time stood still, even for the three watching. Longing, regret, loneliness. Every raw, unbidden emotion imaginable, including affection, Ann convinced herself. He had promised to come visit her frequently, and Ann hoped he would, but they were saying their goodbyes now, here in the cold, before Mrs. Weyman's last trip from the home they had set out to build together when they had left the security of Ontario ten years before.

Boyd choked on his own grief and edged over near his parents. His mother brushed her knuckles over his pimply cheek and smiled a shaky smile. Orville lifted his head and took a deep breath. "Ready now, Grace?"

Grace nodded her chin into the rough wool of his coat.

Grace. What a lovely name, Ann thought.

* * *

On a bright, cold Saturday in November, Ann stood at the kitchen door counting the coins in the palm of her hand. "Coal for heat and fuel for the lamps will be our first concern. Then necessities like sugar and flour." She folded the ends of her scarf over her chin. "What about medical supplies?"

Elizabeth shook her head. "The railway sent everything I asked for. We have enough for years."

"Well, Dr. McRae must have had a lot to do with that. They refused to pay our bill for the fellow with the squashed toe, just as you predicted."

Elizabeth peered through the frost on the window. "I wonder if Dr. McRae will show up for Christmas again this year."

Ann looked up quickly. "Christmas? Did you invite him?"

"No, but we didn't invite him last year either. He came 'lookin' for a wee bit o' Christmas puddin',' as he said."

Christmas pudding. One more thing she'd never made. Ann opened the door and stepped into a blast of cold air. Like a tightrope walker, she followed the sled tracks to Main Street and turned toward Schneider's General Store. Despite the cold snap, the town bustled with shoppers. She pushed her way into the store, welcoming the rich smells and the warm air.

The teachers were ahead of her, searching for red and green crepe paper.

"You both look tired," Ann remarked.

"We continually have new students coming," Iris responded. "And others leaving, with no hope of them seeing the inside of a classroom for who-knows-how-long. Maybe never again. It gets discouraging."

"And we brought headaches on ourselves by suggesting a Christmas concert. Concerts are so much work, but some of the children have little else to look forward to," Lydia added as she dug under a stack of writing tablets.

"A concert? I haven't been to a school concert since—well, my own, when I was a child." Ann inhaled deeply, savouring the aroma of coffee, wondering if she could afford a half pound.

"I wish we had a piano. I don't know how we can have a concert without music," Lydia said.

"Music?" Ann paid for her purchases and waited for the other women.

Outside, squeezed between the barbershop and the hardware store, was a wagon with two emaciated horses tied to its tongue. Three Indians huddled in the shelter of the rig.

"Fish?" asked one.

The three women stopped. Lydia took a step closer. "Pardon me?"

"Fish. Big fish, only five cents."

"Oh, I would dearly love some fish," Ann said wistfully. "It's been ages since I've had fish."

Will Hepburn and Sam Wu were ahead of them, digging through the wagon box.

"Afternoon, ladies." Will leaned into the wagon box. "These are mostly pike, all head and bones. Let's see if they've got anything else." He started throwing frozen fish from the back to the front of the wagon. "Ah. Some nice walleye."

Ann parted with another five cents and jammed a frozen fish into her shopping bag.

"Thanks for your help, Mr. Hepburn," Ann said. "And while we are on the subject of help, the teachers were just telling me about their Christmas concert and their lack of music. What can you do to assist in that situation, I wonder?"

Will looked a little taken aback at first, then understanding dawned in his eyes and he turned to the teachers. "Tell me what you had in mind."

Ann made her way home with her shopping bag, and three oranges in her pockets so they wouldn't freeze. She heard the moaning as soon as she walked in the back door.

Elizabeth bustled into the kitchen looking strained and harried.

"Still bad?" Ann lined her purchases up on the table.

Elizabeth leaned against the doorframe. "There's no doubt she's getting weaker."

"It's much worse than I thought it would be," Ann whispered, and then, because it was all she could offer, "I'll have supper ready right away. Should I make anything for Grace?"

"I don't know if she's awake."

They had tried to brighten the room, with doilies on the night table and a patchwork quilt at the foot of the bed where the dog was curled in a ball.

"I think she's asleep," Elizabeth said. "Come on, Dog, get down."

A weak voice spoke from the bed. "I like her company."

"I wish you had asked James what that dog's name is," Ann whispered. "We can't keep calling her Dog."

TEN

Footsteps echoed back at Herbert as he walked slowly through his hotel. Only shadows lurked in the emptiness that would be the dining room, while the wintry sun struggled over the eastern horizon. The window glass was in and a new man called Ernest something-or-other was down in the basement, stoking up the furnace so the men could paint and hang wallpaper. A corner of Herbert's mind took in the clanging and the smell of coal dust, but his thoughts were caught up with the urgency of getting this all finished in the next four weeks in order to move his own household in before Christmas as he had boasted.

He removed his leather gloves so he could run his hands over the smooth wood of the banister, stopping every third or fourth step on his way up to look back at the spacious lobby. It was a building to make anyone proud—anyone except Beatrice. The sooner he could get her busy organizing the women's department at the store, the better. She had been quiet lately but a little more sociable, visiting with the nurse a couple of times. Just yesterday she had asked if she could hire a sleigh one day to go calling in Plainview. He'd been so surprised he had forgotten to ask who she knew over there.

The top of the stairs opened into the darkness of a long hall that gave way to twelve rooms, six on each side. He took a key from his pocket and put it into a lock on a door directly in front of him. It turned as smooth as silk. He stepped into another stairwell that took him to the third floor, half of which would become what he called the private residence. A sitting room ran the width of the hotel and this he crossed quickly, going to his pride and joy, a gracious balcony with white-painted rails that overlooked the train station and a wide portion of the snow-covered hills beyond. Here he stood on the cold November morning, feeling warm and satisfied. He would be forty years old on his next birthday and a man had to have something to show for his life by the time he was forty.

He lifted his head and squinted. It must be his imagination, but he was sure he heard music floating on the cold air. He walked to the east end of his balcony and held his breath to listen more carefully. There it was again. Fiddle music, the high-brow kind that he didn't usually like, but it sounded fine to his ears today.

With his hands in his coat pockets, he swayed to the music. Nice. The tune changed to something he thought he recognized from when he was a little duffer. A Christmas song, maybe? Who did he know that could play music of this kind? Across from him, Hepburn's flower tubs were full of snow. Now he had a bench out there for folks to sit on and pass the time of day. Herbert made a mental note to have the carpenter put together a couple of benches for the hotel's front veranda.

The music stopped. Herbert felt bereft for a minute, then the door to Hepburn's barbershop opened and Stefan Gregorowicz stepped out, tucking his hands into his pockets. Herbert remembered hearing something about Hepburn taking a fiddle in on pawn.

Herbert saw Will come to the door with Gregorowicz and heard the barber say, "Come again after work, if you like. I'll have the coffee pot on."

Gregorowicz bowed from the waist, then picked his way through frozen manure and entered the hotel.

Will looked up, straight into Herbert's eyes. "Morning, Herb. Your place is shaping up real nice. How long now?"

Leaning his forearms casually on the rail, Herbert answered, "Only a week or so, I guess. Got the furnace going so's the men can work in comfort."

"Well, that's right generous of you," Will chuckled.

Herbert let the comment go. "Come on over for a look around. If you're finished with your music recital, that is."

"I'll do that a little later maybe, on my way for coffee at the Chinaman's." He shivered and went into his shop, closing the door.

Herbert shivered, too. By now the downstairs should be warm. As he turned to go he noticed the sun had risen enough to turn the tent tops across the tracks a rosy colour that looked almost pretty. As long as he didn't have to live in one. He stood a moment longer, surveying the bustle around the train station and realized that, besides being an elegant addition to his hotel, the balcony was a great place for keeping tabs on the whole town.

He found Stefan in the lobby, squatting beside a bucket of varnish. The fumes of turpentine mingled with the smell of coal dust, and Herbert was grateful he didn't have to spend the whole day indoors. He watched Stefan stir the glittering varnish, noticed the long slim hands, like an artist. "Will paying you to play for him over there?"

Stefan rocked back on his heels and blinked up at him. "Excuse, please?"

Another one that couldn't understand half of what he heard. "Wasn't that you playing the fiddle at Hepburn's?"

"The violin. Yes."

"Why?"

The man's gaze was puzzled, but direct. "Why? Is mine."

Herbert felt his hackles rise. Some of these people just didn't understand their place. "I know that. Is that how you pay him back? Giving recitals?"

That got to him. "I pay back with money. I play to practise for children's concert at the school."

"Ah, yes. The concert at the school." Herbert tucked his hands into his waistcoat and admired the way the room filled with light as the sun climbed higher. "Good idea, a concert. Makes everything feel like home, doesn't it?"

Stefan looked as though he didn't know whether he was supposed to answer or not. Finally, he said, "The teachers give me pages of music from the school so I can play the right Christmas songs."

Herbert realized he had those two dowdy teachers to thank for the familiar music he had heard. "Well, good for them. Now carry on with your work."

Out on the street, it occurred to Herbert that he hadn't received the Old Country bow that Hepburn had.

* * *

The dog tore around the parlour in a frenzy of barking before they heard the sound of boots on the front porch. Elizabeth opened it to a stranger who eyed her brazenly, then shuffled his feet and remembered to grab his cap from his head. "There's this fellow in a tent next of ours what's real sick. Been coughing and that for days but now he's just in a bad sweat and gone all quiet-like. He's been bunkin' with one other, but that fellow up and took off when this sickness came."

Elizabeth nodded her head slightly. "So, this neighbour of yours has been all alone? For how long?"

"Can't rightly say. 'Nother neighbour—uh, you know her, I believe—Ermiline? She told me where you was and said you would come."

Ann folded a pillow case with a snap. Ermiline was one of the local ladies of the evening. Elizabeth had patched her up one morning after her escort of the night before had beaten her nearly senseless.

Elizabeth accepted the reference. "How is Ermiline?"

The man smirked, exposing rotted front teeth. "Looks fine to me and she says to tell you, she'll see you get paid. It's not likely this fellow has any money. Hasn't worked since he got here, I don't believe."

"All right, then," Elizabeth said. "I'll get my coat, but I shouldn't imagine I can do much. Someone should have come sooner."

The messenger became defensive. "I didn't know he was so sick. Not my business to watch over every Tom, Dick and Harry." He jammed his cap back on his head.

"Never mind." Elizabeth reached for her coat. "I said I'd come."

The dog fretted around the man's ankles.

Ann stepped closer to Elizabeth, but spoke directly to the man. "It's getting late."

"Two o'clock in the afternoon is not late, Ann." Elizabeth pulled on her leather gloves.

"You know what I'm saying," Ann went on. "I have to stay with Grace so I can't come with you. Take the dog. Like her last owner said, she seems to be a good watchdog. And a guardian angel for Grace."

"The dog will just get in my way in those dinky tents. Anyway, Ermiline will take care of me." Elizabeth followed her scruffy guide out the door, thinking about what she had just said. She was putting her trust in Ermiline; was that so much different from Ann's friendship with Jingfei Chiu?

She paused at the last moment and turned to Ann. "That's a good name for the dog. Angel."

Hours later, Elizabeth sat on a hump-backed chest with rusted metal corners and hinges, listening to the faint rasp of a man's final breaths. As she'd suspected, there had been little she could do for her patient when she arrived but listen to his chest and hear the deep congestion on his lungs. She had asked the reluctant messenger to start the tinny stove and set a galvanized pail of water to boil in the hope that steam would help. Together they had rolled the patient—God bless him, no one knew his name—onto his side and she'd thumped his back until it turned bright red. But the infection had taken a firm hold and, big and young though the man was, it would take him sooner rather than later.

She yawned and stretched her elbows back to relieve her shoulders. The little silver watch pinned to her apron bib said seven thirty. Ann would be worried. She stood and bent over the man on the folding camp cot. Maybe she should look through his trunk for papers or something that would identify him.

A rustle and scratching on the canvas wall made her jump and face the tent opening. Ermiline's brassy red head appeared, followed by a waft of cheap scent layered on top of unwashed skin. "I's just headin' into town. How's he doin'?"

Elizabeth relaxed her shoulders and dropped her voice. "Well, he's still alive but just barely. It won't be long now."

Ermiline eased the rest of her body, decked out in a loud, yellow-and-brown-checked coat, inside the flap. Her gaze flicked nervously to the patient and back to Elizabeth. "I thought sure you'd fix him up. You was so kind to me."

"He was too far gone when I got here. No one can help him now," Elizabeth whispered. "I won't leave him, though. No one deserves to die alone."

"You're somethin' else, you are. Never thought I'd see a fine woman like you spend the night with the likes of him, just so's he don't die alone." Ermiline pressed a pink satin handkerchief over her mouth and nose.

"He's not contagious, Ermiline." At least I hope he isn't, Elizabeth thought. I don't need an epidemic of an infection this fierce. "Do you happen to know his name? I don't even know what to call him."

"One of them was Ed and the other Sherman or some such, but I don't recall which was which. The healthy one run out as soon's this one took sick."

"So I heard. I was just about to look through his things."

"You jus' go ahead an' look away, Nurse. Oh, and," Ermiline dug in her bronze beaded satchel and dropped a silver dollar into Elizabeth's hand, "here's for your trouble." She disappeared backwards out of the tent. From outside, she called back, louder than necessary, "Let me know if I can be of any more assistance."

Elizabeth rushed to stick her head out the tent flap. "There is one more thing, Ermiline."

The woman returned in a huff. "What is it? I gotta get—well, I got people waitin'."

"Would you send someone for the undertaker? Someone who can tell him how to get here?" Elizabeth tried a pleading look. "Thank you so much." She ducked back into the tent.

"She think I'm a missionary or something? Who's supposed to pay for an undertaker?" Ermiline's voice trailed away into the night.

The latches on the trunk popped easily. Someone has been here ahead of me, Elizabeth thought. Nothing of value remained, not even a change of socks or a clean shirt. No one would bother dragging a chest like this to the frontier unless it had held something at the beginning of the journey. On the brown-stained paper bottom was a handful of letters and a battered New Testament. Elizabeth opened the book and read the inscription on a gold-embossed label:

TO SHERMAN HENRY WOODHOUSE
FOR PERFECT SUNDAY SCHOOL ATTENDANCE
GOOD SHEPHERD PRESBYTERIAN CHURCH 1904-05

* * *

Halfway down the path, walking toward town, Stefan was hailed by a loud, flashy woman who waved her arm over her head and yelled, "Hey! You there!" It was Ermiline. Stefan recognized her as the woman Mr. Schneider kept chasing out of his hotel.

He expected the hard part would be finding the right tent, but bad news has a way of getting around. As he tramped through the filthy snow in the camp, wondering how the stink of urine could survive in this cold, he congratulated himself once again on getting his family out of a situation like this. They might be the laughingstock of the town, living in an old train car, but they were clean and warm.

Stefan stood in front of the tent that had been pointed out to him, trying to decide how to knock on a canvas flap, then cautiously pushed it aside and ducked his shoulders to step in.

Elizabeth was sitting on her heels in the circle of lantern light beside a cot. She wiped the forehead of the man on the rough cot and tucked the cover under his chin. "Is that you, Mr. Faraday?"

"No, not Faraday," Stefan answered.

She turned quickly and stared up at him, her eyes looking strained in the shadows of the lantern.

"Ermiline sent me."

"Oh."

Then the man's chest heaved as though he couldn't get enough air and with a steady hand, the nurse brushed his hair back from his forehead. "I'm here, Sherman."

The newcomer almost said, My name is Stefan, not Sherman, so calm was she about the job she did.

"He's not contagious. That is, he won't make you sick, if you want to come in."

Stefan sat on an old trunk and studied the tent. The rusty lantern gave off more kerosene fumes than light and oily scraps of tarpaper covered the floor. "Ermiline said you wanted Faraday?"

She only had time to nod her head. With a deep rattle that sounded as if it must tear his chest apart, the man on the cot expelled his last breath and what little life was left in him. Stefan crossed himself, then looked away—at the ceiling, the little stove and eventually back at the nurse. She sat as though defeated, her hands folded gently in the lap of the blue-and-white-striped dress and white apron that Stefan liked so much. Finally she ran her hand over the man's face, closing his sightless eyes.

Without turning in his direction, she said in a steady voice, "Stefan? Could you go for the undertaker now, please?"

He came back with Faraday, who grumbled, "Who's going to pay for this, I'd like to know?"

Stefan helped Elizabeth into her coat and took her elbow to guide her out of the tent, leaving the undertaker to his job and his griping.

"Thank you for your help, Stefan. It was good of you."

He wanted to tell her she shouldn't have gone there alone in the first place, that some people in the town talked about the nurse and her housekeeper doing things that weren't considered proper. But he said nothing, just walked with her as quickly as they could toward the light on the hill.

"Oh, dear." Elizabeth looked at the dark outline of Ann pacing in the light of the parlour window.

The door opened for them as they climbed the front steps and from behind Ann came such groaning that Stefan couldn't help shuddering. Is that all these women had to fill their day, he wondered. Moaning, dying people?

* * *

Ann heard the plaintive cry from downstairs and in total darkness stumbled into the small bookcase under the window. A book thudded to the floor. She'd lost track of hours and days; sometimes there was light streaming in the windows, at other times darkness impeded her rush to help their patient.

Her heels ached from the cold, even through the thick socks she wore to bed. She finished shrugging into her robe as she skimmed down the stairs toward the yellow light from the sickroom. She went immediately to the pile of diapers on the nightstand and prepared to change the woman who had shrunk to the size of a child.

"I'm going to tidy your bed, Grace. Then I have your medicine so you can sleep. Down you go, Angel. There's work to be done." The dog gave her a long-suffering look, and hopped down.

Grace stared at Ann from eyes that were lost in their hollow sockets. "Where's Orville?"

"He's at home with Boyd. It's the middle of the night and you are at the Evans's house. Remember?" Ann gently removed Grace's diaper, then yanked at the soiled linen that covered the rubber sheet they used to protect the mattress. Covering the frail body with the quilt, she hurried into the kitchen where she scraped the bottom of the reservoir with a dipper for the last drops of warm water. She shook the grate with a rattle and a burst of ashes, then fanned the sparks to life with a scrap of newspaper.

In all it took only about twenty minutes. The sedative eased Grace into a quieter agitation that Ann now recognized as their patient's most settled time. Absolute peace appeared to be too much to hope for. The mantel clock chimed five times as Ann bundled the used bedding into the washroom. The kitchen had begun to warm up, so she filled the kettle and pushed it over the heat, then splashed cold water from the bucket into the copper boiler on the back of the stove before going back upstairs. Her first chore, once she had dressed, would be to carry out the slops and bring in several more pails of water from the pump outside.

The days and nights ran together like a long, troubled sleep with one bad dream. Ann and Elizabeth lived with piercing screams and pathetic whimpering, and the need to handle the fragile body again and again to keep it clean and warm. Keep *her* clean and warm. They tried not to snap at one another, often apologizing, until the constant, "I'm sorry," worked on their nerves as much as anything. For hours at a time they simply laboured without a word.

A weak light crept over the eastern horizon as Elizabeth came into the kitchen. She stood blinking out the window. "My goodness. We have feet of snow."

Ann stopped with a bucket of water on her way to the washroom. "It's been accumulating for several days. It's nearly the middle of December. The frost on the trees is pretty, isn't it?"

Sometime before noon, they heard heavy steps on the back porch and a banging on the door. Angel shot from the sickroom like an arrow, her hackles standing on end. Ann was surprised to find Orville and Boyd staring in through the frosty window. They had not been near the house for weeks. They clumped into the house without saying hello, never mind taking the time to remove their dirty boots or hats.

In the kitchen, Orville wordlessly stuck a fist toward Ann, a fist holding a gunnysack. She peeled the oily burlap from a shoulder of pork that had gone green and fuzzy with bad handling and poor storage; it smelled like summer carrion. Gingerly, she folded the edges of the sack around the tainted meat and handed it back.

"We don't need meat, thank you, Orville. I'll let you take that home with you. We could however, use some potatoes and carrots— and feed for our horse. You can send Boyd back with all of that as soon as possible." With tight lips she stared directly at Orville and waited with a flutter of anticipation. She felt the need of a good scrap boiling just below the surface.

"I can do that. I sure can." He nodded until his cap slid over his eyes.

Deflated, Ann led the two of them into the sickroom where Elizabeth was trying to coax a thin gruel into Grace from a pap boat. The father and son stopped in shock inside the room before Boyd whimpered and fled back to the kitchen.

"Oh, for evermore," Ann muttered in exasperation as she followed him.

The boy circled the kitchen like a caged animal looking for an avenue of escape, Angel yapping at his heels. Ann ran a weary hand through the loose strands of hair at her nape, then scooted the dog outdoors.

"Sit down, Boyd. I know this must be very hard for you." She opened the breadbox, sliced a thick slab, then slathered it with butter and jam. She set it before the boy and poured him a mug of milk.

He picked up the bread with both hands and shoved most of it into his mouth at once. Saliva and jam drizzled down his chin.

Swallowing hard to keep her stomach from heaving, Ann hurried back to the sickroom.

"She's not really awake right now, Orville, and I don't know if she hears us. I think it would be beneficial for you to sit down and speak to her for a few minutes." Elizabeth rose and pointed at the chair she had vacated.

He flinched as though someone had pinched him. "Beneficial?"

"Take her hand and just talk about the farm, how the animals are doing, the weather—anything."

Orville sat with his knees spread and cautiously reached for his wife's blue-veined hand. He cleared his throat and had to start over once or twice. "Grace? Grace? Boyd and me, we . . ."

Ann left to check on Daisy. When she came back, their visitors had gone, leaving a smear of jam on the table and the stink of manure everywhere. She got out the mop.

* * *

Elizabeth could never be sure how she knew when the end was near; she just did. There came a point when a patient, young or old, rich or poor, stopped fighting to breathe. With Grace there was an additional and even more startling moment of truth.

In the late afternoon, she sat up of her own volition and looked directly into Elizabeth's eyes. "I have to go now. I'm so tired." Then she flopped back on the pillow like a rag doll.

Ann clutched the front of her washed-out blue shirtwaist. "What did she say?" she whispered.

Elizabeth looked from Ann's weary, frightened face to Grace's sunken and yellowed visage and felt an uncanny prickling up and down her arms. "She's babbling. Hallucinating. It's the sedative—I have to give her so much of it now."

Then she took Ann by the arm and led her into the parlour. "I don't believe it will be long now. I can't say for sure, but she is near the end. I hope so, to be honest with you. I know it sounds terrible, but the best thing for this poor woman now is for her to let go of this world."

"I don't believe anyone would fault you for thinking that way. Least of all Grace."

Those were the most civil words they had exchanged for days. They stood side by side at the parlour window, looking down on the town as lights flickered into life in kitchens below them, where other women peeled potatoes or scolded their children. A final sense of waiting settled over them.

"I'm going to find something more solid for supper than soup for a change," Ann said.

"I'll call if I need help." Elizabeth returned to the sickroom to find Grace on her side, curled into a tight ball with her knees drawn up to her chin. Elizabeth tried to straighten her, but she was frozen into the position of a babe in the womb.

The smell of bacon and eggs lured Elizabeth. Ann had brought the brighter gas lantern from the parlour into the kitchen and it hissed from a hook in the middle of the ceiling, filling the room with a white glare that made Elizabeth squint.

They took their time with the meal, eating large portions, like men who had toiled outside all day. Ann had found a precious tin of pineapple chunks on a back shelf and they ate the fruit until it was all gone. Later, Ann washed the dishes while Elizabeth kept a close watch on their patient, both moving deliberately, not as harried as in days past. The hours chimed by on the clock so Ann took the lamp back into the parlour, then nestled chunks of coal into the stove.

Elizabeth made herself comfortable in a chair as Ann stretched out on the sofa.

Sometime later, a hand on Elizabeth's arm shook her whole body. "Elizabeth. Elizabeth."

Sleep had locked her neck in a painful position. "What is it?"

"Angel is fussing. Whining. And Grace—she's so quiet," Ann whispered in a tremulous voice. "I can't hear her breathing anymore."

Rubbing her neck, Elizabeth struggled to her feet. "What time is it?"

"Just after four in the morning."

Elizabeth went through the ritual of holding her breath and listening to Grace's chest, but the relaxed and comfortable position of the dead woman told her all she needed to know.

"We'll have to notify Faraday and then someone will have to ride out to the Weymans'."

Ann stared at the still body. "There's really no hurry now, is there? I'll wait for daylight and take Daisy."

ELEVEN

"I see quite a few people turned out for Grace Weyman's funeral." Herbert rubbed his hands together. "And most of them are hanging around to shop for Christmas."

The Chinaman shuffled over with a cup of coffee for Pietr Severson, then stood with his eyes on the floor, waiting for someone to order something else.

"I'll have a slab of that raisin pie," Herbert said, and waited only a minute for it.

Pulling his chair closer, he pressed his fork into the pastry, running his tongue over his bottom lip. "I think that boy of theirs was a bit of an embarrassment to his mother. Queer, cockeyed kid."

"It's hard to lose someone at Christmas," Alf noted.

"Hard time of year to bury someone," Pietr added. "It took us two days to thaw the ground, burning straw and coal on it day and night."

Herbert kept his attention on his pie. What kind of boy would he have? Would Beatrice's spells be passed along to a child? No, he convinced himself—any boy of his would be smart and strong. Beatrice's moods were just a bad case of homesickness, that was all. He scraped up the last sticky bits of raisin with the flat of his fork and dragged it over his tongue.

Herbert glanced at the Chinaman sitting at his table at the back with a pot of tea. He wasn't alone so much anymore. The last few weeks the fiddler's father, old Gregorowicz, often sat with him in the afternoon, the two of them sipping tea out of little bowls and playing chess. They didn't talk much; when a customer came in, Sam got up and served him, then went back to the game. He always wore what looked like blue pyjamas and black slippers, and Gregorowicz had on a red shirt and sheepskin vest and some kind of contraption on his feet that looked like just leather straps wrapped round and round right up his legs. Strange, foreign pair, thought Herbert.

"All moved, Herb?" Will asked.

"What? Oh, yes."

"And your new department store?" Alf had to pipe up, even though the whole town knew the answer to that.

Herbert felt his collar heat up. "Can't find help. Not for the store or the hotel. Rooms should be all full up, but I can't find chamber-maids or cleaning women."

Cliff Milner from the lumberyard came in and plunked himself down. "Just coffee," he called to the back.

Will pushed the sardine tin ashtray over toward Milner. "Get all those bricks unloaded?"

"Yup. Took four men the better part of a day, but we got them piled out back. Too cold for brick work right now but the bank is going to send some masons out to build the thing when it warms up."

"Sure will look fine, a big brick bank like that," Alf said.

Then they moved on to the subject of who would get a hospital first and worked themselves up over the possibility that Plainview might beat them to it.

Pietr sat quietly with his arms crossed and then added his two cents' worth. "The folks in Plainview will never raise the money any more than we could. They can't levy taxes against anyone but the property owners within the town boundary and they'll never scare up enough that way."

Everyone stared at the Swede and Herbert couldn't help smil-ing. It was God's own truth, but he liked it much better when it came from someone other than himself. For some reason, they listened to Severson and never argued.

Milner frowned. "What're you saying?"

"A hospital would serve everyone for, oh, forty or fifty miles around, but the government won't allow taxation for anybody but the people living right in Plainview, or any town for that matter. So they're blowing hot air, boasting about a hospital."

"Yes, I looked into it myself. They'd have to raise the money by subscription and you know how hard that is. Not like the school where we could levy a tax of five cents an acre for five miles around," Herbert offered.

"You mean they'd be baking cakes and things like that? Why, it would take them years to find the money that way." Alf looked so relieved it was comical, but Herbert understood his feelings. Everyone knew that a town had to keep on top of changes or it would just shrink up and disappear as though it had never existed in the first place.

The door squeaked open a sliver and a little girl slid in, paused to let her eyes adjust to the light, then made a bee-line to the back and hung on her grandfather's shoulder. The Chinaman smiled for the first time that Herbert could recall and reached his long arm to the cupboard for a gaudy tin. He removed the lid and let the little girl choose a cookie. Herbert decided a little girl wouldn't be so bad, if that was all he and Beatrice could manage.

"Looks like school's out." Alf rose to go back to work.

Will shrugged into his jacket. "When are we going to be able to have coffee in your new place, Herb?"

Herbert pulled his attention from the child and her grandfather. "I don't know when the furniture will get here. Ordered it from Chicago months ago, haven't heard a word since."

"Quite an expense, heating that big empty room," Will commented.

"Can't be helped," Herbert muttered. He left with Pietr, just behind Gregorowicz and his granddaughter. Something about the child, the Christmas streamers and Will's reminder that his dining room was empty got him to thinking.

Standing on the walk, his breath coming in puffs of vapour, he addressed Pietr. "I guess the teachers are out of school for the day, too. I was hoping to talk to them about their program."

"Nah, they're probably still working. They never get home before supper these days."

"That so? Maybe I'll stop by there. I always meant to see how things were going at the school anyway."

As he started to walk away, Pietr spoke again. "Another thing. You were saying you needed help?" He pointed his chin at the girl and her grandfather who were picking their way across the tracks on their way to the boxcar. "Gregorowicz woman's been helping Bertha now and then. The young one. Only woman I've ever seen who can out-work Bertha and do it with a smile."

"That so?" Herbert repeated. "Well, I appreciate you telling me that, I surely do." On impulse he stuck out his hand and shook the smithy's.

By the time Herbert reached the schoolhouse, the short December day was nearly spent. His footsteps on the oiled plank floor in the long common cloakroom announced his arrival. Entering the first classroom, he found Lydia Turnbull folded into one of the children's desks near the window, leaning into the last of the wintry sun and trying to mark papers. She raised her head to look at him but stayed seated. The light shone through the tangle of curls around her head, and it appeared almost pretty, but then she blinked her pale cat's eyes and he realized how old and tired she looked. "Hullo, Mr. Schneider."

Instantly, he heard footsteps from the other classroom and turned in time to see Iris Tanner's bulk come into the room.

"Good afternoon, ladies. I hope I'm not taking you away from your work?"

They exchanged a quick look, before Iris answered. "The light is beginning to go on us, anyway. Whatever we have left we'll take home and finish after supper."

Herbert turned on the sole of his left foot and examined the classroom, the colourful alphabet over the chalkboard and the carefully printed lessons for each grade. The teachers followed his gaze and he knew very well that they became more and more uneasy with each silent second that passed. When he thought enough time had elapsed, he bestowed a half smile on them. Now that he took a second look, both women looked worn to a frazzle. But then, they always looked as though they'd dressed in a bad windstorm, he thought.

"I came to talk about Christmas," he said jovially, removing his leather gloves and holding them neatly together.

Iris's jaw dropped. "Christmas?"

"Yes, your Christmas program. That is an excellent idea, by the way, having a little concert and party for the town."

"The town?" Lydia asked.

"We've always had a program for our children at Christmas," Lydia said in a huffy tone. "It's the only Christmas celebration some of them will have."

"Well, that's wonderful. You've had plenty of experience then." He had really begun to enjoy himself, and the prospect of their surprise and delight when he made his generous offer made him tingle all over.

Lydia uncurled herself from the desk and began collecting her pages. "It will be a simple program, Mr. Schneider. Some of the children are still learning English, so we'll present the easiest carols and a few short recitations. I hope the board will find that to their satisfaction."

"You do whatever you deem appropriate, ladies."

"The children have started making a few decorations," Iris said. "Chains from coloured paper, balls from old foil, things like that."

"Well, I'll tell you right out what I had in mind, and I think you'll agree that my proposition will make for the best Christmas celebration in the whole province."

Their faces were mirrors of alarm.

"You know of course that my new hotel is finished?"

"Yes."

"We heard."

"But the furniture hasn't come yet. The dagnabbed suppliers are as slow as molasses in January, so I have all that space, heated and with nice bright gas lights, just begging for a worthy use of some kind, wouldn't you agree?" He slapped his gloves against his thigh.

They stared at him, then at one another and then back at him. For teachers they sure were slow to catch on.

"I'm saying you can have your little concert in the hotel. How would that be?"

"What?"

"Where?"

Why was this so hard to understand? Here he was, offering them the nicest place they'd ever held a concert, he felt pretty sure, and they couldn't get it into their heads.

"In my hotel. In the dining room to be precise. It's empty—well, so is the tavern for that matter but we can't invite children in there, now can we?" He laughed at his own bit of nonsense.

But they both flinched at his hearty laugh.

"Why, I never thought . . ."

"Never even considered . . ."

"We've practised here, gone through the program so many times, the children may not feel comfortable somewhere else." Lydia looked around the room and plucked at her baggy skirt.

Amazing though it appeared to him, Herbert sensed reluctance on the part of the teachers. He had come with the certainty that they would fall all over themselves at the opportunity to move their little do to his hotel. He wondered if he should bother arguing with them, or just go over their heads and tell them the concert was going to be in his dining room and that was the end of it.

But it was the holiday season. "School closes on the twentieth, doesn't it? That means you'd have to fire the stoves up again just for one night. Quite a waste of wood and coal, with the tight budget we're on."

The green eyes widened and the other one sucked in her breath.

In a most companionable manner, he went on. "I'm not sure the board can afford the coal, and the gas for the lamps. Think how nice it will be in the hotel, warm and bright. I've sent some men out to look for the tallest tree they can find and we'll put it up right in the window where everyone can enjoy it." He would get on that first thing tomorrow. "Let the kiddies decorate the tree with their—what did you say? Paper chains?" He stepped closer to the pair of them, the image of his tree clear in his mind.

"B-but, they'll be shy," Lydia protested.

"They've never practised there. They won't be able to perform," Iris went on.

"You'll be able to practise when you decorate the tree." For the love of Pete, did he have to think of everything? "Come every day 'til the concert if you like. How would that be?"

"Well ..."

"It's settled then. I'll tell Mrs. Schneider we'll be having—how many guests for a party?" He chuckled as he drew his gloves back on.

"We have fifty-seven students right now." Lydia tapped what looked like an attendance record.

"And of course, their parents and little brothers and sisters will be attending. The single men usually turn out for these things, too. In fact, everyone for miles around will come, regardless of the weather. So—hundreds, I guess."

Herbert was shocked. "Hundreds! Are you sure?"

"Absolutely sure," one of them answered.

Herbert rocked back on his heels, trying to imagine so many people jammed into his lovely dining room.

"But now that you've put it so convincingly," Iris said, with something of a glint in her eye, "I'm sure the whole community will appreciate a special evening in your new hotel."

"And," Lydia jumped in, "if we came every day to practise on your stage . . ."

"Stage?" Herbert asked weakly.

Lydia hugged herself to stop shaking, even though Herbert didn't find it cold in the school at all. A little warm, in fact. "Of course. What is a concert without a stage? You're quite right, Mr. Schneider—it will be wonderful and the whole town will be thrilled. And don't worry about the food. We have a committee of mothers taking care of refreshments."

"Food?" Herbert's throat felt a bit tight. "I'm sure you know what's best," he said as he went out, slipping down the icy steps. "Couldn't you get a couple of those fifty-seven kids to clean the steps properly?" he grumbled under his breath.

The teachers stood on the top step and waved him into the gloaming. "Tell Mrs. Schneider we'll be there first thing in the morning." Their voices carried on the cold air and he thought he heard a snort but it was probably his imagination.

He entered his new residence to find Beatrice sitting in her favourite old horsehair chair in their near-empty parlour. The furniture from their old place couldn't begin to fill the rooms here but she didn't seem to have any interest in buying more.

Herbert stood for a minute and looked darkly at the sad shape of his wife in the lightless room, but his usual fury didn't rise and for the first time in months he missed Dr. Evans. A man needed another man to talk to now and then.

"Beatrice?"

From the hollow of the chair he heard an indrawn breath that came close to a sob. It was going to be like that again, was it? Her spells of misery were getting closer together, and longer all the time.

With his hands in his coat pockets, Herbert perched on the edge of the sofa and stared out the window as the expanse of sky turned to a pretty shade of royal blue. "I just spoke to the teachers about their Christmas concert. I offered them the use of the empty dining room downstairs and they jumped at the chance to have such a nice place for their little party."

He didn't expect an answer and he wasn't disappointed. He inhaled the faint smell of varnish and his belly grumbled. No smells of food, no trace of supper. He continued to talk, even though he knew he was only talking to himself.

"They'll bring the children over to practise a few times. You'll enjoy that. You can hear the little ones sing." He paused and took a deep breath. "They say they need a stage though. Never thought of that, but I guess I can get a couple of the men to rig something up. And we'll need chairs, too."

He heard her melancholy breathing and a rustle as though she had moved in the chair. He worried a hand out of his pocket and rubbed the soreness out of the back of his neck.

The voice that came out of the darkness had an eerie strength to it. "I don't know where to get chairs."

"I'll take care of the chair problem," he said quietly. "I can get some benches from the church, I expect."

He stared at her outline, saw the glitter of the whites of her eyes and knew she was looking back at him. Sometimes she made the hair stand up on the back of his neck, and at other times, like now, he just felt a bone-deep unhappiness for both of them.

"I'm going to get the men to cut a big Christmas tree to put up in the window down there, make it really special. The teachers tell me that some of the children won't have any Christmas but what we give them."

"Then they should have presents. I always got presents when I was at home."

Herbert was gratified by her interest, but presents? "Well now, that would be nice, but there are nearly sixty children over there, and they all appear to have brothers and sisters."

She sucked a big breath in through her nose. "And candy and an orange."

"Candy, you say?" Herbert thought of the paper-lined barrel of hard candy that he had just received at the store and brightened. "I believe we can consider candy. I can always count on you to come up with the best ideas, can't I?" He weighed the cost against the good will and started to like the idea.

"Tied up in little bags. I remember the candy tied up in little bags."

Wearily, he went along with her. "We have a pretty good stock of small brown bags. You'll have to do the filling, though," he warned. "I can't spare any of the help this time of the year, and I don't know about the tying part. Ribbon gets pretty expensive."

"Wool."

"What?"

"Coloured wool to tie the bags with and hang them on the tree. It will be beautiful."

Herbert laughed aloud. "There you go again with the best ideas in the country. Tie up the bags with coloured wool and put them on the tree for the whole town to see."

"Are you sure there is enough candy?" The worry in her voice was genuine.

Herbert stood with energy. "Get your coat and hat. I'll tell you what we'll do. We'll go over to the store and put all the hard candy away in the storage room to make sure there's enough for our surprise, then we'll head on down to the Chinaman's for supper. I hear tell he fries up a fine mess of liver and onions with mashed potatoes and gravy. You know how you enjoy liver and onions."

Giggling, she loped over to get her coat. "He has a braid, you know, down his back. And I heard he wears his bedroom slippers to work."

Herbert helped her get her coat on straight. "He does for a fact."

They walked down the dark stairs to the lobby, and waved at the night clerk standing behind the curved mahogany reception counter. With one accord, they looked into the empty dining room and then moved on.

On the street, Beatrice said, "Red and green."

Herbert exhaled in a frosty puff of exuberance. "Red and green what?"

In a voice he barely recognized, she answered, "Red wool for girl babies and green wool for boy babies."

His feet felt heavy in the snow. "Babies?"

"Red and green. Green and red," she repeated in a sing-song way.

The hair stood up on the back of his neck.

TWELVE

The wind rattled the windowpanes enough to lift the blue-and-yellow curtains. They were sitting in the kitchen to conserve fuel, Elizabeth reading a novel and Ann poring over a recipe for Christmas pudding, when a loud banging rang from the front door. Angel tore around the house yapping.

"Were you expecting someone?" Ann asked.

Elizabeth shook her head.

They hurried to the front hall and skidded to a stop, shocked by a stark white face framed by black gloves peering in the window at them.

"Merciful heavens," Ann exclaimed. "It's Beatrice and she looks frantic. Do you suppose something has happened to Mr. Schneider?"

In undertones, Elizabeth answered, "No, but I believe I know what this is about."

Ann pulled the door open and Beatrice stumbled into the hall.

"I need to see you." Beatrice pointed her chin at Elizabeth.

"Very well," Elizabeth said curtly.

"I'll light a lamp for you." Ann headed back to the kitchen.

She had only put her hand on a match when agitated voices crackled from the doctor's office. Beatrice's was high and frantic, but Elizabeth's remained cool and composed. Ann finished the business of lighting the lamp and stoking the stove, only then realizing that her hands were shaking. The argument from the front carried ugly words and even uglier implications.

"I will not have any part of it." Elizabeth sounded shocked.

"You have to help me. What will I do? I'll die!"

"Don't be ridiculous. You could go to Calgary and stay close to a doctor there."

"No, I'll die, even with a doctor. I know it, I can see these things. Don't you understand? I see these things."

"I understand that you're overexcited. You should discuss this with Mr. Schneider. Tell him you want the best treatment possible. Why, I'll wager he would even let you go home to Nebraska if that's what would make you feel better."

"Tell Mr. Schneider?" Her voice broke into a squeal. "You're not going to tell Herbert, are you? You're not allowed to do that. This is a private visit and none of his business, do you hear me?"

"Dear God," Ann said to the kitchen stove.

Elizabeth kept her voice quiet and even. "I won't tell a soul, of course. That's your privilege."

"This wouldn't be happening if you'd given me something to prevent it in the first place. I told you last summer I had to have something, and again just a few weeks ago."

Ann thought she might even feel a little sorry for Herbert.

Beatrice babbled on. "I know you have things that could fix this, I've read about them in the magazines. I would have sent for one of those tonics on my own, but that yappy Mel at the post office tells everybody everything."

"He does not," Ann murmured quietly and then thought, Mercy I'm getting as barmy as Beatrice, talking to myself.

"I know you can get that stuff, being a nurse. No one would ask questions. I'd pay you good money, too." Then in a sly and threatening way that made Ann's flesh creep, Beatrice finished with, "You've helped other women, I know you have."

Ann hurried back toward the office.

"I have never *helped* anyone," Elizabeth snapped.

"Here's some light," Ann said with determination.

Beatrice ignored the interruption. "Please, Miss Evans, I won't tell a soul. You probably have some right here, right in these cupboards."

Elizabeth stood up with a crackle of skirts. "I most certainly do not. Come to the kitchen and have some tea."

Between them, Ann and Elizabeth managed to herd her into the kitchen. Ann placed the lamp on the table and shoved the kettle onto the front of the stove.

Behind Beatrice, Elizabeth rolled her eyes. "Sit down, Beatrice. Do you take cream and sugar in your tea?"

Beatrice perched on the edge of a chair. "Just sugar will be enough."

Ann slopped the steaming water as she poured it over the tea and scalded her little finger. "I like sweet things myself," she said.

"I fixed the sweets for the babies. The candy bags."

Ann stopped in the act of reaching for cups and Elizabeth froze with her fingertips resting on the back of a chair.

Slumping back with a grunt, Beatrice studied the hallmark on the bottom of the tea cup. "I'll never live in a nice house again." Her cheeks sagged more than her gaudy dress.

"You mentioned babies, Beatrice." Elizabeth spooned sugar into her tea and stirred soundlessly.

Beatrice lifted her chin and a twisted expression flitted across her face. It might have been a smile. "Mr. Schneider and I went down to the store a few nights ago and hid all the candy in the back."

Ann slid her bottom onto a chair without knowing what she did.

"Then we took little brown bags and some green wool and some red wool. Took it home. Not home, but that place he makes me live in now."

"Bags and wool?" Ann asked.

"The men from the store brought all that candy to me yesterday and I put it in the bags. I tried to make sure every bag got one of each kind and that none got more than they should, you know?"

Elizabeth nodded as though it all made sense to her.

"Then I tied them up with green string for the boy babies and red for the girl babies."

"The babies?"

In sane and level tones Beatrice answered, "The candy is for the Christmas party. It's my Christmas surprise for the boys and girls when they come to our hotel for their party."

Ann tried to relax and offered a weak smile. "What a kind thing to do."

Sliding without effort back into her forlorn and whining voice, Beatrice said, "I wanted them to have what I had when I was little. I always had a surprise at Christmas time."

Elizabeth slid a hand across the table and touched Beatrice's fingers lightly. "And your baby, Beatrice? Will you plan surprises for your baby?"

Beatrice's face convulsed once, as though in a fit.

"You appear to me to have a lot to offer a baby. I mean, nice things from the store, a fine home, and just think, all your wonderful ideas could be put to splendid use for your baby."

"I'm so afraid. I'm not strong, you know. Everyone thinks I am, because I'm such a big woman, but I'm not."

Ann held her burnt pinkie over her lips and blew on it. The kettle hummed a friendly tune on the back of the stove while the clock in the parlour chimed the half-hour.

Elizabeth sounded enthusiastic. "You'll have a lovely time choosing clothes and furniture. Do you have the latest catalogues? Have you seen the pretty carriages and cribs they make now?"

Beatrice pressed her hands over her eyes, as though to avoid looking at something distasteful. "I'm not well enough, don't you see?"

Elizabeth leaned back and spread her arms expansively. "Everyone will fuss over you, bring little gifts for the baby, and ask how you are."

"I should get home now. I think it's nearly dark out there." Beatrice rose abruptly, tipping the chair.

Elizabeth jumped up, grabbed the chair before it hit the wall, and hustled Beatrice to the door. "Now, I urge you to tell Mr. Schneider the minute you get home."

"I look forward to seeing your little candy bags at the Christmas party," Ann said as she held the door open.

"The minute you get home," Elizabeth repeated.

Beatrice turned her frown toward Ann. "Huh?"

Elizabeth heaved a sigh. "Just get home. It's very cold tonight." She shoved the door closed after her patient, turned the key and then leaned against the wall. "Dear God, she gets worse every time."

The spectre of Beatrice's visit hung in the house for the rest of the day, so when they took their lamp and started up the stairs, Elizabeth hesitated only a second before the bottle of brandy that Ann had found for the Christmas pudding.

"I think we deserve a pick-me-up after that, and in real brandy glasses, too."

At the top of the stairs Ann suggested they should decide what to wear to the Christmas party.

"I don't feel like celebrating Christmas," Elizabeth objected. "And the concert will be one of those terrible amateurish affairs that are just an embarrassment for everyone."

"An evening out might be good for us and it will show our support for Lydia and Iris." Ann led the way to Elizabeth's room. She searched through the wardrobe and held a two-piece costume aloft, lifting her brows at Elizabeth.

"That's too lightweight for winter and probably not dark enough. I'm still in mourning."

Elizabeth turned her nose up at three more outfits. "This then," Ann said finally, shaking out a cashmere dress of midnight blue.

Elizabeth looked over the rim of her glass. "Ah, yes, I'd forgotten about that one. I haven't even worn it yet. What about you? You're not going to wear that awful brown thing, are you?"

Surprised, but not hurt, Ann answered, "I thought I would. Is it that bad?" She returned Elizabeth's dress to the wardrobe.

Elizabeth made a face. "You bring the lamp and I'll bring this." She waved the brandy in the air. "You must have something in that mysterious trunk of yours."

Ann followed with a lagging step; Elizabeth bounced onto the bed and cuddled under the satin-covered quilt with Angel snuggled into the curve of her hip.

But Ann didn't open her trunk. Deep in the back of the closet where she had stuffed it, weeks ago, she found a white duck garment bag and, for better or worse, pulled it into the light of the lamp. Slowly, deliberately, she unsnapped the side of the bag, hearing the expensive rustle, inhaling the delicate perfume.

Elizabeth rose to her knees, eyes wide.

Ann held the dress under her chin, letting the folds of sapphire silk fall to the floor, pulling the skimpy bodice across her chest. With a cool eye, she determined that it would be a bit loose. Their weeks of hard work had taken a toll.

"You didn't wear that to school concerts, did you?"

"No." Ann shook the dress out one more time and dropped it over the back of a chair. From the garment bag, she removed a dove-grey wool dress, the high collar trimmed with silk velvet to match the turned-back cuffs on the sleeves.

Elizabeth gave the dress an expert glance. "The grey is pretty enough, too, but where on Earth did Mr. Montgomery take you in that?" She pointed her brandy glass at the evening gown.

Ann hung the grey dress on the open door and moved to pull the shade down on the window. The room had begun to warm up, but she felt chilled through to her bones. She took a gulp of brandy that burned the back of her throat and made her cough.

Elizabeth knelt like a child, waiting for an answer.

"Malcolm could never afford to buy me a dress like that. He was just a simple clerk in an import firm, counting other people's money."

"Import?"

"I have gloves and shoes to go with it." Taking another swig of brandy for courage, Ann hiked up her skirts and fetched her secret key from her underclothes.

There was a mixture of shock and embarrassment on Elizabeth's face for a split-second, then curiosity won out and she wriggled to the end of the bed to watch Ann perform her magic on the trunk.

Ann lifted the tray that held her everyday stockings and shifts, exposing the deep, bottomless layers of her past. From between folds of tissue she lifted a pair of creamy silk stockings, then dropped a silvery blue negligee onto the bed. "There are shoes in here somewhere."

Elizabeth trailed the side of her hand over the stockings. "These are French or Italian," she said quietly.

"Yes, they're imported. Everything in here is imported."

"Imported again." Elizabeth ran her tongue around the rim of her empty glass.

"Some still have the tags on them. Jingfei reasoned that shoppers would be more interested in a garment if they could be sure it came from far away—like France or Italy. I learned about luxury goods, the kind you won't find in the Eaton's catalogue, while I was working at my last job."

The wind moaned around the house, finding its way under the windowsill until the flame of the lamp fluttered.

Elizabeth slid back to the head of the bed and pulled the comforter to her chin. "You have a trunk full of expensive lingerie, but when I hired you in Calgary you didn't even own an apron, did you?"

"No." Ann eased herself onto the side of the bed. She's no fool, this nurse who looks like a little girl.

Elizabeth moved as if to leave, then stopped. "You were married to Mr. Montgomery, and then?"

"And then he died. Less than a year after we were married. My only other relative, an aunt, was sick and even worse off than I was. As I got poorer and poorer, Malcolm's boss kept stopping by with little gifts of food and money. He won my trust, as was his intent, you see, and then he did me the great favour of offering me the position of housekeeper. My aunt and I were thrilled." Ann felt the chill in the room and not one whiff of warmth from the spirits. "He travelled frequently, to Europe and Asia, buying all manner of goods, including expensive women's accessories." She lifted the stockings and let them slip through her fingers. "I lived in his dreary apartment over the warehouse and at first I was simply a housekeeper with not much real work to do. Eventually he gave me some simple bookkeeping tasks, which I enjoyed."

Elizabeth asked in a small voice, "Real work?"

"One day he brought a particularly finicky, but rich, customer to the office where I was working. The man refused to buy anything unless the goods were shown to best advantage. He insisted I model them."

Elizabeth carefully set her glass on the nightstand and slid off the bed. "Not the lingerie?"

"That was the first of many occasions when I was asked to help sell merchandise. It was not a request so much as an ultimatum and I had to make a decision on the spot. I decided in favour of taking care of my aunt."

Elizabeth stood with her head down as though studying the design on the carpet. "You're too smart to get trapped into something like that," she said quietly. "Why, you were no better than your friend, the c-concubine."

"No better at all. I was young and alone and without money. I may appear smart now, but my learning came at a very high cost."

Elizabeth took a few steps toward the door and, without looking back, asked, "Like me, you mean? Alone and no money?"

"Not at all. You have an excellent education and valuable training."

When Elizabeth turned, Ann saw that she could not accept her housekeeper's past, that she wanted a better explanation. No, she wanted a different explanation. Elizabeth did not want to have to accept the fact that a woman, on her own and without money, might have to compromise herself in order to get by. Ann looked steadily back, knowing full well she might have gone too far. "My aunt survived for three more years and I was able to hire someone to care for her. The way we cared for Grace."

Elizabeth started toward her own room.

"Elizabeth, wait."

Ann proffered the stockings. "I know we agreed not to exchange Christmas gifts, but I'd like you to have these. You could wear them to the concert with your new blue dress."

Elizabeth stared at the stockings for a long time, then shook her head. "No, thank you."

THIRTEEN

They started coming in the middle of the day. Herbert scratched at the frost on the store window and watched two oxen lumber down the street, the driver trying to find room to hitch up on railings that were already crowded. Half a dozen youngsters tumbled out of the wagon box before it had even stopped. Up and down the avenue, why, there were children all over! Where did they come from, Herbert wondered.

Herbert revelled in the tinkle of the bell on his shop door as it rang again and again. He tucked his hands in the pockets of his waistcoat. "Merry Christmas, Merry Christmas," he said over and over.

He couldn't remember half their names, but most of them called back something cheerful, the greetings harmonizing well with the *ching* of the cash register and the crisp *whirr* of the new brown-paper dispenser. Feeling like a grand host, and trying to look like one, he strolled the aisles, smiling and greeting people, and checking inventory. Sugar, flour and coffee were going fast, but he had more out back. The specialty goods were moving, too: the boxes of chocolates, tins of liquorice allsorts, fresh oranges and apples—all those things that wouldn't sell worth a darn after the holidays. They would just sit there and rot or collect dust until next Christmas, unless he discounted them.

As the sun began to set, he slipped and slid his way home on the crowded boardwalk, hoping Beatrice had found the time to fix a bite to eat. In front of Porter's, a gang of young men were eating sandwiches in the back of a wagon, laughing and carrying on. Probably had a bottle of holiday spirits in the wagon with them, but what did it matter so long as they behaved themselves? Down the street, the Chinaman was doing a booming business.

Herbert wiped at a dull spot on the hotel doorknob with his coat sleeve before opening it carefully and stepping in. Warmth brushed his cold face, bright light spilled from the dining room along with the crash and scrape of chairs and benches being lined up for the concert. Lydia Turnbull was hollering orders at the two men he had hired to get the room ready. He gritted his teeth and without looking left or right went straight upstairs.

There was a light on at least, but still he held his breath. Beatrice had been acting more oddly than usual. Early this morning, as he had pulled his nightshirt over his head, he had heard her in the kitchen, making strangled sounds as though she were crying or sick. But when he asked her, she just looked at him with dark, glazed eyes and said he didn't have to worry, she could take care of herself.

Quietly, he hung his coat on a hook by the door and then sat to remove his boots. In carpet slippers, he walked through the sitting room, following the shaft of light from the kitchen. She turned from the stove, a grubby apron over a red-and-brown dress he'd never seen before. He had a merchant's eye for what would sell in a small town, and he was pretty sure he'd never ordered anything this ugly.

She plucked at the wide triangular yoke that made her mannish shoulders look all the more broad. "I got a new dress for the party."

"I see that."

Poking a steaming pot in his direction, she said, "I made some soup, because I thought we would get a bit hungry before the supper tonight. Mrs. Matthews said they don't serve supper at these things 'til about midnight."

"Well, well, isn't that fine. There's quite a crowd already." Herbert pulled out a chair, making himself smile at her flushed cheeks. Were they painted? He had never seen her sallow skin so bright.

She glanced at him with the saucepan in her hand. "I hung all the bags on the tree."

He squinted up at her, trying to keep the smile in place. There was no telling where her mind was from one minute to the next. "And you still had time to make soup?"

"It's from cans," she said defensively. "Tomato soup from cans, then I added a can of baked beans and some onions. Mother made it that way."

Herbert gripped his knees. About the only food in the world he hated was tomato soup out of a can; it always gave him indigestion. How many times had he told her that?

She slopped some into bowls and sat down, waiting for him to taste it. He sighed and picked up his spoon just as she jumped to her feet. Startled, he stopped and stared.

"Crackers. I forgot the crackers." She smacked the tin onto the middle of the table.

With relief, he took a handful and crumbled them into the soup. Raw onions had been chopped into the sludge of beans and soup.

She relaxed a bit and sat down, eating with enthusiasm. If she'd had an upset stomach this morning, she certainly seemed better now, shovelling the soup into her mouth as if she were starving to death.

"Do we have some cheese, or baloney, maybe? To go with the crackers?"

"Cheese." She jumped up again and returned with a block of cheese that had hardened on the end. She cut the crusty piece off, looked it over carefully, then stuffed it into her mouth.

Herbert felt his belly tighten but managed to reach for the block as calmly as possible. He kept his face down, eating steadily the cheese and crackers. "Do you think there will be enough bags? Sure are an awful lot of youngsters in town. Wonder if the folks in Plainview heard we were giving away treats and came to help themselves? You know how they are."

"That's where I got my new dress."

Herbert raised his eyes and eyebrows, wondering why the subject had changed to dresses.

"Plainview," she said with glee. In fact, a little giggle came out with the word "Plain" so that it sounded more like "pain."

He sat up straight and felt the heat under his collar. In about an hour he expected to be downstairs, in a clean shirt, giving the whole countryside a look at what a fine establishment he had built.

"I went over to Plainview the other day," she repeated, a scared and haunted look coming over her features.

Without a word, Herbert left the kitchen and went to try to find a clean shirt.

* * *

Stefan tucked the back of his shirt in tightly and pulled at the sheepskin vest. He shouldn't have worn these Old Country clothes. It had seemed like a good idea at home, with Eva and Hilde urging him on, but now, as the room began to fill with young men, some in suits and ties and stiff white collars, he realized how foreign he looked. Even his work clothes would have been better. Many of the men wore work clothes and he assumed that, like him, they didn't have suits.

The room continued to fill with boisterous groups, shaking off the cold and admiring the beautifully decorated tree. Women claimed the chairs and strained forward in their seats to see better; the children received a command to settle down.

At the last moment, the men at the back parted, as though by an order from on high, and two women walked in.

Stefan didn't realize that he was holding his breath until someone jostled him and the air went out of his lungs with a whoosh. Elizabeth wore blue, a deep, soft blue like the centre of a flower, and her hair had been piled in a loose bunch on top of her head. She surveyed the room with wide, solemn eyes, looking more curious than excited.

In the back of his mind he heard the hollow echo of the children's boots on the stage and Lydia saying, "Good evening, ladies and gentlemen, and welcome to the First Annual Aspen Coulee Christmas Concert."

Space miraculously appeared for Ann and Elizabeth to stand at the back, just behind the last row of benches, so they could see clearly. It occurred to Stefan that he was staring, then he glanced around and saw that all the other men were staring in the same direction. And quite a few of the women, too.

Ann's grey dress made her hair turn gold. She had the usual distant smile on her face, and he wondered if she practised it in front of a mirror. Even though the room was crowded, the women stood a foot apart, not one thread of their clothes touching, as though an invisible barrier separated them. Odd. He'd never noticed that before, because in most ways he'd come to think of them as a pair, like the teachers, working and even thinking together.

Stefan turned his attention to the stage, determined not to worry about his clothes. He heard a scrambling of feet and saw the little ones move to the front of the platform and sit with their feet hanging down so the parents could see the big girls behind them as they said their pieces.

Stefan opened his case, withdrew the violin and plucked at the strings. When the older girls, blushing and giggling, moved back, he took the opportunity to practise a few soft notes. There were more recitations, then Miss Turnbull nodded at him and he stepped onto the corner of the stage, not bothering with the little steps. They had agreed that he would stand at the side, and the children would turn a half step his way so they could follow his music more easily.

He tucked the satin-smooth wood under his chin and ran through a few more notes, then nodded at the teacher. She clapped her hands and about sixty little faces stared at him expectantly. The audience was holding its breath. Stefan heard nothing but his own quiet breathing and the throb of his pulse, like a metronome. With one, true stroke, the opening strains of "An American Christmas Hymn" swelled and filled the room. On cue, Lydia raised her baton and children's voices followed, "Oh, little town of Bethlehem . . ."

A satisfied *aahh* came from the audience. Stefan wished he had let Hilde trim his hair the way she had wanted to.

* * *

Elizabeth clasped her hands in the folds of the front of her dress and let the music come to her. Each note was true, and even the children's voices, working hard to stay with the violin, sounded all right. She looked at the crowd, really looked this time, and saw that most of the audience was enjoying the performance, although they probably didn't realize they were being entertained by a true maestro.

Clapping burst around them. Stefan nodded his head before sweeping into the notes of the next song. The children watched him as though mesmerized, working harder, Elizabeth guessed, at staying in time with the violin than they ever had at their lessons. They ignored their teacher with her jerky baton, dressed in her best checked, two-piece suit with a tattered crepe-paper corsage pinned low on her bosom, a gift from one of the children, surely.

The room became hotter and stuffier; the smell of bodies and mothballs overpowered the astringent fragrance of the tree. A mother hushed her crying baby, making more noise than the child. In the front row, Beatrice Schneider winced with each whimper, her head and shoulders shaking visibly. Elizabeth studied the back of Herbert's neck, bulging over his collar. Would they all hear the good news from him tonight?

The children shuffled into silence and Stefan played once more. "Jingle Bells, Jingle Bells." Lydia turned to the audience and motioned for them to join in. Shyly, nervously, a few sang along, with Theodora Matthews's high, clear trill leading the way. Elizabeth patted the palms of her hands together and decided to sing along as well but not too loud—it had been so long since she had heard these favourite old Christmas songs. They all finished with a breathless laugh, turning to congratulate one another. With a great deal of relieved shoving and misbehaviour, the children sat down where they were on the stage.

Lydia, flushed with the success of the program, turned to address the audience. "As some of you may know, and the rest will have deduced by now, Mr. Gregorowicz is an accomplished musician and will now perform for us."

Someone handed Stefan a stool. Along the wall, young men flexed their shoulders and jostled their mates, but he was unaware of them as he perched on the stool, one heel hooked on a rung, the other foot flat on the floor. He took his time while the audience fidgeted, and then fell silent. Elizabeth almost laughed out loud, recognizing a born entertainer, someone who knew how to manage a crowd.

The children on the stage waited with open mouths until, with a flourish, Stefan launched into a rollicking song that Elizabeth had never heard before. An Old Country tune by the sounds of it, meant for dancing, and soon the dining-room floor was rocking again, as everyone clapped along or tapped their feet. Without stopping, he moved on to a reel that was familiar to almost everyone and Elizabeth felt the surge of restless energy from the throng against the wall. They had come to dance and if the chairs weren't shoved back soon, they would take matters into their own hands. Obviously, Stefan knew this, too. With a toss of his long, black hair and a dramatic pause that hushed the room, he swept into the opening notes of Handel's "Halleluiah Chorus."

Elizabeth caught her breath. He seemed oblivious to anything but the magic he was creating, but she became aware of a disturbing sensation that began somewhere below her collarbone, trickled through her body, and settled in a warm puddle at the bottom of her abdomen. In a rush of emotion that she could not identify, she felt her chest tighten until she had to open her mouth to breathe. She'd missed so much, stuck out here. Her heart and soul filled with a yearning that she couldn't have put a name to if her life depended on it.

Stefan looked up from under the hank of dark hair and his eyes, sleepy with the intoxication of his music, looked straight into hers. He doesn't even see me, she thought.

Stefan knew he had captivated her. His habit had always been to scan the audience, find one person to focus on, and play his heart out until that person was in the palm of his hand. He had known exactly where he would look tonight, but the ease and wholeness of his victory amazed him.

He was aware of the police doctor in the red uniform stepping up behind Elizabeth and resting his hands on her shoulders. He saw Mrs. Montgomery wrap her arms around herself as she stared from Dr. McRae to the bronze Indian in the striped blanket and then back at the doctor.

Heads turned and followed his gaze. His father sat up straight, turned stiffly and stared at Elizabeth. He turned back to his son and Stefan saw the sad shake of his head. His mother assessed the little nurse in her costly clothes and nodded her head complacently. He didn't care about any of it.

* * *

The scrape and grate of chairs and benches on his new wood floor made Herbert's jaw ache. He felt sweat pool in his armpits, but the only thing he could smell was the smoky odour that hung over the Indian who trailed after Dr. McRae.

"'Tis a fine party ye've put on for the wee uns, Mr. Schneider."

Herbert held a brown package out to a grubby hand. "It's the only Christmas some of them will have, you know."

McRae looked down his long nose with a slow nod. "I'm sure 'tis."

Herbert watched the children tear at their packages but didn't chastise them. He had already made the decision that he wouldn't let anyone get to him tonight.

"Beatrice?" He looked around for his wife. The crowd pressed at him where he stood by the tree. The decorations were a shambles already.

"Mr. Schneider?" Beatrice looked around the tree at him, her eyes filled with panic as children pressed at her knees, their hands outstretched.

Herbert felt sorry for her. "You've done a fine job, Beatrice. Everything is just as you said it would be."

Louder, in the general direction of a surprised-looking Alf Porter, he said, "This was all Mrs. Schneider's idea. Insisted on having a special treat for the youngsters, didn't you, Missus?"

"And we all thank you. Children forget, sometimes, to say thank you, but we all appreciate it, Mrs. Schneider, we surely do." And with that little speech, Alf poked his hand at her.

Beatrice blinked, drew back, but then came to her senses and shook the man's hand. All the while the lanky doctor watched, his knowing eyes on Beatrice. At his elbow stood the nurse, a small smile on her face.

Elizabeth had sure shown her true colours a few minutes ago, Herbert thought, making a fool of herself over that Gregorowicz, and right in front of the whole town. Too good for the hard-working local boys, but swooning over the foreigner in the girlish shirt.

Jake elbowed his way over to the tree. "Where do we stack the extra chairs? The boys want to get the dancing started."

"Dancing? Is there dancing in the program? Where's Miss Tanner? Miss Turnbull!" Herbert yelled at the back of the frazzled teachers.

He patted a little boy on the head, pressed another on the shoulders to get by. All the young bucks were busy pushing chairs and benches to the wall while the children skipped and played on the stage, giving a much more natural performance now that the concert was over.

"Mr. Schneider?" He heard Beatrice's weak plea, but this was a more important matter.

"Miss Tanner? What's this about dancing?"

Iris swiped a strand of hair off her face. "I have no idea, Mr. Schneider."

"Come on, Herb. You know that a half-dozen country boys can't get together without a dance breaking out." Will Hepburn grinned like a clown. In fact, he looked like a clown in his bright yellow waistcoat and checked suit. Where did he get those silly duds, Herbert wondered.

"Dance? But there's no orchestra." Herbert grasped at his last hope. "What will they do for music?"

The words weren't out of his mouth before Ernie Hoffer stepped onto the stage with his wheezy accordion. A cheer went up from the crowd. The old rancher tried to sit on the stool that Gregorowicz had used, but it was too high for his bandy legs so someone tossed him a chair. Tossed!

"What the . . ." Herbert sputtered.

More cheers arose as one of the railroaders jumped up beside the rancher, took Hoffer's battered black Stetson, plunked it on his own head, and played the first few notes of some kind of jig on a mouth organ. Herbert felt that his tasteful little party was turning into a side show.

"C'mon, Gregorowicz!" someone yelled and the rest took it up. "Gregorowicz! Gregorowicz!"

Will laughed and slapped Herbert on the back as Stefan perched on the stool again. "Well, that makes two more pieces of a band than we usually have."

The sweat ran down Herbert's back. But what could he do? He had insisted they come and he wasn't going to let anything get to him tonight. "Well, they've come out in the cold. We might as well make a party of it."

Guests came by to compliment him, then got down to some serious dancing. The doctor waltzed by with Elizabeth as the Indian stomped out a dance of his own invention in the corner. Ann and Hepburn sailed past. Maybe it wouldn't be so bad after all. It might scuff the floor a little, but it would get scuffed eventually anyway. He saw the tree rock dangerously and went looking for Beatrice.

Herbert fought his way to the tree, found Beatrice backed into the window, and led her to the chairs along the wall. A couple of young men got up and let them sit. He grunted a thank you and lowered himself to the seat, sweat running freely down his forehead. He flapped open a new white hanky and mopped his face.

They kept at it for hours. The lights flickered and the floor shook, but the enthusiasm of the dancers never wavered. McRae and Hepburn changed partners. About midnight, just as Beatrice had said, the music stopped and the women opened hampers of food. Children, who had been playing under benches and in the lobby, rushed at the table like a pack of coyotes.

Bertha Severson bellowed at them. "Get back and wait 'til things are passed around." She cuffed a couple of boys on the ears. One stuck his tongue out at her and Herbert chuckled.

An hour later, the floor was smeared with spilled coffee and squashed tuna-fish sandwiches, but the music started up again. Herbert held a piece of cake in one hand and a cookie in the other. He turned to Pietr. "There's more dancing?"

"Ya. The people that live a distance won't try to go home 'til dawn. They can't risk losing their way in the dark. In this weather, they'd freeze to death before morning." He shrugged his shoulders. "So they'll keep right on dancing as long as someone will play for them. Myself, I'm getting old, I guess. Two, three in the morning is about all I can take."

"Dawn?" Herbert echoed weakly. Nothing is going to bother me tonight, he reminded himself.

To everyone's surprise the doctor traded places with Stefan and played the violin. He wasn't nearly as talented, but he did a respectable job of a couple of pieces, including a waltz that allowed Stefan to have a long dance with Elizabeth. Strands of her hair had fallen loose and floated around her flushed face, making her look quite pretty. They circled the crowded dance floor as though there were no one else in the room, not touching any of the other bungling couples, barely touching the floor, it appeared.

Herbert glanced around the room and saw that most of the others were watching them. Ann sat between the teachers. She had relaxed her stiff back, he thought, but then maybe she was just tired like everyone else. The teachers looked as though they wouldn't have the strength to walk home.

"Tired, Beatrice?"

She nodded. Her eyes glittered in the lamplight and her flushed cheeks had gone a sickly white.

"Go on up, then," Herbert said magnanimously. "Lots of folks are heading home. No one will think it rude or anything."

But she shook her head. He wished he could go up himself.

"I wish I could go up, too," he said out loud. For some reason that made her look worse.

Impatience stirred in him again, but he was too tired to try to find out what had been working on her nerves these last few days. Nothing was going to get his goat tonight. The baby asleep on the chairs beside him smelled as though it had filled its diaper and he had chocolate cake stuck to the sole of his boots. Out of the corner of his eye he saw the Indian still dancing, but no longer by himself. Ermiline, her bronze hair flaming, stomped around with him, bulging out of a red-and-brown dress identical to his wife's. Before he could stop himself, he heard the roar of his own voice. "Who let the floozy in here?"

FOURTEEN

Herbert left his store, empty except for one bored clerk who pretended to sweep behind the counter, and stepped onto the street. The whole town was quiet. It wasn't just his business. One week into the new year, folks were staying close to home.

A mild spell they had enjoyed had been replaced by a cold snap that turned the wet snow to humps of ice on the boardwalk. Herbert slipped and caught himself, then swore under his breath as he turned his collar up against the wind. The streets were a disgrace. The community well, with the banged-up horse trough in front of it, had a mound of brownish ice growing right out onto the street. The youngsters liked to play on it, but it looked terrible. In fact, the whole street was a mess, with dirty snow and horse droppings layered one atop the other.

He crossed the intersection to his hotel just as Elizabeth breezed around the corner, toting her father's medical bag.

"Good morning, Mr. Schneider," she said pertly. "I hoped I would run into you."

"You did, did you?"

"Yes. The streets are filthy. If the town doesn't take care of this problem now, we could have a serious outbreak of illness when it melts." She tilted her face toward him with a tight smile on her lips and the expectation of an answer in her eyes.

If it had been almost anyone else, Herbert would simply have admitted that he didn't like it either, although his reasoning had more to do with appearances than sickness. But the bold confidence of this young woman had always rankled him. "Do you have the money to hire a crew to clean these streets, Miss Evans?"

"It's not my duty to assign town work, Mr. Schneider. I believe that one of your responsibilities as overseer is that of sanitation officer, is it not? I feel I should warn you that this mess could lead to big problems in the spring. Just the smell and the flies will be a deterrent for people to come shopping."

He gritted his teeth and stared into her shrewd eyes where he saw the unmistakable twinkle of a challenge. He scrambled for something to say, some smart answer to throw back at her.

But she waved her little mittened hand and continued on her way. "Well, good day to you, then. I have to see to another injured railroad worker. I think it's time I sent them another big bill."

"You leave those gentlemen alone, young lady!" He watched her cross the rutted street as the first snowflakes stung his cheeks, her small figure looking like that of a child. She hadn't been much of a child at Christmas, he remembered, throwing herself at the music man with the women's shirt. And yet, for some reason, that made her more acceptable to the people in town, even the ones who were so set against her a few months ago. One way or another, he wanted to find a way to put this girl in her rightful place.

Herbert's mood lifted as he entered the hotel. The dining room now had some furniture, enough to feed twenty men at suppertime, and there were usually a few lined up waiting for a table to empty. The floor that had been scuffed from the dancing looked even more used, but that didn't matter as long as everyone got served. His problem now was to find people willing to work for reasonable wages.

In his office, he took off his coat and relaxed in his chair, listening to the rustle of activity overhead. The Gregorowicz women were cleaning rooms, making beds, doing laundry and mending.

He could faintly hear their foreign chatter. His shoulders stiffened when he realized that he didn't hear Beatrice's voice. He had asked her to take more interest in the running of the place and she had reluctantly agreed to supervise the cleaning staff. He snorted out loud—the worst housekeeper in the territory seeing to the cleaning staff.

At ten thirty Herbert snapped the cover on his pocket watch closed and put his coat back on. Out on the street he bent into the cold north wind and hurried toward the Chinaman's. He'd tried to cajole the men into meeting in his dining room, but the first and only time they had come the cook had still been drunk from the night before.

Heart-warming smells met him even before he got through the door: pipe smoke, doughnut grease and coffee. Too bad it couldn't be in his dining room. He stomped the snow off his boots and looked around. Most of the regulars were already there and, judging from the raucous laughs, they were in fine humour.

"Coffee and a doughnut, Sam," Herbert called before he reached the table in the middle where they always gathered. He hoped no one was in a hurry to leave so he could enjoy his food before bringing up the issues that needed to be discussed. By the time he had thrown his coat over the back of the chair, the Chinaman had set the cup and plate in front of him.

"Old son of a gun," Will Hepburn said to Alf Porter and smacked him on the back.

Herbert forked a chunk of spongy doughnut into his mouth and looked at Porter, who was red-faced and grinning.

Pietr Severson folded his arms over his chest, smiling across the table. "Hell of a way to get help in the store, Alf. The rest of us have to go out and hire people."

Herbert grinned and stabbed another hunk of doughnut. It felt good to have them razz someone else for a change.

"How many will this be?" Cliff Milner asked.

"Mrs. Porter is expecting another little Porter. Number six, isn't it, Alf?" Hepburn grinned from ear to ear.

They all guffawed again and Alf looked like the cat that had swallowed the canary, but Herbert had to work hard to swallow his doughnut, thankful that no one expected him to say anything. Six children. Herbert felt a hollow spot in his stomach open up and each time he thought of one of the Porter children, healthy and bright, it got bigger. With the tip of a moist finger, he ate the crumbs from his plate one at a time, watching the celebration from what felt like a great distance.

The door opened and a blast of cold air swept across the floor. Three people yelled at once. "Close the door, Kenny."

Herbert perked up. Kenny had a horse-drawn scraper called a Fresno, a metal bucket used to dig basements and cellars. It might do the job of cleaning some of the dirt from the streets. He pulled out the chair beside him. "Sit here, Ken."

Kenny took the chair with a smile, then stopped before sitting and stared at Herbert. "You decide not to go over to Plainview after all? Smart of you. Like I told Mrs. Schneider when she came to rent the cutter, the weather's turning fast today and it's eight miles each way."

Feelings of confusion and something more ominous froze the smile on Herbert's face. He didn't have any idea what Kenny was yapping about, but he couldn't admit that out loud. The faces around the table had got all the fun they could out of the proliferation of Porters; they stared from Kenny to Herbert with undisguised curiosity.

And yet that empty place in Herbert's gut didn't fill with anger and shame the way it usually did when Beatrice pulled one of her stupid stunts. She'd been getting worse and worse by the day; crying one minute, giggling the next, and then sitting for long hours at a time, staring at nothing. And now, what was this about renting a cutter?

Herbert became aware of the men exchanging glances, digging in their pockets for change, polishing off the last of their coffee. He had expected a serious attack of teasing, but their silence hurt more. It said quite clearly that they all knew what a trial Beatrice was, and even more painful, that they all felt sorry for him. Porter might have to put up with their teasing for weeks about creating a half-dozen children, which was something Beatrice couldn't manage to do even once, but all Herbert could hope for was their pity.

As the three of them stood to leave, tossing money on the table, Kenny shuffled his feet and stammered, "I'm glad you didn't go, Mr. Schneider, but seeing as how you didn't, where's the rig and horse? I'd hate for the little mare to be standing out all morning if she doesn't need to." ·

Four faces stared at him. Herbert had thought he could get out of here, go home and lambaste Beatrice a good one, then wait for tomorrow to invent an explanation. "I'll see to your damn horse. You'll get her back."

Kenny flinched and sat down with a thud. The others hiked on out as fast as they could. Herbert rose slowly from his chair without looking at Kenny, who had his head bent over his cup. He took his time fastening the buttons on his coat and easing his hands into his gloves. As though he had all the time in the world, he sauntered out of the Chinaman's and down the street.

Trying not to look obvious, he searched the hitching posts for a cutter and mare. Two farm wagons stood in front of the train station and he saw only three saddle horses, one in front of the post office and two outside his own store.

By two o'clock the storm had picked up a momentum that prairie people recognized with foreboding. Iris and Lydia let the children go home early and the livery was emptied out of sway-backed draft horses, hunching homeward with three or four children huddled on their backs.

"It might be days before we can go back to school," the little Gregorowicz girl told Herbert shyly. "That's what my teacher said."

He looked at Hilde and Eva as they stood in the doorway of his office, the child with her cheeks red from the weather. "I am soon finished the beds. She should not try to walk home alone. She will wait on that chair and not move." Hilde pointed to a chair at the back of the lobby.

"The child is no bother, Hilde, but she should sit up front here, away from the tavern. A tavern door is no place for a little girl." Herbert turned sideways in his chair and stared across the street at the blur of snow where he would have been able to see the station on a clear day. "Just finish what is absolutely necessary and get on home. You can't see your hand in front of your face out there."

"Thank you. I will work more hard tomorrow."

But Herbert continued to look out the window, his cleaning woman's gratitude falling on deaf ears. He felt old and tired and quite muddled in the head. It stemmed from his inability to decide what to do. Beatrice was not in the hotel, the store, or even, he was beginning to believe, in town. The cutter and team had not been returned to the livery stable the last time he had gone down to ask, and that was only an hour ago. Weariness weighed him down as he realized that the only thing he could do at this point was go door to door and ask if anyone had seen her today.

With a heavy tread, he climbed the stairs to the apartment. It was still filthy, even though he had asked—no, demanded—that Beatrice get up this morning and get to work. Tomorrow he would send Hilde up here to clean it and not put any more demands on Beatrice right now. He searched through the clutter for a heavy cardigan to put on under his coat and some thick wool mitts instead of the gloves. From the floor of the closet he retrieved his good fur hat, gently brushing the pile forward and back, then pulled it over his ears and went out the back way, down the narrow, snow-covered steps at the rear of the hotel.

Hoots of laughter and a cloud of tobacco smoke filtered onto the street from the back door of his tavern. They'd propped it open an inch or two again, even though he asked them not to waste the heat like that. Crews had been sent home early because of the blizzard, but home, to most of these men, meant the tavern. Herbert turned his back on the open door and ploughed through the snow down the back lane. Where could he even start?

He decided on one more visit to the stable. With his head down, he passed the empty stores along the street, feeling the cold bite into his face and toes. At the forge, smoke curled out of the chimney. He peered through the small, sooty window in the door and was drawn to the cheery blaze and the smell of hot metal. Pietr was bent to his work, his heavy leather apron, moulded from years of use, black across the thighs. Herbert felt a deep yearning for the smithy's life, for his simple craft and his sane, steady wife. Good God man, he chided himself, get a grip on yourself. How could you possibly feel that Bertha would be a bargain?

Pietr looked up quickly and stared into Herbert's eyes. Without either man uttering a word, Herbert saw the dawning in Pietr's eyes before he dropped his tools and reached for his coat and knit cap.

Pietr closed the door of the forge and clapped a big hand on Herbert's shoulder. "She's not back."

He knows, Herbert thought. He shook his head. "I was just going to check the stable one more time."

Pietr turned with him toward the stable, the warm weight of his hand staying on Herbert's shoulder. "You left your apron on," Herbert said.

"Doesn't matter." Pietr opened the side door of the stable and they stepped into the warm horsy smell of manure and ground feed.

Herbert, who had never been fond of horses, wanted to crawl into one of the hay-filled mangers, curl up and sleep until spring. With Herculean effort, he picked up one foot and then the other as Pietr guided him to the back where two men sat over a wooden crate, playing checkers. Kenny saw them come, looked from Herbert to Pietr and simply shook his head.

They started with the three of them, Pietr, Kenny and Herbert, but by the time they had fanned out over the town, a dozen men were knocking on doors, searching henhouses and calling up and down alleys. As more people became involved, Herbert withdrew into himself, numbed by the shameful exposure of his personal life as much as by the deadly temperature. Pietr stayed with him, uttering only those words necessary to ask at each house if anyone had seen Mrs. Schneider.

At the Evans house on the hill, the two women looked in alarm from Herbert to Pietr as the Swede explained their search.

Elizabeth exchanged a glance with Ann, then addressed Herbert. "Has Mrs. Schneider discussed her condition with you at all, Mr. Schneider?"

Herbert cringed. Then he thought, what difference does it make now? "It's not an easy thing to talk about. I just kept hoping that she would get interested in different things, you know, like the concert, or the store, to keep her busy. Involve her mind somehow."

Ann stepped closer to the nurse, prodded her with an elbow. Elizabeth clasped her hands in front of her and even in his befuddled state, Herbert could see she was finally at a loss for words. She took a deep breath and cast a sideways look at Pietr.

"I meant, has she told you recently of any other, uh, medical news?"

Too weary to play games, he only shook his head and pulled his hat back on.

"I think I should tell you that Mrs. Schneider has been to see me a few times."

"I know that." Herbert turned toward the door.

"Do you know why?"

The anger he had kept tamped down all day like a smouldering cinder burst into flame, scorching his belly. He felt as though someone had been beating on him and now he wanted to fight back. Towering over the little nurse, he asked, "What are you trying to say, woman? My wife is sick? Sicker than, well, what we all know? Is that it? Is that what you want me to say?"

Pietr tugged at his arm. "C'mon, Herbert. Let's go."

Ann stepped forward. "No, Pietr, wait, please. Elizabeth isn't trying to hurt anyone. She has been begging Mrs. Schneider to speak to her husband, but it's a private matter . . ."

"Nothing about my life is private anymore, don't you see that?" Herbert fairly bellowed at the woman. "Whatever secrets you seem to think I should know you can spit them out." He stabbed his finger at the floor. "Here. Now. To me and Pietr, so we can get on with our search and find my wife."

Both women shrank back, then the nurse looked him straight in the face. "If you insist. Mrs. Schneider is expecting a child, Mr. Schneider. Probably in about six or seven months. I haven't been trying to hide anything—it's a wife's privilege to give her husband that kind of news. You know how some new mothers want to wait until they are really sure before telling anyone. But as you can guess, she is very worried about it. I thought if she told you immediately, then you could share her concern—reassure her, let her go to Calgary or Edmonton, or even home if that would make her feel better."

A baby. His child.

They must have taken leave of the two women, because Herbert realized they were moving through a swirling vortex of snow. He stopped and looked around. "Where are we?"

"Almost at the hotel," Pietr answered from beside him.

"I appreciate your company," he said formally to the man who didn't fuss at him to move or hurry. He wanted to add that he was grateful for his silence too, but his face and mouth were too stiff to make the words.

In the lobby of the hotel, grim-faced searchers gathered, some with the white spots of frostbite on their cheeks. His cook, cold sober by the sickly look of him, had rustled up some coffee, steaks and gravy. For once his dining room smelled like a real restaurant, but Herbert wasn't hungry. The others ate with a minimum of muted conversation.

The last to come in was Jake, a sputtering Ermiline behind him. "Go ahead," Jake said. "Tell them."

Herbert looked into her red face and shifty eyes.

She tried to bluff it out, but that wasn't easy with Jake shoving her forward. "Tell them."

"I suspect your missus has gone to Plainview. Gone to see the woman above the millinery shop." She tried to glare at Herbert, but her flat, broad features twisted in an expression that reflected more fear than anything else. "You know the one."

The quiet talk dwindled away. Most men kept their eyes on their plates, but Herbert knew they were hanging on every word the woman said.

"What makes you think my wife went to see her?"

"Beatrice," she said, using the familiar name with a bravado that was clearly insulting, "Beatrice came to see me a few weeks ago, just before Christmas. She said she needed the services of an experienced midwife and that the nurse wouldn't help her, so I told her what everyone knows. The only other person in this part of the country who sees to women's problems is Grandma Malkin."

Women's problems, Herbert cringed. Beatrice had gone to this scent-soaked harlot for advice on her problem. His child was a problem to her. The dark fragments of dread that had gradually entangled his mind all day began to take on a cold clarity. Beatrice had found herself to be pregnant and, frightened and confused as she often was, had gone to the Evans woman for help. But of course, that superior little snip had merely told her to speak to her husband and then get herself off to Calgary or back to Nebraska. But why hadn't Beatrice gone to one of the other women in town who had children, like Mrs. Porter or the preacher's wife? Someone who could have talked sense to her? Herbert knew the answer to that but couldn't bring himself to think about it.

He stared at the puffy, painted face in front of him. It took every bit of the strength left in his weary body not to beat her to a pulp. "Get her out of here."

Muffled conversation started up again as the men finished their coffee. Some stood shuffling their feet, wanting, Herbert surmised, to get home to their own whole, safe families. He sat over his cup and watched them leave until only Pietr, Will and Jake sat around the table with him.

Will took a deep breath. "You know what that old lady Malkin is best known for, don't you?"

"Not now," Pietr said.

"I think we have to talk about it now. Right, Jake?"

Jake's face turned purple, but he managed to speak. "Ermiline says that Mrs. Schneider asked for some pills. Female pills to, uh, make women regular. Ermiline said she didn't have anything and it's against the law for the nurse. So she sent your wife to the old lady in Plainview and I guess she, uh, doesn't bother with pills."

"The point is," Hepburn went on quickly, "we can put two and two together and figure out that Mrs. Schneider has gone to Plainview.

I'm pretty certain the storm would have started there about the same time it did here and she would just stay with the Malkin woman."

Pietr nodded his head. "Will's right. The best thing for you to do now, Herbert, is get some rest and we'll see what tomorrow brings. The storm will probably blow itself out overnight and your missus will strike out when the going is clear. You could even rent a saddle horse and head out to meet her as soon as the wind lets up."

"I guess so." Herbert stared into his coffee mug. "Everything will straighten itself out tomorrow." He didn't believe a word of that, and from their pitying expressions, neither did any of them. But right now he needed to be quiet and alone, to think this thing through. Because, as sure as he had just gone through the worst day of his life, someone was going to pay for his grief.

FIFTEEN

Almost half of the front page of the very first edition of the *Poplar Press* was taken up with the news of the tragic death of Beatrice Schneider, wife of prominent businessman Herbert Schneider. According to editor Pritchard she had lost her way in a blizzard after spending the morning visiting a friend in a neighbouring town. Amazed readers also learned that she was a social leader in the community and had recently arranged a lively Christmas pageant for the town.

What was not in print was that the first alarm had gone out the day after the blizzard, when the little mare from the livery stable had wandered into the Belanger brothers' homestead with tatters of harness and rigging dragging at her heels. The Mounties arrived by train the next day and assembled a search party, but it was the same two brothers, investigating a flash of colour on a windswept hilltop, who found Beatrice's frozen remains, clad only in her gaudy Christmas dress. Her coat and galoshes were nowhere to be found.

The gruesome gossip about a blood-soaked cutter did not make the press either, but Bertha swore up and down that Kenny went out to the Belanger place with a can of kerosene and burned the cutter to ashes in the middle of the snow bank where it had become stuck.

Ann and Elizabeth pored over the paper on the morning of Beatrice's funeral, avidly reading aloud every scrap, from lost animal postings to announcements of the next meeting of the Central Alberta Stock Growers Association, and a bitter article about the inequity of freight rates to the West. They couldn't help but exchange glances when they flipped the paper over and saw a half-page advertisement of all the bargains to be had at the January sale at Schneider's General Store. They read it carefully, mindful of their own diminishing resources.

Finally, Ann rose to take her porridge bowl to the basin. "We're going to make it through 'til spring, one way or another."

"I really loathe this feeling," Elizabeth said. "Always worrying about money and wondering if we'll survive."

"I don't like it either but I've spent much of my life doing just that."

"I can almost see why some women accept the first proposal that comes their way," Elizabeth mused thoughtfully.

Ann shook her head. "Don't be tempted."

Elizabeth heaved a sigh. "I'm not. I could never spend the rest of my life with anyone unless I felt some kind of attachment to him."

"I'm glad to hear that."·

"Well, this case I'm going to today will help with finances. Jean Summers doesn't appear to present any complications in her pregnancy and her husband promised he would make my visit well worth my while. If you have enough to see you through while I'm gone, we'll be in a better position."

"Don't worry about me." Ann put a lunch of hard-boiled eggs and bread and butter in a cookie tin for Elizabeth to have on the train, which could almost be counted on to stall in a few snowdrifts at this time of year. Elizabeth packed a small grip and her well-used linen drawstring bag.

They layered heavy gabardine skirts over petticoats and wool combinations, then shortly before one in the afternoon, Ann led the way to town, breaking trail through the drifts. Their skirts crusted with snow, they stomped into the station and left Elizabeth's suitcases in the baggage room before hurrying to the church.

They were too late to find a place to sit, so they stood with a crush of people at the back of the unheated building, not warmed in any way by the choir's melancholy rendition of "Rock of Ages." The service was over in less than thirty minutes.

In the churchyard, they flinched at the chilling rattle of frozen soil thrown onto the lid of the coffin. Reverend Matthews droned into a bitter wind, his words scattered and lost before they reached the congregation. People shuffled their feet to keep warm; the wind caught the ashes from the fire that had been burning for three days to thaw the ground and sifted it, along with dirt, into the open grave. With unseemly haste, the mourners fled the windswept cemetery and flocked toward the Schneider apartment in the hotel.

Herbert sat near the window on an old, worn horsehair chair, its original colour darkened by dirt and age. Stefan entered with a chair under each arm.

"Ah, good man," Will said.

"I just take them from the dining room," Stefan said. "I can get more."

"Let's do that," Will suggested. "We're going to need them."

Ann envied the men for having something to do, then saw Hilde in the kitchen pouring coffee, and made her way through the crowd.

Embossed olive-green paper covered the walls and a darker green carpet with frayed edges had been placed on the floor, leaving a bare wood rim around the border. It looked as if the Schneiders had just torn it out of their old home over the store.

"This place isn't even clean." Bertha swiped with a dingy rag at dried food on the table.

"Can I help?" Ann asked. "I need something to do to shake this strange mood I've been in for days."

Bertha nodded sagely. "It's probably just the waiting."

"Waiting?"

"You know—waiting for the third one." Bertha tried to match cups to saucers.

"Third one?"

"Death. Death always comes in threes. Everyone knows that."

Ann shuddered. "I never heard of such a thing."

"First Grace Weyman, then Beatrice Schneider, now who will be the third? It's a fact. Death always happens in threes. And that's all I have to say on the subject."

The next hour dragged into what felt like a day as Ann strained to hear the train whistle. A plate of cornbread was passed around and she forced herself to eat. After two cups of coffee with extra cream and sugar, she began to feel warmer. When she heard the mournful bleat of the train, only twenty minutes late, she set her cup on the table and didn't even offer to help with the dishes. There didn't appear to be a clean cloth anyway. She and Elizabeth bundled up and clattered down the stairs like children released from school, dashing across the street as the locomotive squealed to a stop.

Ann left Elizabeth to board the coach and made her way to the engine. She flapped her hand at the hissing steam and squinted up at the engineer who leaned out of his cab to hear her. "The nurse is getting off at the water tower ten miles from here—you'll be sure she's picked up, won't you? You can't just put her off there in this weather."

"I'll wait a couple of minutes, but I got a schedule to keep."

She bit her tongue to keep from saying that he had never kept a schedule yet as far as she knew.

After the train had rumbled on its way, Ann stopped by the post office and was rewarded with a bright red envelope from San Francisco; she hurried home on numb feet. Upstairs, she gathered her flannelette nightgown, a sheet, a wool blanket and her satin comforter, and spread them before the pot-bellied heater in the parlour to warm. She closed the doors to the office and the treatment room to conserve precious heat, then did the same with the washroom. Only after half an hour did she remove her coat. The house crackled from the cold as it settled for the night.

Ann locked the doors and closed the curtains against the cold, dark night. She made a pot of buckshot tea, undressed quickly and wrapped herself in her comforter. With a sigh, she broke the seal on her letter, stopping as she always did, to sniff the wax.

"Miss Ann . . ."

That can't be right. Daughter—she always calls me Daughter. Does she have a new letter writer? Ann checked the envelope, but the handwriting and stationery were the same as all the others.

"I have with much regret to write to you . . ."

Ann was startled by a moan and realized it came from her. Angel jumped onto her lap and stared with worried eyes.

"The doctor came too late."

She hugged the dog to her chest and buried her face in the animal's silky neck, but all she could smell was sandalwood and a hint of opium.

In bits and pieces, she managed to read the rest of the brief letter. The gossips in the market said that lawyers had poked through Jingfei's belongings before the movers came and packed everything away in boxes. They would search through her papers for family; everyone has relatives, the writer said.

"Everyone but Jingfei," Ann whispered aloud. And me. She reached for her tea and discovered it had grown cold but she drank it anyway, like bitter medicine.

For hours she lay with the letter in her hand, staring at the lamp, her mind as murky as the smoky glass globe, crowded with memories.

Some recollections were happy—rice wine and dried fish that had been marinated and fried into savoury morsels that tasted much better than they looked. Some memories were painful, but Ann brought them out to look at anyway. Her delight the day Jingfei gave her the old Chinese wedding chest that she used as a trunk, and her shock when the old woman told her what the gift was for.

"He make you dress up in those clothes and he tell you keep records of how many. Bring some to me here and we put in trunk. A nightgown one time. Underwears another time. He won't know if you make the records look right—you know what I say? Soon you have enough fancy clothes to open your own shop. Nothing wrong with being a shopkeeper."

Ann knew it was wrong, but it was just a lark at the time, an excuse to visit more often, to hear more of Jingfei's outlandish stories and to be with someone who cared about her. One day she would return it all.

Another time Jingfei said, "Bring names and addresses. Where you can buy these things, who will buy them from you. Take all his business from him." Then she'd cackled and smacked her knee in glee.

Ann still didn't take it seriously, but she did as she was told. It pleased her to entertain the old woman with her own tales of larceny and deceit. She even managed to sneak a few dollars into her silk pouch.

Then they would drink tea and discuss how and where she would start her own business. That's what they were doing that day in April of 1906 when shock after shock of an earthquake levelled the shabby buildings of Chinatown, and dust and panic had penetrated Jingfei's padded world.

They took to the streets with thousands of others, fleeing the fires and choking on smoke, pushing handcarts or wheelbarrows with a few belongings, only to be driven back by men posing as authorities, people who didn't want the Chinese ghetto anywhere near their neighbourhoods.

After only a few hours, Jingfei sickened, probably, Ann realized later, from lack of opium, so they had simply turned back, into the devastation that had been Chinatown. Miraculously, her friend's house was almost intact and they had hunkered down to wait for whatever was going to happen next. More Chinese straggled back and by the time the fires had been put out three days later, makeshift stalls were selling vegetables and fish as usual.

That was when Jingfei had told Ann, "Go now. No one look for you. That man, he just think you dead like everybody else. Run now. Find a ship."

A few days later she was in Vancouver, Canada, with her trunk and the clothes on her back, spending precious money for a ticket on an eastbound train, numb with exhaustion and fear, not knowing where she would end up.

SIXTEEN

Herbert spent sixteen or eighteen hours a day in his office or the dining room, most of the time writing letters, but when the tavern closed and the whole town slept, he had to drag himself upstairs and try to rest in his cheerless home. He tolerated it for a week, then one morning he moved his clothes one floor down to the biggest guest room at the front and sent for some carpenters. They told him they could convert his apartment into a dozen small rooms in about two weeks. He took a few keepsakes to his office, including his silver hip flask and a framed picture of the Grand Canyon, and sat down to figure out, at a dollar fifty a night, how much income the rooms on the third floor would earn each month, now that his establishment was full most of the time.

He waited for the bartender to come to work at eleven o'clock and stopped him on his way through the lobby. "I'm having some alterations done upstairs and I need to empty the place. I'd appreciate it if you could find anyone who needs household effects. Get whatever you can out of it."

The man's mouth dropped open before he stammered, "Sure. Whatever you say."

At noon Herbert walked over to the post office and down to the Chinaman's, surprised at how mild the weather had become. He lowered himself onto a chair across from Will Hepburn. "It looks like we've got our January warm spell."

Will looked startled to see him, but recovered. "Yup. Change feels good, doesn't it?"

"Better than it was, that's for sure."

"Even the worst of it breaks sooner or later," Will agreed.

Taking a deep breath, Herbert pointed at Will's plate and asked, "What's that you're eating?"

Will poked at the stuff on his plate and stabbed a piece of something that looked like chicken. "Chop suey."

"What the hell is that?"

"Some kind of Chinese stew, I think. Real tasty."

Sam appeared silently at his shoulder. "I better try a plate of that suey stuff," Herbert said.

* * *

Ann stood on the back porch with her arms folded, too amazed to enjoy the weather. She stared from Elizabeth to Mr. Summers and back to Elizabeth, who looked as though she couldn't decide whether to laugh or cry.

In high spirits, Mr. Summers and a boy about ten years old were unloading a cow from the back of their wagon. "Prime young heifer, she is," the rancher boasted. "And bred, to boot. She'll be dropping a calf about the end of March."

"A calf?" Ann managed.

The boy opened the door to the stable while his father tugged the heifer down a ramp made from the end gate of the wagon.

"Mr. Summers has paid me for my services with a cow." Elizabeth looked at Ann helplessly. "It's very generous."

"Well, you brought me another boy, Nurse, same as your father did a year ago. Never have enough boys, ain't that a fact?" He clapped a hand on his son's shoulder.

"But, we don't have enough feed for it," Ann protested.

"Ah, you can pick up some feed from the livery. In a couple of weeks she'll be able to dig through the last of the snow and graze a bit."

Ann glanced quickly at Elizabeth who simply shrugged her shoulders. They thanked Mr. Summers as sincerely as they could and waved him on his way.

After supper, they talked into the night—about the birth of the Summers's boy, Herbert Schneider's move out of his apartment and the death of Jingfei. But their thoughts and conversation kept coming back to the cow in the stable.

"Pick up some feed?" Elizabeth repeated. "We can hardly afford to feed our horse."

"Or ourselves. Still, she must be worth thirty, maybe forty dollars if she's going to have a calf," Ann said. "We'll have to sell her."

"She's very quiet. Mr. Summers said she would make me a good milk cow. A milk cow! Can you fathom such a thing?"

"Have you ever milked a cow?" Ann asked.

"Never in my life."

"Nor have I. The only reasonable thing to do is sell her."

"But wouldn't that be something of an insult to Mr. Summers? Like looking a gift horse in the mouth?"

When they stopped laughing, the solution seemed obvious. Hilde would know how to care for and milk a cow, but she didn't have a fence or shelter and couldn't build one until the ground thawed in the spring. They would keep the cow for now and hope that Hilde would eventually be able to buy it.

* * *

Stefan didn't know what to say. A cow?

Elizabeth sat across the table from him, drinking tea. Eva sat on one side with her head bent over her schoolwork and his mother quietly did needlework near the window, but their attention was really on the talk between Hilde and the nurse.

He tried to see the boxcar through the nurse's eyes. The walls were a pale yellow and embroidered curtains brightened the windows. The plank floor had been painted dark green and was decorated here and there with rag rugs. To him, it looked nice, but she had everything new and modern.

"You will only need to pay us a small amount at a time, over many weeks," Elizabeth explained.

Many weeks to pay. Like his violin. Even though he was working for the railway again, he had to help Hilde support their family and try to pay Will Hepburn a bit, too.

"A milk cow! Butter and milk—everything we need!" Hilde folded her hands over her heart, then dropped them and her shoulders sagged. "But we can not, Miss Evans. It's too much."

"Please, call me Elizabeth. You can come and take care of her in our little pasture for now, until you have some place to keep her."

"Ach, yes, a pen," Hilde said, and Stefan could hear the yearning in her voice.

Elizabeth looked directly at Stefan. "It would help us too, if we could make this arrangement, because we don't know anything about cows."

Stefan looked back into her blue eyes, saying nothing, wanting nothing more than to give her anything she asked for, but feeling the yoke of responsibility settle more heavily on his shoulders.

She leaned toward him. "Neither of us even knows how to milk a cow. We're not farmers," she finished with a little laugh.

He had to smile back, remembering that she said the same thing about him not so long ago. She waited and watched. What could he say? That a cow was exactly what Hilde needed? Or that a cow was one more thing to tie him to this place?

"Miss Evans . . . ," he began.

"Elizabeth."

"Elizabeth . . ."

She stood up with her hands folded in front of her as though she was praying. "Please, think about it. I have to go now or Ann will worry."

Stefan helped her into her coat and then shrugged into his own.

"Hilde was the first person to come to mind when we talked about what to do with the cow."

His own mind, which never rested, had planned and calculated constantly for the better part of a year. In a few months, a year at the most, he hoped to have his violin back, and Hilde, well, it was amazing how well Hilde had done.

"Hilde has done very well, Stefan," Elizabeth said quietly.

He laughed. She looked at him quickly and slipped on the snow. Stefan grabbed her arm so she wouldn't fall.

"She has," she insisted.

"I only laugh because I think the same thing at the same time. Hilde does very well."

"Will she keep on working at the hotel in the spring, or will she just grow her garden?"

Stefan shrugged. "She likes to work at the hotel. Mama sews a bit there so they are both busy and Papa gets a little work helping with all the new buildings. Papa talks about planting in the spring. I think he is not so homesick and will be a help to Hilde. Maybe even file on his own land some day."

Late in the afternoon like this, with the town so quiet and a coyote yipping off in the distance, Stefan felt as though he had been here forever. Some days he felt a panic to get away, to find enough money to leave, and at others, like now, walking with this woman who had worked her way into his family and his heart, he wondered if he could be content to stay. He dared to take her bare hand for the last few steps to the back porch. She didn't protest.

They could hear the dog barking inside. Elizabeth rose one step ahead of him on the stairs and turned, making no effort to free her hand. "You must bring Hilde tomorrow to see your cow."

The step brought them almost eye to eye. "You will try to make me into a farmer?"

She laughed, a warm contralto that made him smile. "I wouldn't dream of it."

"You don't dream?"

"Dream?" She shook her head as though waking up. "Oh, that's just an expression."

"But you have dreams, yes?"

"Yes, I have dreams."

"I don't mean the ones at night. I mean the ones for the rest of your life."

She shivered. The light was not bright, but he was sure he caught a look of panic in her eyes, before she glanced away.

To ease the moment, he said, "I feel your heart beat, here." He pressed the tip of his index finger gently on a spot on her wrist that thrummed like a perfect note on his violin string.

"Pulse," she said.

"Pulse? Not your heart?"

"It's almost the same thing."

He curled his own hands around her small fists and cradled them against the front of his coat. "Your heart is in your hands?"

Her eyes glittered up at him, but she merely shook her head and muttered something.

"I can't hear what you say."

She turned her hands over in his. "I said my heart is in your hands."

No English words came to him. For a few seconds, which felt like forever, they stayed still. Then he felt her take a shaky breath, sensed her begin to pull away. "Don't go."

"If I don't go soon, I'll never go." The panic that he thought he had seen in her eyes was now in her voice.

* * *

By the second week of March, Herbert had nearly forgotten his life in the apartment upstairs. If he were forced to admit it, he would have to say that he quite liked his new room and new freedom.

His office shone with a cleanliness that he tended to himself. As efficient as the Gregorowicz woman was, he trusted no one with his things. He wrote copies of all his correspondence, including the ones to all the medical schools in North America, and then when the refusals came he attached them to the original and locked them up.

He did the same thing with the letters he wrote enquiring about a wife. Bride, they called them in the newspapers. If a town could send for a doctor, why couldn't a man send for a wife, a mother for his children? Herbert creased the paper carefully into three equal folds and slid it into a crisp envelope. If the postmaster pawed through everything that went out of Aspen Coulee, and Herbert would bet his last nickel on it, the snoop would just assume the town was still searching for a doctor.

He planned on taking more care in the selection of a wife than he did with a doctor. If the man had finished his medical schooling, Herbert didn't really care where he came from or what he looked like. Any wife of his, on the other hand, would be from a good family, a healthy family. How he would determine that had not bothered his mind, because no one had answered his letters yet. And of course she would have to be young enough to produce a good-sized family, not someone pushing middle age like the teachers or the widow.

Herbert stood, tucked his chair into his desk carefully and brushed a speck of dust from his overcoat before pulling it on. He put three letters in his breast pocket, locked his office door behind him, and went out into the glare of spring sunshine, only to be met by the ripe stink of manure. Some equally ripe language followed as a driver tried to free a rig floundering hub-deep in a sea of mud and filth.

"I can smell the rot right into my shop," Will Hepburn fumed at his elbow. "What are we going to do about it?"

"Who's going to pay for it is what you're asking, isn't it? We know what to do about it."

"It means the same thing to me. If businessmen can't scrounge up enough money, someone is going to have to advance it, with interest if necessary. It's getting easier all the time for people to go somewhere else to shop. They can't even drive down our streets without getting mired in muck."

Herbert sighed. "I'm going to the Chinaman's for a bite as soon as I see to some other business," he said importantly. "We can discuss it then."

"Discuss, b'damned. There's nothing left to discuss. We have to get this taken care of."

"It isn't just the money, you know. It's real hard to find the help right now. Probably take a half-dozen men and a couple of scrapers to get the job done. We may have to do it ourselves." Herbert was satisfied to see Will draw in his horns at that thought.

"What use is it to whine about it? Still needs to be done." And with those rude comments, Will stomped down the street toward the Chinaman's.

"Whine?" Herbert stared after him. He'd noticed that the kindness he had enjoyed after—well, when he was recovering from his deep tragedy—was wearing thin.

By the time he had picked his way across to the post office and back, Herbert was kicking slop off his pant cuffs and feeling tempted to do a bit of cursing himself. He swiped at a splatter of slush with his hanky and looked up to see the nurse hiking her skirts up to mid-calf and marching straight in his direction.

She was a hundred feet away but steaming right down on him, mad as a wet hen, and it warmed his heart. They could torture him with hot splinters before he would admit it out loud, but here came the reason behind his stalling; this superior little tart with her strident demands. Herbert knew she'd left his dear wife to worry on her own, and he was damned if he would go out of his way to help her.

She gave him a look that matched the filth in the street and swept on past. With a tight little smile, he turned to watch her pass, but the smile faded and disappeared as Miss Uppity-Nurse jerked open the door to the Chinaman's. Herbert hustled after her.

When he got there, her palms were braced on the table and she was lambasting Kenny, Alf, Will and even the preacher, who occasionally got away from his wife and mob of unruly children to join the men. The nurse was working up a sermon that would have done one of those old temperance witches proud, thought Herbert. "Polluted drinking water and children sick with fevers."

Will kept right on chewing, but Alf and Kenny stared at her as though she had cast a spell on them. Sam stood frozen halfway to the table with a coffee pot in his hands.

Elizabeth straightened her narrow back and stabbed her finger at each one in turn. "It's on your heads. Don't claim you weren't warned."

She flounced past Herbert without a glance and slammed the door behind her. Everyone in the place jumped and then started to breathe again.

Herbert gently folded his coat and placed it over the back of an empty chair. He knew they were all staring at him, knew also that he could no longer base decisions on his dislike of the nurse.

"Where can we find the men?" He rubbed his hands together in a businesslike way. "When can we start?"

SEVENTEEN

Fever. With great effort, Ann stopped herself from spreading her palm across her own forehead. "How can you be sure?"

Elizabeth peeled the sleeve covers down her arms and dropped them into the laundry basket in the washroom. "I recognize that smell. It's like mouldy, mouse-infested hay."

Ann willed herself to be calm as she poured hot water from the kettle into the hand basin for Elizabeth, then added a dipper of cold. "Mouldy what?"

The nurse's shoulders sagged with fatigue. "That stale odour the body gives off with typhoid. Once you've smelled it, you never forget it. I thought it was gone from my mind, but as soon as I stepped into that tent, it came back to me like the worst possible nightmare. I've only had to deal with it once before, during my first year of training, but it's branded in my mind forever." She plunged her hands into the warm water. "The disease could spread all through that filthy camp, and the one down by the river, too. We can only hope to stop a serious epidemic by warning everyone, by convincing them they have to take all possible precautions."

"Is there a chance it's just influenza? Not typhoid fever?"

Elizabeth looked up at her with a wry grimace that tried to be a smile. "I've been playing the same hoping game, Ann, but there's no point in fooling ourselves. This is the second case in the past week, both of them in the camp across the tracks. First it was the immigrant child, Susan, and now the youngest of the Long brothers. Could you hand me the carbolic, please? We're going to have to be extra careful with our washing."

Ann shook the container. "This is all we have left."

"Can you find money for more?"

"I can." Ann considered the dwindling stash of coins in her silk bag.

"I need to speak to the children at school about boiling their water and washing their hands. Especially since that child attended classes right up 'til last Tuesday."

"Let me go. You've been up all night and you need some sleep."

"It will carry more import if I go. Then I can stop to see Mr. Schneider and find out which one of us should be reporting this."

"I'll come with you." Then Ann realized what Elizabeth had said. "What do you mean, reporting?"

"The authorities need to be informed of an epidemic of a contagious disease. We haven't had a death yet, but it may be just a matter of time."

A robin hopped sideways down the porch rail, and two gophers played on a stubborn mound of grainy snow beside the woodpile. Mild air touched the women's cheeks, but the hopeful lustre had gone from the late April day.

At the school, Ann stood at the back of the stale classroom, overly aware of the closed, unwashed-body smell of the place. Rows of stiff little backs strained toward the nurse, open-mouthed faces reflecting the seriousness of her words.

"Explain to your mothers that all drinking water must be boiled to a rolling boil for eight to ten minutes," Elizabeth instructed.

A girl of about seven years wrung her hands and another flung her head onto her folded arms and sobbed outright. When Ann and Elizabeth left, the children were busy taking dictation from their teachers—letters to their parents with instructions on sanitation.

Ann asked, "Will it do any good?"

"If their parents have any sense at all, they already know what to do. It's been common knowledge for several years that typhoid is spread in drinking water."

"They have sense, Elizabeth," Ann said quietly. "And they will do whatever it takes to keep their children safe."

"I know, I know. And I'm sorry. It isn't the parents of the children I'm angry at, it's the town that let that quagmire grow and pile up until it reached such a wretched state. And I suspect the squatters out by the river are in just as big a mess. I haven't been out there for some time."

Their first stop was the general store where they bought more carbolic solution and looked for Herbert Schneider, but he wasn't in. Elizabeth led the way to the hotel with a stubborn set to her chin. The word OFFICE had been printed in gilt letters on the frosted window of the door that she rapped on. It's just as well Mr. Schneider can't see through, Ann thought, because if he saw who wanted to talk to him, he wouldn't answer the door. They heard the shuffle of papers, a drawer slamming shut and the unmistakable click of a lock. Elizabeth rolled her eyes heavenward and knocked again.

The amiable expression on Herbert Schneider's face stiffened the moment he saw Elizabeth. He held the door open only a few inches, no sign of invitation in his stance. His eyes shifted from Elizabeth to Ann and he drew back.

"Come in, ladies," he said with an insulting inflection on the word "ladies" as though he didn't really believe they deserved the title.

His ornate oak desk was a model of efficiency, like an illustration in a catalogue. He presented them each with a straight-backed chair across the room from him. Although he had a tray with coffee and doughnuts on a library table near at hand, he offered them nothing but a place to sit.

Lowering himself ponderously into his armchair, he asked, "What can I do for you?"

Elizabeth's face was white with strain. "We have come to ask if you know the proper provincial office to which we should report an outbreak of a serious and contagious illness."

Herbert laughed through his nose. "Really, Miss Evans, we cleaned up the streets long ago. There is no need to come around with your silly threats."

"I don't have the time or the energy to make threats, Mr. Schneider. If you don't know the names of the authorities, I can just go to the telegraph office and have them find out for me. I thought it would be faster and more efficient if we co-operated on this."

Herbert puffed up and turned red, but he stood his ground. "I know very well who to notify, Miss. I just don't intend to do it, not based on your say-so, and that's a fact."

"It's the law, Mr. Schneider. The ordinance respecting public health states clearly that, as a nurse, I must report certain illnesses and typhoid fever is one of them. In fact, it's probably at the top of the list, just after smallpox."

Ann saw a fleeting look of alarm which was quickly replaced by anger before Herbert's small, pale eyes narrowed at Elizabeth, his thick fists clenched on his desk.

Through his teeth he said, "You don't know what you're talking about."

"I do know what I'm talking about," Elizabeth retorted. "There are two cases that I know of to date, both in that filthy slum across the tracks. One is a six-year-old child and the other is a young man twenty years old."

"How do you know they have typhoid? Are you a doctor?" He poked his purple face in Elizabeth's direction. "Huh? Are you pretending to be a doctor now, Miss Know-It-All?"

Elizabeth drew back, then forged right on without a quaver in her voice. "I know because I've seen it before and I just read up on it in my father's books. The distinguishing symptoms are the distended abdomen which indicates lesions on the spleen and intestines, and the rash of course. That's the easiest symptom to recognize—the small raspberry-type rash on the chest and stomach."

"Read about it in your daddy's books, did you?"

Some of the fight went out of the nurse's shoulders and Ann had the urge to shout, don't let him see you weaken, even if he drags your father into this!

"Yes," Elizabeth answered. "But you don't have to take my word for it. Most women out here over the age of thirty have seen and cared for someone with typhoid. This isn't the kind of thing that stays quiet for long, Mr. Schneider. You can try to discredit me all you like but it won't stop the spread of this disease, or the dread that goes with it."

He jabbed a finger at her. "You're going to start a panic if you go around talking like that. That's just plain irresponsible, Miss, and I don't want to hear any more about it until we get a real doctor out here. It's probably just the flu or measles anyway."

"I'd be delighted if you'd send for a doctor, Mr. Schneider. I'm going to need all the help I can get. And even if it is just influenza or measles, it's still going to spread like a prairie fire in that cesspool of a tent town with only one water well, cheek by jowl with the outhouses."

He flapped his hand dismissively. "Tell 'em all to boil their water. You'll see, the two that are down sick will be up in no time and you'll look pretty darn foolish."

Elizabeth stood to leave. Herbert remained in his chair. "I hope so, Mr. Schneider. I'd much rather look foolish than have to deal with an outbreak of typhoid. In the meantime, I'll wait for your doctor. When will you wire for him? Will you notify the proper authorities at the same time?"

Herbert slid farther back in his chair and pulled his puffy chins in until they folded over his celluloid collar. "I'll do what I need to do without taking orders from you and I'll thank you not to go alarming the population with talk of deadly sicknesses."

Halfway out the door, Elizabeth said, "I've just spoken to the whole school, Mr. Schneider. I've informed the children what precautions to take, and what to look for by way of symptoms."

He came off the chair in a boiling rage. "You had no right!"

Ann pushed Elizabeth ahead of her into the lobby. At Herbert's booming attack, silence fell over the half-dozen or so people who milled about.

Elizabeth called back over her shoulder, "I have every right, Mr. Schneider. The whole of Aspen Coulee will be discussing typhoid fever by suppertime."

A collective mutter was followed by a deathly quiet before every single person in the hotel lobby took one big step back from the two women.

* * *

A week later, Herbert sat at his desk and faced two more women with stiff backs and stubborn chins. The world was a much better place in his youth, he thought, when women stayed home and kept their mouths shut. Take Lydia Turnbull, here; her mouth hadn't managed to close for more than a second since she had come in, and when she did stop to breathe the other one took over.

"Only about half of them have attended school this past week as it is. Their parents are afraid to let them come in contact with other children, even though the nurse says typhoid isn't spread through the air like a head cold."

"A doctor is on his way here from Calgary. I'm meeting the train at one o'clock and then we'll find out the truth about this so-called typhoid and whether or not the school needs to be closed," Herbert stated.

Iris blinked at him. "So-called?"

"What this town needs right now is the opinion of a level-headed man of medicine." He was sick and tired of all the women running around like chickens with their heads cut off, terrifying one another and all their children into the bargain. And he had that high-handed nurse to blame for most of it, he was pretty sure.

Lydia made a humphing noise in her throat. "Typhoid fever is quite recognizable to the women who have had to attend to it, Mr. Schneider."

He just stared back at her impertinence. He didn't have to sit here and argue with the likes of these two. "My decision is final. As chairman of the school board, I say we wait until a real doctor gets here before we make any hasty decisions about closing the school."

They glared at him for a full thirty seconds and then stood as one and marched out of the office without so much as a fare-thee-well. Good riddance to them.

An hour later, when he took his usual stroll up and down First Avenue, he heard the ring of hammers and caught the sweet smell of sawdust on the spring breeze, but the hitching posts and boardwalk were unusually deserted. He wandered east for two blocks to watch the masons work on the new bank. What a fine edifice it would be.

Before turning back, he dutifully looked across the tracks to the sprawl of shacks and tents that had the nurse all riled. It didn't look so bad to him. Oh, the usual litter that shows up after a spring thaw, but that happened everywhere. To hear that nurse tell it, only Aspen Coulee ever had a problem with spring runoff. Herbert thought of taking a walk over there, but a gust of wind came in from the south and he wrinkled his nose. It could wait another day or two.

He enjoyed a quiet two hours in his store, arranging packets of vegetable seeds in a nice display at the front. Women would be swarming in soon to get their gardens started and it was satisfying to take a hand in the actual work of the shop. It was a fine idea to let the clerks see him in his shirt sleeves now and then, too. At noon he put his coat back on and decided there was time for a bowl of soup at the Chinaman's before the train came in.

He arrived in time to take the last chair at his usual table. Will was missing, but Pietr, Kenny and Alf were in attendance. "Don't usually see you in here this time of day, Alf," he said.

"Wife's got real touchy, with the house full of bored children from sun-up 'til sundown," Alf complained.

Herbert ordered soup, coffee and pie. Kenny had finished eating and leaned back to have a smoke.

"Got the family home all day?" Pietr asked.

"Yup. Scared of the fever, like most of the women."

Kenny snorted. "Most of the women and Will Hepburn."

"I see Will's shop is closed," Herbert commented.

Alf nodded. "He told me he was going to the mountains for a few days' rest."

"Typhoid is nothing to fool with," Pietr said.

"Is that what this is all about?" Herbert snapped. "I'm sure fed up with all this gossip about fevers and sickness. It's time the town got back to the business of running businesses. Locking up and leaving town—what will we hear of next?"

Alf slathered butter on a piece of bread. "Isn't that why the doctor from Calgary is coming? To investigate the fever we have here?"

Herbert wiped his spoon on a clean hanky and slapped it onto the table. "No, he's coming to put a stop to this nonsense once and for all, not to nail quarantine notices all over town. If he does that, we might as well board up our businesses and take a holiday like Will."

"I heard there were six cases of it at last count," Pietr said. "Both the Long boys are real sick in that old tent with no one to tend to them. We don't have a spare bed anywhere, else we'd try to help out."

Not unless the boys have the money to pay your wife, Herbert thought. "We need another doctor," he grumbled, trying to change the subject.

No one bothered to offer an opinion so Herbert concentrated on his chicken soup. There were some things that Chinaman could sure cook and chicken soup was one of them.

Pietr and Alf tagged along with him to meet the train, which was right on time for a change.

A young, fair-haired man with a brown leather grip and what looked like a medical bag strode down the platform toward them. "Mr. Schneider?"

"My God, he's just a boy," Pietr said under his breath.

Herbert's heart sank. Somewhere in the back of his mind, he had harboured the hope that they would send a reliable, mature man who would be interested in setting up a practice here. This young man, with his hand outstretched, even had freckles over his nose.

"Doctor?" Herbert croaked.

"Burns. Dr. Fred Burns, Mr. Schneider. We met when Dr. Evans died, if you remember."

Herbert didn't remember. "Of course. Well, you'll want to come on over to my hotel and rest. It's up and running now and I reserved a nice quiet room for you."

"I'll just drop my grip off, thanks, Mr. Schneider. Then I'll have you take me to the patients. Two of them, I believe?"

"Uh, well, is there a hurry to . . ."

Pietr cleared his throat and stuck out his hand. "Pietr Severson, Doctor. And it's up to six now, according to the nurse."

Dr. Burns started across the avenue to the hotel so quickly that the rest of them had to hurry to keep up. "Six is it, Mr. Severson? Well, I'm not surprised. And how is Elizabeth? I thought she'd be back east by now."

"She's doing a fine job for us, Doctor," Alf said.

Herbert wanted to trip Alf onto his mealy mouth. Fine job? After what his Beatrice had to suffer? "Maybe you would like something to eat or at least a cup of coffee."

"I brought a lunch on the train with me. Let's get down to business. I have to head back south on Thursday."

Pietr smacked Herbert on the back. "Mr. Schneider likes to take care of business. I have to get back to work myself, so I'll let him show you around."

"Good of you to come, Doctor," Alf said and disappeared as fast as the Swede.

"Would you like to start with the children?" Herbert asked weakly.

"My thinking exactly," Burns answered in a jaunty way that Herbert didn't care for. "We're going to get along just fine, Mr. Schneider."

Twenty feet inside the tent camp Herbert wanted to turn tail and run. How could so much filth exist out here in the wide open spaces? He had to ask some grubby children who should have been in school where he could find the little girl with the fever.

Susan was holding her own, with a frantic mother to watch over her. The children were clean and there appeared to be a considerable supply of tinned goods in a box on the table. Herbert took in snatches of conversation while he looked around, but mostly he just wanted to be back in his own office.

"Cool sponge baths. You should probably boil the water that you sponge her with, just to be sure."

"The nurse told me the same thing. I been so worried—will the other children . . . ?"

The doctor gestured widely. "Get out of this fetid place. That's what will keep your other children safe."

"My husband's on the homestead now, trying to get a house up."

Bluntly the young doctor snapped, "Never mind a house. Get a good well."

Outside, the doctor paused, opened his leather bag and withdrew a large, bright yellow sheet of cardboard. Using the stub of a carpenter's pencil with its thick black lead, he printed the words QUARANTINE and TYPHOID, then signed it with a signature as compact and neat as the man himself. Next he smeared strong-smelling glue on the back of the paper and slapped it right by the door of the tent.

"Is that necessary?" Herbert asked, knowing the answer before it came.

"Yes. Any deaths yet?"

Herbert shook his head, aware of eyes staring at the notice, ears listening through cloth walls. He wanted to tell the doctor to mind his mouth, but thought better of it. Somewhere in the back of his mind, he had known all along.

"Tomorrow we'll look at the source of water. And what about outhouses? Got enough? Far enough away from people? Another week or two and this place will be swarming with flies."

Herbert puffed along behind Dr. Burns, trying to keep up with the questions and not step in anything too disgusting.

The second child they visited was older, but sicker and in much worse living conditions. Oddly enough, the doctor was less blunt and took more time.

Darkness was creeping up on them by the time they finished with all the children and found themselves at the Longs' patched tent. Herbert thought it must be getting on toward suppertime, but he doubted if he would ever be hungry again. The stink of rotting garbage was almost a relief from the stench of diarrhea and something mouldy and evil that lurked in the corners of the tent.

They had to bend double to get in; Herbert gagged, swallowed hard and felt a wave of dizziness. He stayed hunched by the door, ready to flee, his composure completely gone.

The doctor lowered his voice. "Ah, Elizabeth. Our paths have been crossing all afternoon. Quite a little epidemic you have on your hands here, eh?"

She looked up from where she was kneeling on the floor between two beds which were just mats spread over poplar poles, her striped nurses' dress soiled from the dirt of the floor and Herbert could only wonder what else. Her sleeves were shoved past her elbows as she slopped a generous amount of water over the bare chest and belly of the older brother.

Herbert averted his eyes from all the nakedness, wondering how a gentleman like Dr. Evans could have produced such a brazen hussy, or why any young woman would want to demean herself like this. He promised himself that no daughter of his would ever be allowed to sink this low.

With tired eyes Elizabeth stared at the doctor before she seemed to recognize him. "Dr. Burns. I wish I could say welcome, but, as you can see, it's not a very welcoming situation we have here."

The doctor squatted beside her, but he appeared more interested in the tired face and messy hair than he was in the two sick men. "How are you managing?"

"Not well. These two, for instance, are from somewhere in South Dakota. I've wired their family, but who can tell when anyone will be able to wire back?" She lifted one man's head and tried to pour water over his lips. "I've just been thinking that I would like to get them up to my house so my housekeeper can help with them. Then I'll have more time to get around to the others."

"Any of the other women able to help?"

"Help of any kind is hard to find. Most of the women are mothers of young children and they're terrified of carrying the illness home to their families."

Burns started to speak again but the man the nurse had been bathing suddenly began writhing around and babbling nonsense. His brother started to cry. Herbert shrank back toward the flap of the tent, wondering how he could get out of there without looking like too much of a coward. Burns pressed the delirious man back onto the stained mattress.

The nurse tried to calm his brother and Herbert had to admit she had a nice way with the sick boy. But the next moment she was whispering to the doctor, "These two cases have taken a different course. Bobby didn't experience any of the delirium . . ."

The doctor nodded and started a lecture on typhoid that Herbert didn't feel he wanted to hear. When footsteps crunched in the garbage outside and the tent flap opened, Herbert had never been so happy to see anyone in his life.

"Here, Gregorowicz. I was just leaving. You can fit in here."

It occurred to Herbert to ask the doctor if he was ready to leave, but he looked back long enough to see the man's fair head bent close to Elizabeth's, and her hanging on every word. If he wasn't feeling so sorry for himself, exposed all afternoon to this kind of pestilence, he would have felt sorry for Gregorowicz, staring at his little nurse on her knees between two near-naked men, gazing transfixed into the eyes of a third. Nosiree. No daughter of his would ever be in a compromising situation like that.

EIGHTEEN

Under the precious letter in the breast pocket of his patched work shirt, Stefan's heart missed a beat. Someone had soiled himself, and Elizabeth was down there on the floor in the middle of it, looking dirty and worn out; he wanted to grab her and run, but she hung on every word spoken by a young gentleman in a three-piece suit who knelt beside her. Squatting near the entrance, Stefan had time to study the man as the two of them discussed something in medical terms he didn't understand. Fair hair, well cut. Smooth, strong-looking hands. Intelligent blue eyes full of admiration for the woman in front of him. Stefan knew that if he held up a mirror he would see the same expression in his own dark eyes.

She looked his way and blessed him with a wan smile. "Stefan. I was just thinking of you."

He almost forgot the other man. "Do you have to do this?"

She nodded. "That's why I wanted to see you. I need to get these two men up to the house so Ann can help me."

"Dr. Burns," the man said and offered his hand to Stefan. "I have to disagree with Elizabeth on this matter. I don't think it is in the best interest of the town for her to be living with her patients."

"This is my friend, Stefan Gregorowicz," Elizabeth said, as Stefan returned the firm grip.

"I see." Then Dr. Burns's bright eyes flicked from Stefan's face to Elizabeth's. "I see."

Still, Stefan was prompted to ask, "Dr. McRae couldn't come?"

"Who's McRae? Oh, with the Mounted Police? It would take too long to find him. I've been appointed to the position of medical health officer whether I like it or not, and I'm here for 48 hours only, so let's see if we can solve some of your problems before I have to leave. Mr. Gregorowicz, have you seen any large tents around? Sometimes the railway uses them."

"Yes."

"I'm going to appropriate one from somewhere. I have the authority to do that. We'll set it up some distance from here and get a makeshift infirmary going. Then you, Elizabeth, can organize the women to take care of the patients in proper shifts. You'll be the matron, as it were. Sound like the best solution to you?"

She slumped back on her heels. "Why didn't I think of that? What about disinfectant, Doctor? I'm not sure the town has all that much left, and I don't know if the patients can afford to pay for what they use."

"Then let's get started. Mr. Gregorowicz will find someone with the railway and tell him the doctor has ordered them to donate a tent. Elizabeth, make a list of everything you need, and if necessary, I will send it back from Calgary as soon as I get there. And before I go to bed tonight, I will beard the lion in his den."

They both stared at him with a puzzled look.

"Mr. Schneider. He's having a little trouble accepting this, I think. He's going to be even more upset when he finds out what I intend to do about that well and the outhouses and this whole fiasco." He spread his arms to indicate the camp. His last comment before they headed to the store was, "And then of course, we will present him with the bill!"

The three of them grinned at one another. Stefan thought he could like this man, especially since he was leaving town the day after tomorrow.

To appropriate, Stefan realized, meant that the doctor could help himself to anything he needed and wanted in the whole town. Jake stood with his big hands hanging uselessly by his side as his tent and stove disappeared. He scratched his head and asked a few other puzzled men what or who a medical health officer was.

"I'm going to borrow your man, Gregorowicz, too," the doctor told him, and Jake nodded without a word.

In the general store, Stefan carried two large sacks while Elizabeth emptied the shelves of borax, quicklime and carbolic acid. As an afterthought, she threw in two dozen plain white towels and twice as many washcloths. At the counter, a young clerk totalled the list, then looked on with trepidation as Dr. Burns signed his name with a flourish.

"The government will pay. Send it along to the office in Calgary when you have a chance. No hurry," he said to Schneider's quaking employee.

"The government will pay?" the man repeated in disbelief.

Elizabeth hoisted a box of washing powder. "I think we should have some washtubs, too. The linens need to be soaked and washed separately from uncontaminated clothes. I can't ask anyone to take them home and do them with their family wash."

So they moved on to Porter's store and bought more supplies, again with the doctor signing.

The sky was completely dark by the time Stefan walked Elizabeth to her house and remembered the letter in his pocket. "I have a letter from Montreal."

"I think we'll need to separate the women from the men with a sheet or something," she said, then as an afterthought, "What letter?"

"From a university in Montreal."

She looked as though she didn't understand. "Montreal?"

"There is a good music school there."

Finally she smiled. "Ah, yes. Music schools. That's wonderful, Stefan, and when I have time, I want to hear all about it."

The letter stayed in his pocket like a promise.

The next morning, Dr. Burns supervised the assembly of the tent and stove, then considered the cold, damp ground before stalking off in search of a floor. Stefan followed him into Sam Wu's restaurant a few minutes after the businessmen had gathered for lunch.

Cliff Milner sputtered in his soup. "Borrow lumber? Who ever heard of such tomfoolery? And all those people with the fever? Who's going to want it after that? Take it. Use it. Then burn it!"

The others stared at the doctor in terror, wondering what he was going to demand of them next.

They set the tent up in tall grass on an open patch of prairie between Elizabeth's house and the church. Four men, including Stefan and his father, nailed the floor together on two-by-fours so it would be off the ground. A sparse stock of cleaning supplies was stored on the floor under the tables. Then they had the backbreaking chore of digging a hole for a new outhouse. By nightfall on the second day, the infirmary stood waiting, smelling of green lumber and a hint of creosote.

As Stefan and his father dragged their feet toward home, they encountered the tidy figure of Dr. Burns, caught in the midst of a group of men who all seemed to be talking at once.

Herbert's face was purple. "How do you come by the authority to turn our town upside down?"

"The provincial government has asked me to take care of your epidemic. And," the young doctor went on, as though he were discussing the weather, "I have the authority to fine anyone not complying with the Public Health Ordinance. I think it is fifty dollars for a first offence."

That shocked everyone, even Herbert, into silence until Pietr said, "Let's hear what the man wants."

"I want the pump in the camp pulled and the well sealed off."
Dr. Burns looked from one face to another, but got no response, either
for or against. "Then the outhouses have to be knocked down and
burned and the holes treated and filled in. And if you want this epidemic over with before midsummer, I recommend moving that whole
transient village to a new location. One that's higher and drier."

Herbert couldn't keep his temper in check. "That's just ridiculous!
Where do you propose we move it to?"

The doctor shrugged his well-clad shoulders. "I don't care."

It was obvious from his tone that he didn't. And that was the
undoing of the men, especially Herbert. They were still yelling and
arguing when Stefan and his father left. The doctor stood, bright-
eyed and unconcerned, in the middle of a noisy row.

By the time the train pulled out on Thursday with a tired but
unruffled Dr. Burns, Stefan had assisted in the demolition and burning of two outhouses and the closure of the camp well. The future of
the camp itself was still in dispute, but Herbert stood on his side of
the avenue and ordered the construction of two new toilets not far
from where the old ones had been.

* * *

Just before eight o'clock on the morning of May 10th, Ann draped
a blue-and-white-checked cotton square over her forehead and
tied the ends at the back of her neck, covering her hair completely.
When she glanced in the mirror at her blue cotton wash dress and
bibbed white apron, she thought she could pass for a nurse herself. She nearly stepped on a crocus as she hurried across the dry
brittle grass toward the tent and when she bent to pick it, she saw
with regret that her knuckles were red and raw even though she had
rubbed them with petroleum jelly before she collapsed into bed late
the night before.

She stepped softly onto the wooden floor of the tent so that those poor souls who had managed to fall into a troubled sleep wouldn't waken. Several times a day for the past three weeks, they had scrubbed the floor until a fine layer of wood had actually been worn off, but still the smell made her throat close and her stomach lurch. She found Elizabeth bent over one of her many notebooks, scrupulously recording the progress of her patients.

Leaning against the table, Ann picked up one of the dog-eared books. It described, in Iris Tanner's perfect script, the night that had just passed. "I'm not sure why you have to keep such detailed records," she said quietly to Elizabeth.

"Habit," Elizabeth answered absently. "It's interesting that the sickest people are the ones who were the healthiest before they became ill. Did you notice that?"

"I haven't given it much thought, to be honest. I just assumed the ones who end up here are men who don't have families to take care of them. Like Orville Weyman. Can you imagine Boyd trying to nurse his father through this?"

"I think Boyd would still be hiding in the barn if Mr. Porter hadn't gone out to get him. Now I'm told he spends most of his day hanging around the hotel. Mr. Schneider puts him to work sweeping floors."

"I hope he doesn't develop the fever. He'd be so much harder to care for than the other sick children around town."

Elizabeth stared thoughtfully out the open end of the tent. "Yes, at least the three children have their mothers to fuss over them. Children don't seem to suffer as much as the men, for some reason. And the woman, the bride from Nova Scotia, she has a lighter case, too. I wish I knew why."

Ann checked the water boilers on the stove to make sure they had enough for morning baths and then noticed the tired hunch of Elizabeth's back. "Did you get any sleep at all last night?"

"Yes, I went home after midnight and slept until about five. Orville has been delirious most of the night, and you know Mrs. Nelson, she's so timid sometimes I think she'd be more help staying home and making custard for us, like Mrs. Porter. You'd think a grandmother of her age would be used to sickness by now."

"Well, we have to make do with whoever we can get. Poor Iris, she must be exhausted. Who will be here today?"

"Bertha and Theodora."

With genuine feeling, Ann responded. "Good. We'll get a lot done. There's a heap of soiled linen soaking out there."

On pleasant days, and this promised to be one of them, Elizabeth insisted they open both ends of the tent and let the breezes blow right through because even the air needed to be cleaned. At night, when dampness settled on the grass, they closed the tent. The constant demand for hot water meant the stove was never allowed to die out, so by morning the heat and smell inside were unbearable. Each night shift ended with the throwing open of the tent.

On the trampled grass behind the tent, Iris was resting on an old bench that had been brought from the school, her elbows propped on the rickety table that served as a resting spot for the women. Stefan's father had constructed a wooden stand for washtubs and a long clothesline that was never empty.

Mrs. Nelson perched on a backless chair and Bertha stood, arms akimbo, scowling at Iris. "All I can say is that in my day, spinsters didn't attend to the personal needs of young men."

"Oh, Bertha," Elizabeth exclaimed. "That kind of thinking is what has kept medicine in the dark ages for centuries. If Iris feels there is anything she shouldn't do, she can let Mrs. Nelson take over."

"I have two younger brothers," Iris said wearily. "And I can't remember how many boys have had accidents at school that I needed to help them with. I'm not exactly an innocent babe, you know."

At that moment, Theodora Matthews breezed around the corner of the tent. "Good morning, all!"

Ann couldn't help smiling. The preacher's wife was as welcome as the spring sunshine. "Hello, Theodora. It's lovely to see you."

Theodora wore a loud floral apron and had her hair tied up in a piece of the same material. The first time Bertha saw her in it, she swore the costume had started life as a tablecloth. Elizabeth had said she didn't care what the rag on the woman's head was made of because the woman herself was the most valuable of all nurses—a survivor of typhoid fever. She proved to be far more than just immune to the disease. She worked hard at even the dirtiest task and never lost her smile. In fact, her constant, and increasingly bawdy, sense of humour kept them all from bursting into tears on many occasions.

"It's lovely to be here," Theodora sat beside Iris. "Lovely to leave my bored and restless children with Mr. Matthews again. I don't know how you do it, day in and day out at school, but frankly, I think it's good for our men folk to see what we have to put up with."

Iris chuckled. "You come here every day looking and sounding as cheerful as a robin."

Theodora beamed. "I love it. I truly do."

And because it was not in the woman's character to tell anything but the truth, they all grinned at her, even Bertha.

Ann turned her face to the blue expanse above and inhaled deeply. "It's going to be a fine day. I can feel it in my bones."

"Then let's get started on it." Theodora smacked her thighs and stood with energy. "Let the graveyard shift go home."

Ann felt as though a cloud had passed between her and the sun. She glanced superstitiously down the hill at the graveyard and shuddered. "I wish you wouldn't use that expression. Ever since Norman Long passed away on the night shift the first week we were here, his brother Bobby has a real fear of nights."

"Sorry, dearie." Theodora looped her arm in Ann's. "I'll try to remember. But this terrible illness will take its toll, you know. Norman won't be the only one."

Six narrow beds, three on either side, lined the tent walls. Like everything else, including the cup that held the crocus, they were cast-offs from local citizens or even, as in the case of the rickety table out back and one of the beds, actual garbage scrounged from the dump. One bed stood conspicuously empty.

They started with the sickest first. Orville Weyman had moaned and thrashed until it had been necessary to fashion sides on his bed with padded boards. They cleaned his soiled bedding and washed him from head to toe, then Ann left Theodora to massage glycerine into his heels and along his spine. When she was done, she tied his wrists and ankles to the bed again with strips of cloth so he couldn't climb out.

The first time Elizabeth had asked Ann to tie a patient to his bed, she had panicked, the thought of someone being confined like an animal too much to bear. She had never been able to bring herself to do it, but Theodora could deal with anything.

Bobby Long had recovered well from the first stages of the illness, although he suffered from melancholy following his brother's death. Ann supported him down the path to the outhouse and showed him once again how to scoop lime into the hole afterwards. "A generous amount now, to kill all the germs. It's not expensive and better to be safe than sorry."

He gave her a pathetic look, but she did not give in to the temptation to help him. He was gaining his strength nicely and Elizabeth insisted that pity was the last thing he needed. Next she helped him wash himself, checking to ensure they used the two percent solution of carbolic acid. "Some buckets have a stronger, five percent solution for the laundry. I don't want you to get that on your skin."

By the time the sun had climbed high overhead, yards of bedding and towels flapped on the clothesline. Ann stood in the warmth and pressed her hands into the small of her back. "I would love one of Theodora's massages," she said.

"Be careful what you wish for," Bertha responded. "Only the sickest are getting that kind of attention."

Later, Ann looked up from trying to feed Orville and saw Elizabeth beckon to her. "Aren't we low on water?"

In surprise, Ann answered, "A little, but I can get it."

"Why don't we get some now?"

Ann pointed her chin at the two women in the tent. "Theodora and I can do it later. You look exhausted. Go on up to the house and have a rest."

Elizabeth jerked her head toward the house. "I will. Walk along with me and bring some water back with you."

Ann got the hint. "Oh." Then she called to Theodora and Bertha. "I'm going for some water."

To make conversation until they were out of hearing range, Ann said, "It's a good thing our well is high and clean, isn't it?" Near the house she looked at Elizabeth's strained face and asked, "What is it?"

"Mr. Schneider hailed me when I was in town."

"Oh, Elizabeth! You can't let that old goat get under your skin."

Elizabeth responded with a small tired laugh. "He didn't want to get under my skin. He showed me a letter he had received from a lawyer in Calgary."

Ann dropped the bucket and clapped a hand to her throat. "A lawyer? What is he up to now?"

With a shake of her head, Elizabeth said, "I'm not sure he's up to anything other than trying to find a doctor. That's just it. This lawyer has an offer from a doctor who is interested in coming to Aspen Coulee."

Ann's heart missed a beat. "Isn't that what you wanted?"

"I thought so. But since this epidemic, and with Stefan"—her cheeks actually turned pink—"I don't know." She looked at her house as though seeing it for the first time. "It seems I have a place here now."

Me, too, Ann wailed to herself. She looked more closely at the tired face. "What is it? There's more, isn't there?"

"This new doctor will only come if he can find a suitable house. A house large enough to provide a dwelling as well as an office, modern and convenient—my goodness, Ann, the man described my house to the last shingle."

"He wants your house, too?"

Elizabeth nodded. "And he has made a very fair offer, according to this lawyer. If I'm interested, the lawyer will arrange a meeting with my lawyer, Mr. Macdonald, and the terms will be discussed at that point. Mr. Schneider was so polite and eager it was laughable, but I have to take this seriously." She looked at Ann with pleading eyes. "Don't I?"

"You do. Absolutely you do."

Ann stumbled through the afternoon in a haze. Sweat soaked the band of her kerchief and trickled down her back. She welcomed exhaustion like an old friend as they mopped and scrubbed, carried water in and slops out and treated everything with disinfectant, the dust of lime powdering their shoes. Nothing would ever feel or smell normal again. If she worked hard enough, Ann felt, she wouldn't have to think about what was to become of her. She developed a dull headache with the worry of it. Elizabeth had gone to share her news with Stefan. Stefan, with his acceptance letter from a school of music in Montreal.

Supper consisted of a thin gruel for the sickest men and bread and cottage cheese for those who were able to keep solid food in their stomachs. The evening routine was a repeat of the morning, with bed baths and massages to prevent sores. Bertha left them to attend to her own household, and Theodora and Ann took turns sponging Orville with cool water to try to lower his raging fever.

A rare quiet settled around the tent. Their chores complete, the two women flopped on the bench outside and enjoyed the silence. The haunting call of a nighthawk drifted in from the hills. Ann peered through the dusk and remembered how frightened Beatrice Schneider had always been by the empty prairie. "It's lovely at night, isn't it?"

"Indeed, quite wonderful. I believe I smell a hint of wood smoke, though," Theodora said. "A brush fire, perhaps."

Ann propped her tired feet on the broken chair and leaned back on the table, wincing at the ache in her muscles. She should be used to working this hard by now.

Theodora sat beside her, her dress sagging between her knees. They had a full five minutes of peace before Bobby Long crept out of the tent to join them.

"Did you hear if there was any news for me? Did my mother send a wire?" Under the protection of near-darkness, he made no effort to hide his tears.

Ann slid over on the bench. Homesickness and grief were going to kill this eighteen-year-old even if the fever didn't.

Theodora answered first. "No, m'dear. But she will, you know that. And we will let you know straight away."

"Sit with us." Ann slid over. "Here, beside me. Keep us company."

They heard footsteps coming toward the tent. "Must be the grave-yard—I mean, evening shift," Theodora said.

But Bobby picked up on the morbid reference. "I'm so scared sometimes. I feel so weak and with Norman—well," he whispered, "maybe I could die yet, too."

The footsteps crunched closer and Ann assumed they belonged to Mrs. Nelson. She couldn't help reaching out to touch Bobby's hand.

"We're not going to let that happen. Elizabeth will take care of you during the day, and Mrs. Nelson, here, at night and . . ."

"And," Theodora said emphatically, "Mrs. Montgomery is every bit as good a nurse as Miss Evans. Miss Evans says so herself, every day. Listen to Mrs. Montgomery, she tells us, because she knows as much as I do. Neither of them will let anything happen to you."

"There ye are, son. Safe as a babe with all these lasses to tend tae ye." The voice at Ann's shoulder spoke with enough assurance to cure the whole town.

NINETEEN

It was as though he had never gone. The battered saddlebags and dusty uniform were as familiar as the ease with which he moved back into their lives. He strolled from bed to bed, following Theodora and her lamp, and the men who had been too weak a short time earlier to hold their own spoons struggled to sit up. Ann couldn't help smiling herself; his mere presence was a balm to all of them. She sat down to a notebook at the table and carefully entered the details of their afternoon.

Dr. McRae saved Bobby until last, helping him into bed, then pulling up a chair and stretching his legs in front of him as though he had all the time in the world. Surreptitiously, Ann watched the doctor take the boy's pulse and neglect to let go of his hand, holding it as it lay on the covers. His quiet, steady lilt filled the room, the words distinguishable only to Bobby, yet Ann heard two or three other men sigh deeply before drifting into an easier sleep than they had had for days.

With Bobby settled, Dr. McRae brought his chair back to the table and stood looking down at Ann. "Ye've had a hard time of it."

There was no denying it. The proof was in her rough hands and her soiled and sweat-soaked dress.

"We've had some excellent help." Ann glanced at Theodora sponging Orville once again. "You really do see the best in people at times like this, don't you?"

"That ye do, lass. That ye do." He slid onto the chair, his knee brushing hers.

She pushed an open notebook toward him, noticing too late that it was upside down. "We've kept excellent records if you would like to read them."

He put a palm on the book without looking at it. "Am I still welcome up at the big house? I put my horse away, but no one was home."

Startled, she said, "Of course. Why would you even ask? I sent Elizabeth home hours ago so if she's not there, she must have gone to see Stefan. She puts in such long days. But your—that is, the doctor's room is always ready. And there's room for Horse Child, too."

"My friend isna travellin' with me anymore." He looked directly at her and she saw that despite his light-hearted manner, something in his life had changed.

Ann let her pencil drop. "I'm so sorry. What happened? Not this . . . ?"

"Fever? Nay, Horse Child has never been sick a day in his life. We needed tae go our separate ways, that's all, the both of us. We got called back to our own people, Horse Child up tae a place called Lac La Biche, and me to make that miserable voyage across the Atlantic."

She blinked dry, tired eyes and tried to follow what he told her. He'd gone somewhere. Across the Atlantic to his own people—in Edinburgh if she remembered correctly. Before she could stop herself, she blurted, "But you came back?"

The tension drained from his shoulders and something that looked much like contentment settled on his features. "That I did. My father, rest his soul, passed on and I had to clear up some business matters."

"What will you do without Horse Child?"

He startled her by covering her hand with his own, then graced her with the boyish grin she remembered from Christmas. "Find someone else tae be my keeper."

Slowly she pulled her hand back, not even trying to hide the raw knuckles. With effort, she squared her aching shoulders. Her face felt stiff and sore; her stomach tightened and actually hurt. A keeper.

All day her mind had struggled with her future, with the thought that Elizabeth might soon be gone, in the same way that most of her money was gone, and she would be left without work. But for some reason that her tired brain couldn't explain, the word "keeper" from this man felt like a slap in the face.

As his smile spread to his crinkly eyes, he went on. "A housekeeper. Someone tae do for me—to fix my coffee the way I like it, tae stay on at that brae big house and help with patients. D'ye know anyone?"

The clatter of her chair shattered the calm as she stood and, in one motion picked up the notebook in front of him, turned it, and smacked it onto the table so that it was right side up. Straining to whisper so as not to frighten the patients, she mimicked his accent. "D'ye need a keeper then, laddie? An' for what? Tae show ya what's up an' what's doon?"

He blinked at the notebook, obviously seeing it for the first time. "What?"

But Ann felt the room tilt, and her throat hurt from having to whisper. She made what she hoped was a haughty exit, grabbing the bucket of quicklime on her way. It might not be dignified, but there was no shame in cleaning an outhouse.

When she had done everything she could think of outside, she returned to the tent and heaved a sigh at seeing only Theodora and Iris. "Where's Mrs. Nelson?"

Iris made a face. "Late as usual."

"You go on home, Theodora," Ann said. "I'll wait for her."

They closed the tent and turned the lamp as low as possible to keep the moths away. Normally, Ann enjoyed a quiet half-hour visit with the teacher, but tonight her mind couldn't stay with any one thought. Close to nine o'clock, Mrs. Nelson showed up at last, and Iris urged Ann to leave.

"You look terrible tonight," she said with her usual bluntness.

The night air washed over Ann like a bucket of water from a very cold well. She chided herself for getting all sweaty and then walking home without a wrapper. The lamplight from the windows of the house wavered, faltered and danced far, far away, then came closer as Ann hoisted her heavy feet toward the back door. With one foot on the step, she doubled over, but had enough wits about her to realize it was the last symptom, the final confirmation, before she hurried down the path to the outhouse.

Several minutes later she crept into the house and poured herself a basin of water. She thought of the times in her past when she had wanted to die and couldn't catch as much as a cold. She heard voices in the office: Elizabeth's, high and excited, the doctor speaking only a word now and then. Ann closed the washroom doors and under cover of darkness, opened her dress and scrubbed herself as well as she could. When she was done, her hands shook so badly she could hardly bring a glass of water to her lips. She gulped the water down, poured more and drank that too, then with supreme effort she tiptoed past the office door and started up the stairs with the dog at her heels. She would have made it but for the clicking of Angel's toes.

With three steps to go, Ann heard Elizabeth's voice. "Ann! You're home. Dr. McRae is here and I have the most amazing news. Come back down and have a cup of tea with us."

Slowly, carefully, Ann turned. "I'm very tired," she said. At least, that's what she wanted to say but it sounded different somehow.

Elizabeth's frowning face floated up to her. A wary-looking Dr. McRae stepped out of the office and watched the two of them without a word. Ann propped her hip against the banister.

Elizabeth started up the stairs. "You know that letter Mr. Schneider told me about? Well, it turns out that—Ann? Are you listening? It turns out that it's Dr. McRae who wants the practice! Can you imagine? Ann?"

A great weakness in Ann's knees forced them to fold and slowly, with what she hoped was some fragment of dignity, she sank until her bottom made jolting contact with the top step.

"Ann!" Cool hands smoothed her cheeks. "Oh, dear God!"

Dr. McRae took the stairs two at a time, towering over Elizabeth, blocking all light. Ann grasped the railing and made one final effort to get herself to her room. She felt Elizabeth's arm around her waist and had an overwhelming rush of affection and trust for the nurse.

"Elizabeth?"

They had made it as far as the little sitting room. "What is it, Ann?"

She was aware of the tall, silent man who followed them, so she whispered to Elizabeth, "Please don't tie me up."

"For the love o' God! What's she goin' on about?"

Elizabeth snapped the covers down on the bed. "We had to tie a couple of the men to keep them in bed. Ann could never bring herself to do it."

"Please, Elizabeth."

In a firm voice Elizabeth answered, "I promise, Ann. You're not going to be that sick, anyway. I just know it. Let me help you into some cool nightclothes."

Dr. McRae knelt to untie her boots but she drew them away from his hands. He stared up at her as the lamp flickered to life.

"They're filthy," she said.

He gripped her foot again and in seconds her boots were yanked off and her skirts thrown above her knees. With a frozen expression, the man at her feet slid his hand up her thigh and peeled first one stocking and then the other from her legs.

Ann sat in her plain cotton drawers and chemise, shivering so hard the bed shook. Painfully, she turned and saw that Elizabeth had somehow managed to open her trunk and was up to her shoulders in a froth of silks and satins, releasing a suffusion of incense and perfume into the pure air of a prairie night.

"What the hell have you got there?" Dr. McRae demanded.

"Lightweight nightclothes," said the nurse matter-of-factly, tossing a negligee onto the bed as though she did the same for all her patients.

Ann reached for the gown and held it to her chest. From a great distance, she heard her own voice, frighteningly weak. "Jingfei?" Jingfei would get her out of this situation.

"No, Ann. It's me and Dr. McRae. I'm going to ask him to leave now while I get you into bed."

But he hauled Ann up by her underarms and propped her against himself so she wouldn't fall. "Dinna be daft, Elizabeth, ye canna lift her on your own. And dare I ask who this Jingfei is?"

I recognize that lovely accent under my ear, Ann thought. "Dr. McRae?"

He went totally still. "Ann? D'ye know me?"

She flopped her forehead onto his chest. "I can't do for you. I'm sorry."

"Elizabeth," and his voice brooked no argument. "Get on downstairs for cold water. This fever is rising by the minute."

"But—she won't like it. She would want me to undress . . ."

"Do as you're told, Nurse."

"Yes, Doctor," Elizabeth said, in her cross-little-girl voice. "Come, Angel. We're in the way here."

Cold air washed Ann's body where her chemise had been, then just as quickly her drawers were drawn down her hips and dropped around her ankles. Silk slithered over gooseflesh. If she didn't stop shivering soon, her bones would fly out of her skin and her teeth would crumble in her clenched jaws.

"Intae bed. Easy now."

Flat on her back on the sheet, she felt long, warm hands at her throat, down her neck, pressing and probing. Then, under her gown, fingertips exploring her stomach, her abdomen and finally the hollow place between her belly and her hip bone. With the last scrap of strength in her body, she opened her eyes and looked straight into his. She didn't flinch from his look or his hands. In her confusion, she found something comforting and familiar about his touch, like a very old memory, and she felt neither fear nor revulsion. Painfully, she tried to focus. "Malcolm?"

"Ewan McRae."

"Of course." She thought to tell him in no uncertain terms that she couldn't be any man's housekeeper ever again, but strangely, she heard herself say, "I'd love to do for you, Ewan, but I promised Jingfei. Because it wouldn't just be coffee, would it?"

If she squinted hard she could make out the blue of his eyes and she saw a flicker of something—shame, perhaps.

"Quiet now," he said. "I'll hear nae more."

Her heart cramped and so did her stomach. She moaned like an animal. "It hurts so much."

He slid his left hand under her tailbone and spread his right over her abdomen, gently rubbing the top hand in large circles. His shoulders heaved in a huge sigh. "Aye, it does lass, it does."

Elizabeth clattered back into the room, the joy of the last few hours completely gone. Dr. McRae turned toward her, his face a study.

"Is she sleeping?"

He nodded. "For now."

"Thank God you're here. How do you always manage to turn up just when we need you most?"

He ignored her question. "Can ye tell me what all this"—he waved at the open trunk—"is about? How well d'ye really know this woman?"

Elizabeth set the basin on the dressing table and picked up a hand-carved jade comb. "I know her as well as I need to. I can tell you that Ann has had a difficult and complicated life. I can also tell you that she is as true and loyal as anyone I have ever known. But don't ask me to give you the details of her life because I don't know them all, and if I did, I wouldn't reveal them."

The doctor stared at her until she squirmed, but she held her ground. "Ann's not just a housekeeper, you know," she said defiantly.

"Nae, she's not, lass. But we have tae treat her like a patient for now." He settled onto a chair with the look of a man who intended to stay awhile.

* * *

In the morning sun, Elizabeth watched the shock and concern on the faces of the circle of women who had made her work almost bearable. "As you know, the first seventy-two hours are the worst. Dr. McRae and I will take turns staying with her, but we would appreciate any time you can spare for us. If you can take over here, it will give me more time to nurse Ann. We assume from her condition that she passed through the first stage while she was here amongst us." She wanted to relieve their fears but keep them on their toes at the same time.

"That would not be out of the ordinary. We're all tired and overworked, so things like headaches and general aches and pains get overlooked. We're all very conscientious about scrubbing. But"—and here she paused for effect—"it would not be unusual for a second wave of fever to break out, especially with the heat and flies. We have to be vigilant." News of Ann's illness had spread through town and two new faces had shown up to help this morning.

"I tell Mr. Schneider I'm not back until Mrs. Montgomery is well. He said nothing, so here I am." Hilde stood with her sleeves rolled up.

Looking nearly as defiant but mostly uncomfortable, Ermiline said, "I can help as well as the next."

Red-faced, Bertha opened her mouth to give her two cents' worth, but not before Theodora acknowledged Ermiline without batting an eye. "Every pair of hands is a blessing, that's what I always say. A pure blessing. I surely could use your help on my rounds today."

Even Bertha was not willing to fly in the face of an attitude like that and Elizabeth had the urge to giggle about the alarm on Ermiline's face at the thought of spending the whole day with the preacher's wife. If Ermiline only knew—well, she would by the end of the day.

Every reaction to Ann's illness was different. Predictably, Mrs. Nelson swooned onto a chair and Elizabeth decided she might as well let her go. "I would appreciate it if you could take over the cooking chores. That's how you could help most. You can do your cooking and baking at home and bring it to us."

"Now? Today?"

Elizabeth had no sooner nodded than the woman was on her way down the knoll.

Theodora and Bertha would take over the management of the infirmary tent, with Elizabeth supervising as much as possible. Dr. McRae would visit patients in their homes and keep office hours at the house.

"Dr. McRae will be here if we need him, but typhoid is a nursing job," Elizabeth said. "And you're the best bunch of nurses I've ever worked with." Without thinking, she laughed. "I wish I could take you all with me." Her cheeks warmed when she became aware of them all staring at her with their mouths open.

Back up the hill, her shoulders tensed as she entered the house, listening for sounds from upstairs. All was quiet. With two rare lemons for which she had paid a princely sum, she made a crockery jug of lemonade. She poured a tall glass and started up the stairs on tiptoe.

The curtains fluttered in from the open window in Ann's room. His coat was gone, replaced by a simple homespun shirt with no collar, but other than that, Dr. McRae looked as though he hadn't moved since she had left him at midnight. His legs were stretched in front of him, his hands folded over his middle and his chin sagged onto his chest above his stethoscope.

Ann's hand plucked at the pillowcase by her ear. With quick, efficient motions, Elizabeth dipped a cloth in the basin at the bedside and wrung it out. She sponged her friend's forehead, face and neck, before rinsing the cloth once again. This time she lowered the sheet and untied the neck of the wrinkled and sticky gown. Working quickly so as not to chill her patient, she swabbed her chest and especially her underarms. The attention agitated Ann, stirring her to moan and thrash.

Elizabeth didn't hear the doctor leave the chair, but she knew he was standing behind her as she eased Ann's head forward and coaxed some lemonade past her dry lips.

"She's burning up."

"Aye, it's still at its worst. Let's get her in tae dry linens."

And so the cycles of Ann's disease dictated their lives. During times of relative quiet, one of them would stay with her and the other would carry on with duties around town. When evening came, they sat on either side of her bed and talked of the future, of when he would move to Aspen Coulee and give the citizens what they wanted most—a reliable doctor they could call their own.

"They don't know how lucky they are," Elizabeth said as they sipped some of the lemonade. "They'd better appreciate you."

He chuckled. "Did they appreciate your daddy?"

"Yes, they did," she had to admit. "Maybe he did the right thing after all, coming out here."

"He'd be more'n pleased to hear ye say that. It worried him considerably that ye were unhappy here."

"Will anyone appreciate what I'm trying to do?"

"I wouldna lie tae ye, lass. Many folk dinna tak to a young female doin' what ye do, seein' what ye see."

She sighed. "Do you ever regret coming way over here, making a life so far from home?"

He took a long time to answer. "I left m' home looking for excitement, adventure—a measure of freedom from family dictates. I found adventure in Asia, and more excitement than any man needs in Africa. But freedom seemed tae be the figment of a young man's imagination. So I came here because I had what they needed—a military background and medical training." They sat in silence for several minutes. "Tae my surprise, I found what I was looking for in the first place, or at least as close tae it as possible on this Earth."

"You did? Here?"

"Aye. For me it's all here."

TWENTY

On day two of Ann's illness, with a hot wind blowing from the southeast, Orville Weyman succumbed to the congestion in his lungs. His death was a grim blow on top of the news that four more cases of typhoid had been diagnosed since they had put Ann to bed. The second wave was upon them. Bertha took Boyd by the hand and led him, howling with grief and fear, toward the forge. "Pietr can keep him busy for now. He's going to be a nuisance around here."

That evening, as she attended to Ann, a knot of dread began to build in Elizabeth's stomach. The pattern so far had been that the older patients had been the sickest. The children and Bobby Long had suffered only mild cases and recovered fastest. How old was Ann? Thirty-four? She wished Dr. McRae would get home.

He eventually retuned in a rage. "Why in the name of all that's holy didn't young Burns have that camp moved? It's a bed o' vermin—mice, lice and all manner o' pestilence."

"He tried. Mr. Schneider wouldn't allow it. He wouldn't let them move onto any land that might be sold for a profit, and the railway was building on their land and, well," she said wearily, "you know the excuses men can come up with when they don't want to do what's right."

He stared down at her as she poked at her supper. "I heard ye lost another, lass. Ye know you canna take these things home wi' ye."

She had just enough energy to wave an open hand at his furious posture. "Of course not, Doctor. Where would I pick up a habit like that?"

He gave a snort. "Cheeky wee thing. Who's tending our patient?"

"Hilde, bless her heart. She made this meal, the first decent one we've had in days. There's a plate for you under that towel. The flies are terrible."

He started through the dining room. "I'll have a look upstairs first."

"Good. Oh," she called after him, "and Stefan has taken care of the outside chores, including your horse."

"A useful kind o' lad, isn't he?"

"Cheeky thing," she repeated with the closest thing to a smile she had managed all day.

By the third day, they couldn't even make an attempt at humour. They passed one another on the near-run, trying to grab a bite to eat, always aware of the need to sterilize, disinfect and scrub. Stefan kept the water boilers full, looking grimmer as the noon temperature climbed even higher than the day before and the hot wind moaned through the coulee and flattened the prairie grass.

By mid-afternoon, a faint haze settled over the town and the whiff of smoke replaced the stink of diarrhea in Elizabeth's nostrils. Hurrying across the tracks from the camp, she saw people standing in hushed groups as though waiting for something. "What is it?" she asked Alf Porter.

He shook his head. "Don't look good."

Elizabeth could not spare any time to fret about smoke. At home, Ann still thrashed in a state of delirium, her skin waxen, her belly distended and hard. Elizabeth spent the afternoon sponging her with cold water and changing her once again. After supper, she left Hilde sitting with Ann and went back to the tent. All six beds were full, as well as two mats on the floor.

Bertha knelt on the wooden floor, sponging a man whose name Elizabeth didn't know. "As if our work wasn't backbreaking enough as it is."

Elizabeth rested her hand on the woman's shoulder before opening the daily logbook. "Do the best you can. That's all anyone expects."

"Well, they got the best from you, and I'm happy to be the first to say it."

Startled by the vehemence in Bertha's words, Elizabeth stared at her. "Wh-at?"

"This town. You've given them fine service all these months since your father passed on, and my guess is no one has bothered to mention it."

Elizabeth couldn't decide if Bertha's face was purple from embarrassment or from the strain of lifting her patient. "No one needs to mention it," she lied.

Bertha blustered some more. "Well, it's my opinion that they should. And that's all I have to say on that subject."

Theodora winked at Elizabeth.

Ermiline looked ready to collapse. "How long have you been here today?" Elizabeth asked.

"Since I came, I think," the bedraggled woman responded.

"Don't tell me you haven't been home? Go. Get some rest."

The orange hair disappeared into an unnatural orange sunset as Ermiline hurried down the hill. Then two things happened almost simultaneously as Elizabeth stood and watched her go home to bed: flames licked for the first time out of the smoky blur in the west and the wind changed.

As capricious as a restless spirit, it fluttered back and forth from east to west, then twirled and danced to the west, ruffling rosebushes and stirring up dust devils in the baked ruts. As people gathered wordlessly outside their homes to gaze in awestruck terror at the fingers of flame, the wind completed its tease and settled down to a hard driving force from the west. The prairie fire raged straight at them.

"Dear God," Elizabeth prayed as she stood outside the tent with Bertha, Theodora and the two teachers. Think. Think. "Bertha, you'd better get home. You too, Theodora. Iris and Lydia, you're as well off here as anywhere. If we have to evacuate the tent, we'll bring the patients up to the house so I'll need you here. Keep everyone calm if you can."

How could anyone be calm? "Stefan," she whispered as she ran toward the house. "Where are you?"

Hilde stood on the front steps, her face ashen, straining toward her little boxcar house.

"Go get Eva and your in-laws," Elizabeth ordered. "Bring them here." Before the words were out of her mouth, Hilde was running like a man, her elbows pumping.

"Where's Dr. McRae?" she asked a whimpering Angel. She let the dog into the house and gave her a pan of water before running up to Ann.

Halfway up the stairs, her heart froze. The housekeeper stood, balancing precariously at the top of the stairs, the wind from the front screen door blowing her robe out behind her, exposing the long length of her bare legs. "Fire," she whimpered. "Dear Lord, fire. Jingfei, we have to get away from here."

Holding her breath, Elizabeth hiked her dress to her thighs and took the stairs two at a time, careful not to make any loud noises. Ann teetered above her, babbling about fire and no place to go.

A few minutes later, or maybe it was hours, Hilde returned with her mother-in-law and Eva. "All the men in the town are called out to make a—what they call it?"

"Firebreak," Eva whispered.

Elizabeth forced herself to ask. "Stefan?"

"He is with his papa and the others, making the firebreak."

"And Dr. McRae?" Was there a day, not so long ago, when she had only herself to worry about?

Hilde shrugged and shook her head.

Elizabeth nodded. "Fix coffee, sandwiches, whatever you can find, Hilde, please. There are going to be a lot of hungry people to feed." If there is even a town standing by morning, she thought.

The fire rampaged toward them, thickening the air with smoke so she closed the windows, capturing the stifling heat inside.

About midnight, as she hurried back and forth between the tent and her house, she found the Gregorowicz women standing on the porch. "It is stopping," Hilde shouted. "See, the flames are not coming closer."

Elizabeth had to agree. "It's quieter. Maybe the wind has dropped."

But the light breeze caught its breath in one last gasp of spite and bellowed down on them for another ten minutes. Ten minutes was all it took to devour the tent town.

In helpless horror the women watched the dark shapes of people rushing in every direction, flailing wet blankets and tossing impotent buckets of water until finally the railroad right-of-way and the dry expanse of First Avenue stopped the fire before it reached the commercial buildings. A few sparks sputtered across the width of cinder and steel but they were quickly squelched.

Within fifteen minutes, the first of the burn victims, women and children, began arriving at the door. Elizabeth sent Mrs. Gregorowicz upstairs to try to contain Ann and enlisted Hilde's help to spread ointment on singed hands.

Over the wail of frightened, burned children, Elizabeth heard the grim story from haggard women she had never met.

"The men were called away to build a firebreak around the round-house and when the fire came at the tents, it was only us, women and little ones, left to try to save our things."

"Now it's gone, everything up in flames."

"Nothing left . . ."

Despite their grief, she had to ask each woman, "Have you seen Stefan? Dr. McRae?"

They shook their heads.

Shortly after one o'clock, Stefan and his father arrived, filthy and exhausted. "Your house is saved," Stefan told Hilde with a feeble smile. "The firebreak we made for the roundhouse saved your house, too."

Elizabeth studied the haunted eyes in his blackened face. "But?"

"But, two people from the tents, they are not found."

By two in the morning, the last of the burns and injuries had gone, along with the coffee and sandwiches. Hilde begged to see her house for herself. "Take them home," Elizabeth told Stefan. "Come back in the morning and tell me all about it."

As the others started down the steps, she reached a hand to smooth his matted hair.

He grabbed her hand fiercely. "I will take you away from all this soon, I promise."

"No hurry," she responded.

He started to say something more, but a scream came from upstairs and she dashed inside, calling over her shoulder, "Look for Dr. McRae. I need Dr. McRae."

It was still dark when he came into the bedroom. Elizabeth was wrestling with an increasingly feverish Ann, sprawling herself right across her friend. Dr. McRae grabbed Ann's flailing hands, then took her pulse and bent over to listen to her chest.

"I heard—some people—missing," Elizabeth panted.

"A few singed whiskers, but only one actually died, as it turned out. The lady who's known as Ermiline."

"Ah, no! Damn it all to hell!" Elizabeth swore and dropped her head onto the pillow beside Ann.

Dr. McRae spread his long arms across both of them, embracing the two women. "Lass, dinna take on so. How do you know her anyway? She was the town . . ."

Elizabeth struggled free. "Don't tell me what she was! She was one more woman who worked her fingers to the bone for this town, for that selfish, miserable Schneider who wouldn't clean up that hell-hole when I told him to, and for the railway company that worried more about their roundhouse than the people fighting the fire!"

"Yer nae makin' sense."

"She was at the tent for two days, helping us. I sent her home to sleep—she was exhausted, of course she would sleep through anything." The days and weeks had taken their toll and her tears fell.

A weak hand stroked her hair. "Don't cry, Elizabeth. Everything will be fine."

Elizabeth and Dr. McRae sat bolt upright and stared at one another, then at Ann. But their elation faded.

"Help me," Ann whimpered. "Malcolm, I can't find my trunk. There's no place for me here." Her head twitched from side to side, her round eyes searching for something she couldn't find.

A haggard Dr. McRae repeated, "Malcolm again?"

"Malcolm was her late husband," Elizabeth said gently. "He was the one man in her life who was good to her."

"One man?"

"I need to sponge her again. You'd better go now."

"I need tae have a wash myself, then I'll be back. Yer a sight, too, lass. Ye need tae rest."

Twenty minutes later, he padded into the room in bare feet and navy flannel trousers carrying a basin of fresh, cold water and more towels. "Away ye go then, lass."

Elizabeth awoke the next morning to the blessed sound of rain and rolled from her bed with a grunt. Throwing open the window, she filled the room with the smell of wet ashes, then made a face at the heap of soiled clothes on the floor. She dropped a summery green wrapper over her bare skin, brushed her hair down her back, then wriggled her aching feet and rejected the confines of footwear.

In Ann's room, Dr. McRae was stretched out on his back, sound asleep with Ann curved along his left side, the fingers of her left hand curled under her chin. The faint blue of a bruise ringed her wrist where they had held her down.

Tiptoeing to the side of the bed, Elizabeth placed a palm on Ann's forehead, stiffened and ran her hand down the cool cheek. Ann's breathing was deep and regular. Elizabeth wanted to shout or sing, but it would be cruel to wake the two of them so she found a fresh sheet and spread it over them before opening the window partway to let in some damp air.

She went downstairs with Angel and out the back door, where she sat on the top step listening to the rhythm of the rain and envying the antics of the dog in the puddles. She was tempted to join in her play when the barn door swung open and Stefan leaned against the door jam, looking like the serious gypsy of—how long ago?

"I come to take care of the animals. The rain is nice."

"Yes. Silver linings."

"What is that? Silver linings?"

"It means that even in the worst times, some good can be found."

"One thing is not so good, I think, with this rain."

"What? Who?" Dear God, not more tragedy.

Still and serious, blurry through the rain, he answered, "You are on the wrong side of it."

"I am?" I am, she thought, I definitely am.

He nodded, not moving. "Come here."

"I can't." She scrunched her shoulders like a little girl and pointed to the puddles between. "No shoes."

In a few steps he reached her, bent at the waist and tossed her over his shoulder. A few more steps and they were in the shelter of the barn.

TWENTY-ONE

On Thursday, July 7, 1908, Elizabeth Evans stood before the altar of the crammed Methodist church and promised to honour and care for Stefan Gregorowicz for as long as she lived. It was eleven o'clock and the sun angled through the east windows, warming Mason jars full of wild honeysuckle, brown-eyed-Susans and bluebells.

Elizabeth had never been one to moon over an imaginary wedding the way some young females apparently did, but on the one or two occasions when the big day had crossed her mind, it certainly had not included wildflowers torn from a tangle of prairie wool, nor a rag-tag choir howling off-key. Nor, for that matter, a bridesmaid ten years her senior and a Paul Bunyan-sized best man who took up more than his fair share of breathing space in front of Reverend Matthews who had managed, so far, to get things right.

She slid a glance sideways at her fiancé. Even her wildest imaginings could not have conjured up a bridegroom this handsome. He returned her glance and winked slowly without moving another muscle on his face. Flustered, cheeks warm, she realized that Reverend Matthews had directed something to her.

"Yes," she said, because it seemed the logical thing to say.

The congregation chuckled, like a roomful of doting parents. Reverend Matthews blinked twice and then decided her response would do.

In the end they must have said and done all the right things because they signed a few pieces of paper and were on their way down the aisle when Pietr Severson said, "Congratulations, Mrs. Gregorowicz," and the enormity of the moment overcame her.

Good heavens, what a name. She had to take a deep breath and continue on her way, out into the glare of a cloudless day. In Old Country fashion, the wedding party and guests, which included most of the community decked out in their Sunday best, strolled to the house on the hill. Children and dogs ran hither and thither across the rectangular shadow of crushed prairie grass where the infirmary had stood not long before. Yellow blossoms of wild mustard and twisted clumps of prairie sage, dry and antiseptic underfoot, had already crept into the scarred patch.

Along Main Street, men were installing telephone poles and a couple of blocks over, masons were putting the finishing touches on the new Merchants Bank of Canada. Aspen Coulee was forging ahead to keep up with the times.

Laden with the latest in photographic equipment, Will Hepburn hurried ahead of them. "All set here, Stefan, Mrs. Gregorowicz."

"Do you think Mr. Hepburn knows what he's doing with that contraption?" Mrs. Porter asked.

"Claims he took lessons in Winnipeg when he was there," her husband answered.

Will herded them all toward two parlour chairs brought out to the front yard for the occasion. "We'll have one of the happy couple first. Sit here, Stefan, and Nurse, I'll have you stand behind him with your hand on his shoulder."

But Elizabeth was not about to hide her dress behind Stefan in his black suit so she stood to the side of the chair. As it was too hot for silk or satin, she had found a lovely ecru lawn fabric in Calgary that was only a touch lighter in colour than her mother's lace gloves. And being too small for flounces and frills, she had sewn, with Ann's help, a simple costume with a bit of yellow ribbon on the bodice to match the velvet roses on her hat.

With his head to one side and his thumb hooked into his bright green waistcoat, Will made a great show of assessing his subjects. "Ah, nice." Then, with the flourish of a magician, he disappeared under the folds of a black cloth, with only his checked backside sticking out.

One by one, the women bustled away to lay out an early lunch on the trestle tables that had been set up in the shade at the side of the house. Ann drifted toward the back door to help.

"No, no, Mrs. Montgomery." Will gestured for her to come back. "We need the whole party now. You too, Jake."

Jake, sweating mightily in his tight wool suit, protested. "No one wants my ugly mug in a photograph."

Ann returned to stand dutifully beside Elizabeth, with Will fussing around them like a bee, checking the angle of the sun. He returned to the tripod and made a great clatter by shuffling photographic plates before ducking under the black cloth again.

The guests wandered into the shade, sitting on chairs and blankets spread on the ground, eating crustless sandwiches, tomato aspic and peppery radishes the size of a fingernail. Will switched to a box camera and moved among them, taking more photographs.

Shortly after one o'clock, Elizabeth grabbed Ann and rushed her upstairs. "Help me change." She shimmied out of her wedding dress and stood in the middle of her bedroom in her drawers and chemise. "I don't know where anything is."

Ann threaded her way through the boxes and suitcases that covered the floor and reached into the closet that was empty save for Elizabeth's travelling suit. "I'm glad you're not going to try to take all this with you today."

"As soon as we have an address, we'll have Dr. McRae send it to us." Elizabeth pressed Ann onto the bed. "Put your feet up. You should still be resting every afternoon."

"Don't worry about me. No one lets me do anything."

* * *

Herbert strolled with the crowd toward the station. He was carrying his new tan gabardine suit coat folded over his arm, but he hadn't rolled his sleeves up like the bunch of young bucks who had started a pick-up game of baseball on the patch of grass where the infirmary had been. He wondered what the hot and unsuspecting passengers on the train thought of the spectacle of the citizens of Aspen Coulee parading toward the station, cheering the bride and groom on their way.

The nurse scrambled up the metal steps after about a dozen pieces of matching luggage. Gregorowicz carried his violin tucked under one arm and a battered canvas bag over his shoulder. Steam hissed across the platform and the conductor called, "All aboard!"

As the train started its laboured *chug, chug,* Ann Montgomery walked alongside. Elizabeth and Stefan leaned out the open window, laughing at the shenanigans of their friends and waving goodbye to the old folks. Before the engineer could muster much speed, the nurse stretched her hand to take Ann's and their fingertips touched for a second.

Ann kept on walking to the end of the platform, staring down the tracks until the caboose disappeared and the ground stopped shaking. Then she straightened her thin shoulders and turned back to the station. The women had all gone home to do their chores, but some of the men hung around the barbershop, staring in her direction and not pretending otherwise.

Will Hepburn stepped toward her. "May I walk with you?"

"I was hoping to just go by the church for a minute," she said wearily.

He stopped. "I understand."

She looked directly at him. "Thank you, though, for letting me contribute to the violin fund. Did you get enough to cover the whole debt?"

"Ah, sure, don't worry about it. When will you leave us?"

She shaded her eyes from the sun with the back of her hand. "Elizabeth wants me to rest for at least two more weeks before I travel."

"We'll miss you. Any plans, now that you're a wealthy woman?"

Ann dropped her hand and glanced away, then back again. "I'm not wealthy. I just won't have to worry so much anymore."

"I'm glad to hear that. But I'm sorry you had to lose a friend—in San Francisco, was it?"

She let her eyes flick over the rest of them—Pietr, Kenny, Jake, Alf, Herbert and even the new doctor, leaning against the barber pole as though he'd been one of them for years.

Ignoring Will's question, she said, "Maybe we could have lunch with Sam Wu one day before I leave?"

Now that was darn nice of her, Herbert thought, even though she just said it to get rid of Hepburn. They watched her walk past the rusted skeleton of the tent-town pump with its charred handle sticking out of the mess. New green growth sprouted between mounds of sooty rubble and rusted tin cans and in a few more weeks people would forget it had even been there. That's the way things were out here.

"It will be a long time before any of us forget her," Herbert thought, and then realized he must have spoken out loud.

"Well, she's not gone yet," Alf said.

"She's changed," Pietr mused. "When she first came to stay with us, I thought she was the classiest woman I'd ever seen."

Will nodded. "She's still classy."

"Couldn't believe she was just a housekeeper," Pietr went on.

"What did ye think she was?" the doctor asked quietly.

"Pietr's right," said Alf. "She's aristocratic in her way, but different somehow, too."

Herbert snorted. "Aristocratic."

"Used to scare the b'jaysus outta me." Jake pulled his tie off and stuffed it in his pocket. "Went up there once to get a tooth fixed."

"What did ye think she was?" McRae repeated.

"Can't rightly say," Pietr said. "We've followed the settlement right across the prairies from Manitoba and I've seen a few fetching women, teachers and all, but none that stood out like Mrs. Montgomery."

"But ye say she's changed?"

"I see that, too," Jake agreed. "She always had that straight, lady-like way about her, but she's more like one of the rest of us now, you know?"

They watched as the wind wrapped the thin stuff of her dress around her long legs and Herbert could see how frail she appeared. Near death's door according to some, and only the sheer willpower of the nurse and McRae had pulled her through.

"Could be," Kenny speculated, "she was a dance-hall girl or an actress or something."

"Don't be coarse," Alf said.

"Not bein' coarse. Heard tell a real smart store owner up north used to be . . ."

"Just 'cause *you've* got a shady past doesn't mean everyone does. There's no need to start a bunch of stories that serve no purpose." But Will gave Kenny a calculating look.

"Ah, hell, I only spent a couple o' weeks in the clink." Kenny thumped his chest. "And look at me now. Got m' own livery."

The doctor seemed to get a kick out of that.

Ann climbed the steps of the church slowly and disappeared inside.

"Well," Pietr said, "some of us got work to do."

The doctor walked back to the hotel with Herbert. "Your room suit you?" Herbert asked, just to make conversation. He knew his rooms were comfortable because he checked them himself.

"Aye."

Herbert tipped his head in the direction of the yellow house. "You got plenty of room up there for the two of you."

"Dinna like to compromise Mrs. Montgomery."

Herbert thought he sounded tense. "Compromise?"

The doctor reached around Herbert with his long arm and opened the door. "Ye know how folk in a small town can talk."

Herbert stepped up onto the threshold, the lobby inside shady and quiet, and looked Dr. McRae straight in the eye. "They'll do that anyway, Doctor, whether you invite it or not. Always have and always will, so you two might just as well do what works best for the both of you. She needs a bit more taking care of right now, and down the road a piece, you'll need a helping hand too—and you can take that to mean anything you like." He turned to the sanctuary of his office. "There'll be something new to gossip about next week anyway."

Dr. McRae didn't seem to have an answer. For a change.

* * *

The church was dim, but not as cool as Ann had hoped. She stayed inside long enough to take the flowers from two of the jars before stepping back out under the cloudless blue dome.

The only thing sadder than an empty churchyard was a full one, she thought. At Dr. Evans's grave she laid a branch of honeysuckle, and hoped he knew his little girl had found happiness. Grace and Orville Weyman received bluebells and the promise that the town would take care of poor Boyd. Norman Long's grave was still raw, so she left a cluster of brown-eyed-Susans in the soil with the child-ish hope that they would take root and grow. She had a hard time deciding which flowers would please the frightened spirit of Beatrice Schneider, since they were all wildflowers and the wilderness had been her undoing. She left one of each. By the time she reached the last grave, she had difficulty seeing for the tears in her eyes.

She knelt on the new sprouts of grass beside Ermiline's simple wooden cross. The sun beat down on her bent shoulders and bowed head, but she spread the remainder of the bouquet across the grave like a blanket, arranging and rearranging the wilting flowers, then placed the last three bluebells near the cross.

"These are for you, Jingfei. The lawyers told me where you are buried and I promise to come with food and drink to soothe your spirit as soon as I can. And you, Ermiline, what will soothe you? Or me, for that matter? The shanties of Chinatown, the tents of railroad camps, the warehouses of San Francisco—they're basically all the same, aren't they?"

Only the wind whispered back.

With a damp handkerchief and heavy steps, she walked slowly toward the house on the hill. She'd done a pretty good job of avoiding Dr. McRae all day and if she could just get through a few more minutes she wouldn't have to remember awakening from her fever with him right on the bed with her, watching her, eyes full of questions.

It had been a relief, really, to tell him everything—the soul-numbing years of doing what had to be done to get by, the trunk of stolen finery to be used to initiate a new life—all of it. Then she had described the earthquake that had flattened the warehouse district where she lived and where Jingfei had befriended her, and how she had taken the split-second opportunity to run without even thinking where she would run to.

On a ship. Far from here.

He'd listened without comment when she told him that she had found herself in Vancouver and from there on a train, finally stopping in Calgary to try to think. He'd made her drink many glasses of water until she had talked and cried herself back to sleep and when she arose, hours later, he had disappeared again. Until two days ago.

Angel met her in the washroom. "Are you all alone, little one?"

The curtains had been closed against the afternoon heat. From what she could see in the shadows, the women had tidied the kitchen and put left-over food from the wedding lunch under a bowl for supper. She walked through the dining room into the parlour. With trepidation, she called, "Hello?"

Total silence answered her. She heaved a sigh of relief. With luck, Pietr would come for her trunk before the new owner of the house returned to claim his property. Upstairs, she paused in the sitting room she and Elizabeth had devised to help them through the train wreck. The geranium hung heavy with blossoms. She stood before the half-open window that looked east over the rolling hills and beyond, trying to steady her tired mind enough to realize that if she was careful with her money, she could choose her own future, go anywhere she liked. Yet something about the hills and coulees, silvery green groves and emerald-fringed ponds made her yearn to just walk the prairie forever.

She heard the back door open and close. Pietr would knock. Angel sat up at her feet and flopped her tail against the wooden floor.

"Traitor," Ann said under her breath, but in her heart she was relieved that the dog would have a good home right here.

She heard him walk through the house, recognized his tread on the stairs, knew exactly when he stepped into the landing and stood behind her. She hugged herself and continued to stare straight ahead at the hills. They gave her strength, somehow.

"Ye must be tired."

There was no point in lying to him. "Yes, I am."

"Take a rest, then. There's nae more tae be done here today."

She focused as far out on the prairie as she could, because if she looked closely at the window glass, it showed a reflection of her pink-rimmed eyes and messy hair, and the blur of a red coat behind her. "Pietr's coming soon for my trunk."

"Nay, he's not." More of him filled the reflection and his voice came from just over her head.

"He's not?" Her voice trembled at the thought of having to find someone else to do her work; she simply didn't have the strength to lug that thing down the hill.

"He came earlier, an' I sent him away."

"You did what?"

"I told him ye would be bidin' here for a time."

She pressed her forehead against the cool of the glass and closed her eyes. "Why would you presume to do that?"

"I'm comfortable at the hotel. I wouldna feel right, chasing ye from yer home these last days."

When she lifted her head, a trick of light created a mirage-like illusion of the two of them in the glass. They blended into one. "It's not my home."

"Oh? Our Elizabeth told me ye love the place."

"Our Elizabeth talks too much." When she squinted, their images seemed to dance and swim out over the hills, side by side.

"That she does. And a nasty edge she has tae her tongue, too, when she's riled."

"Riled? With you? I can't think what you could possibly do that would upset Elizabeth."

"Can ye not? Well, hurtin' her friend, her best friend in the whole world, was how she put it, upset her considerably."

Her chin dropped and so did her voice. "I was delirious. The bruises on my wrists faded in no time. We all did wh-whatever we had to. Do we have to talk about this?"

"Nay," he said reasonably. "But I'm speakin' about an earlier time, before I knew up frae doon."

She braced herself with her fingertips on the low bookcase that stood under the window. Why did this man have to be so nice? "You have to understand that the term housekeeper may sound innocent enough to some, but . . ."

"Aye, so you told me."

She looked up into his worried reflection.

"We dinna talk enough, maybe."

"There's no need to say more. I'll be gone soon."

He heaved a huge sigh that could only be described as exasperated, then bent to look out the window. "As ye please, but I'm told I owe ye an apology. That's what I'm wantin' to do here, if ye'll let me."

"No one owes me anything."

"I wonder about that." He leaned his forearm against the wall and peered out. After a long pause, he asked, "What is it ye see out there, Ann?"

"I see hills that have been battered by raging thunderstorms, made sterile by deadly cold and scorched barren by fire. And yet— one gentle spring rain and life floods back." She shook her head. "It's truly a miracle."

"Aye, it's the gentle part that makes the difference." He turned and rested his back against the wall, arms folded over his chest. "Ye love it, too, don't ye?"

Too. Go away, she screamed inside her head. Take your soft, charming ways and leave!

He rolled around on his shoulder so he could see the vista again. Conversationally, he asked, "How will ye feel, Ann Montgomery, when there's no gentle green hills outside yer door every morn'?"

"Jingfei told me once that the best way to lose myself would be right in the middle of a crowd. Find a big city and just blend in, she said. I was looking for a crowd when I landed here, almost by accident, like lots of other people have done. But Aspen Coulee is not a big city and I will never blend in."

He turned back to her, watching her intently, but she still stared into the hills, unable to face him.

Finally, he said, "Ye're no a woman to blend in anywhere, lass, city or town, so why not stay here, where ye've been happy?"

She ignored him. "I have to leave. I only need a bit more time to rest."

He sat sideways on the bookcase and took her wrist in both hands. "Ah, time. Time is what we do have, at least a few weeks of it. Isna that what yer wee nurse said? Ye'll rest awhile an' we'll talk."

She dared to meet his gaze. "The last time I talked you disappeared. You're very good at disappearing."

"It was a lot tae hear."

She looked back at the hills, and nodded. "I'm sorry," she whispered.

"Aye. Is there more I need tae know?"

"Do you know that you deserve better than a rather mature housekeeper with a questionable past?"

He snorted. "Ann, m'girl, I've seen a great deal of the world by now, m'self."

"Do you know they'll talk? Will already has his suspicions, I think."

He slid a palm from her wrist to cover her hand. "Aye, and Schneider has some thoughts o' his own."

She groaned.

"But I have it on good authority that ye wouldna be on the tongues o' the townsfolk but now and then."

"What?"

"S'truth, lass. Ye know that yerself if ye think on it. Once they take ye into their hearts, they'll nae cast ye out. Haven't ye seen it often enough out here? E'en Mrs. Schneider, wi' all her problems an' as much as they talked, they grieved o'er the nasty way she died, and speak of her with their own brand of fondness to this day."

Her tired mind struggled with what he said. They knew about her? Or guessed? And it didn't matter that much? Her legs threatened to give way.

"An' I'll no be disappearin' agin. I'm a landowner now, a businessman and a stakeholder in this brae new land." Then he grinned the boyish grin that shaved ten years from his face.

"You're hopeless."

Serious once more, he said, "Nay, lass. I'm full o' hope. And that pretty speech ye gave about the hills out yon? Those were the words of a woman who will ne'er lose sight o' hope."

She was a woman of hope and pretty speeches? Not just a handsome face, a soft figure—a housekeeper? She began to shake, her knees giving out. He steered her gently onto his lap and they sat, without speaking, listening to the whisper of the aspens outside the window while the coulees filled with shadows.

ACKNOWLEDGMENTS

One of the pleasures of writing historical fiction is the opportunity to spend many hours in libraries, archives and museums, all invariably staffed by patient, helpful people. My thanks to:

the City of Edmonton Public Library, the University of Alberta Libraries, Fort Edmonton Park, the Royal Alberta Museum, the Provincial Archives of Alberta, and the Alberta Legislative Library, all in Edmonton, Alberta;

the Glenbow Museum and Archives and Heritage Park Historical Village, both in Calgary, Alberta;

the Royal Canadian Mounted Police Heritage Centre in Regina, Saskatchewan;

the Saskatchewan Western Development Museum in Saskatoon, Saskatchewan;

The Manitoba Museum, Winnipeg, Manitoba;

Lower Fort Gary National Historic Site, St. Andrews, Manitoba;

Canadian Museum of Civilization, Ottawa, Ontario;

and the Canadian Railway Museum in Saint-Constant, Quebec.

My thanks also to on-line sources:

the Canadian Pacific Railway Archives, at archives@cpr.ca (www.cprheritage.com) and Paul Pettypiece, Central Alberta Rail Historian, at www.ForthJunction.com.

Born and raised on the Canadian prairies, Freda Jackson is the author of *Searching for Billie*, a novel set around the historical immigration of Canada's Home Children. Her writing has been published in the *Edmonton Journal* and *Western Families*. She is a member of the Historical Society of Alberta, the Edmonton & District Historical Society and the Writers Union of Canada. Freda lives in Edmonton, Alberta. *For a Modest Fee* is her second novel.